I0685845

Stop The 'Pocalypse!
I Wanna Get Off!

Christopher Ritchie

Thump the chump before it's too late!

First published in 5 Episodes 2016 to 2017 (Kindle)

Published by GB Publishing.org

Copyright © 2016 Christopher Ritchie

All rights reserved

2017

ISBN: 978-1-912031-53-5 (full version paperback)

978-1-912031-52-8 (full version eBook)

No part of this publication may be reproduced, stored in a retrieval system or transmitted in any form or by any means without the prior written permission of the publisher. Enquiries concerning reproduction outside of the scope of the above should be sent to the copyright holder.

You must not circulate this book in any other binding or cover and you must impose the same conditions on any acquirer.

Names, characters, businesses, places, events and incidents whether in a future context or otherwise are entirely the products of the author's imagination and/or used in a fictitious manner with no intent to cause any defamation or disrespect or any other harm to any actual persons or party whether living, dead or yet to come into being.

A catalogue record of the printed book is available from the British Library

Cover art © Derek E Pearson

GB Publishing.org

www.gbpublishing.co.uk

This is a tale of life, love and loss. It is dedicated to all living beings. And among those billions who have passed on, to my mother.

Acknowledgement

Sincere salutations to the idiots who grease the cogs of our governments; to Derek Pearson for the art; to George and Bee for their enduring support; and to my wife and our offspring – wonderful reminders of the majesty of existence. Special thanks to my moral guide, GDR, and also to those whose support fuelled my fire: Nick P., Tim O., Alan H. and Andrew T.

CONTENT

Other works by Christopher Ritchie

PART 1

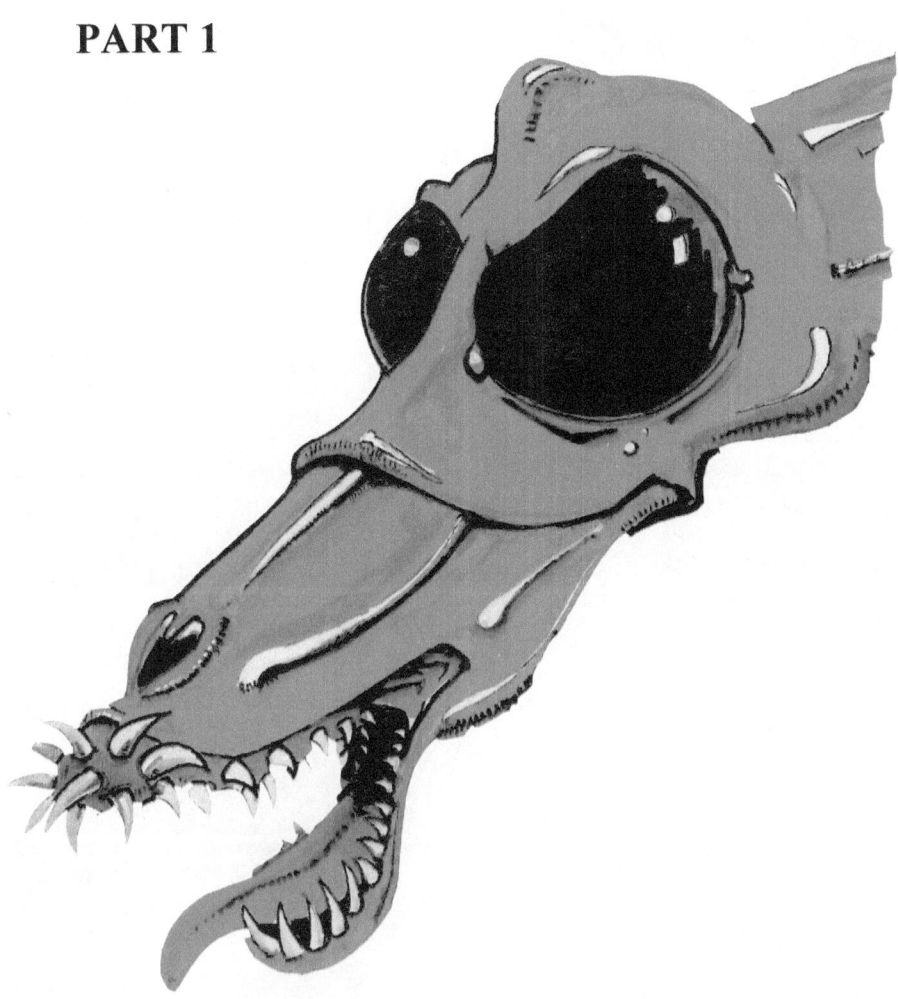

1

I'm nothing special. Never was and never will be. Well, I suppose you could say I played a key part in the biggest story of the last three thousand years, but that ain't more than a single pixel in history. It's down to one's perspection.

Anyhoo, I'll tell you one fact of the matter, as a matter of flying fact: it's all true as blue. Real as my own eyeballs what witnessed this shit: the monster, the slice of Hell, the Rapture... and although I may from time to time over-egg the egg, by which I admit myself to some slight exaggerationism, you must understand I was – I mean am – a showman at heart. I can turn a room with a tune. Does that make me special? Yeah, okay, maybe it does. Just a little.

Today I ain't singin'. No time for that. This story's long and I need you to pay attention. See, this could happen again, and I might not be around to stop it next time. So listen. I tell you again, because I know this plays on your mind: everything I tell you I saw, or I did, or someone else did, that's the truth. The fact I'm here right now proves it all. I ain't one for pulling legs. Let's start at the start. Ready?

She was just a kid, so it seemed, an innocent caught in a world full of darkness that wanted to swallow her up. Who? I'm coming to that. Now while I appreciate I started out as one, I never had much in the way of a calling to make my own kids, although certain women have fed the horse of love. I still ain't got much affection for the little ones, but that's largely irrelevant, I suppose, and I guess it's gonna make less sense as my story unfolds.

Anyhoo, there I was, smoking my pipe outside The Oubliette, right under that neon sign, the 'i' bang-snap in the middle as a matter of fact. It was late, almost the turn of the day, and I could hear the thrum from the Oub behind me, sending a little rub up my bones.

Some folks came and went. I puffed on my pipe. And then I heard that noise that started it all, at least for me... *a scream*. A *child's* scream. Coulda been a car taking a corner in the near distance. Maybe it was someone's TV up too loud. No – there was a clarity to it. Authenticitation. Not that I was overly familiared with screaming, children or not – although now I can profess of myself to being something of an expert – but the point I am trying to make is I *felt* it rather than just hearin' it.

I took my pipe from my mouth and tapped the bulb out. Charred tobacco landed at my feet. Then I scanned this way and that. It hadn't been raining, but the neon reflected a little off the street, and further down each way it streaked in lines, the colour kept alive by the street lamps a few yards apart. There weren't no children in sight, not so surprising for that period of proceedings.

Besides, that ain't a street for children at any time. Just in my view there were three whorehouses, two Aug shops, a Narcosuite and one of them new Nuface places I ain't ever set foot or face in. I like my face just as it is.

'Fuck on.'

The familiar voice pulled me out of my funk. 'Fuck on,' I replied politely to the manageress. She was a rough diamond, that girl. An English rose, dark hair around a pale but pretty face, weather-beaten but still beautiful in a dim light. Respectful of her elders, too. That shit went a long way with me.

'Good set tonight,' she said, lighting up. She took a fat drag on her Digidrug.

'Thank you, Sally. I always aims to please.'

I looked square into her eyes and watched her pupils flop. She offered the Digi over.

'No thanks, ma'am. I'm... watchin' my weight.' Course that made no sense but she smiled anyhoo, then took another bolt for herself. Then I heard that sound again. That scream. Sally started to say somethin' and I shooshed her, holding up my hand to her face. That kinda behaviour ordinarily pains my polite soul, but that scream came louder this time. I felt it again, deeper I guess.

'Ya hear that, Sal?'

'Wha-'

And then she *did* hear the next one. Our heads turned up simultaneousish to the second storey across the street. Mosta the windows up there were dark but one was lit up a bit, a dirty curtain or somethin' hangin' down loose.

What happened next curdled me up bad. The curtain folded over itself and this head appeared, but just the back of it, and then a little hand came up and folded the curtain back. We stood transfixed, watching that head, the hair pressed up against the window. And then all of a sudden, that curtain flew

4

back, ripped away, and the head turned around and we saw a little girl's face and the terror streaked across it. Her two hands reached to grab at the window, but then she was lashed back and out of sight, and another scream came out – longer and... I dunno, *screamier*.

I bolted, leaving my case behind, straight across the street and dashed into the Aug shop. Sally was right behind me. Georgio – he was the proprietor, an old acquaintance of mine too – looked up from his counter. He'd been fixin' somethin' by the looks of it. He saw our expressions, returned one not dissimilar, and shrugged.

'Can't you hear that?' Sally pointed up.

Georgio increased the level of his shrug somewhat.

'How d'we get upstairs?' Sally slapped her palms on the counter. She musta put her Digi away already, or dropped it. I never asked.

Georgio hesitated as he noted the distress in our faces, then: 'Not through here. It's sealed for security. Round the back, down the alley.' He pointed left. Me and Sally dashed out again, turned left and made for the alley two doors down.

Georgio got there just after us, as we heard another scream. The three of us ran into the alley, instinctivisely rounding the corner and then stopping out the back of Georgio's shop. There were three storeys on top of his, but we all looked up at the second floor. That's where the window was, round the front anyhoo, so it musta been round the back also. Logic, that is.

Sally was first to run up the steps, then me. Georgio didn't come with us. I never got to asking him why. Now Sally's augs were auged. That is to say she was like *double*-auged. And those augs were legit. A licensed licencee, someone who ran a nightclub was permitted to have those kind of augs, because they were kinda essential tools for running a 22nd century establishment dedicated to those night-timers. Obviously.

Sally fired up her ThermAug. She used that to detect bodies in the club, particuarly NoBodies. In the Oub those NoBodies had caused enough trouble for to make it a worthy investitude. ThermAug was military grade too, but at Sally's level it was damage control. All those bastards wanted to do was steal and blow their gains on Digis. NoBodies bein' out of the system and all, they don't get to buy and sell in the traditioned ways.

'Nothing.' Sally looked back at me. 'There's nothing there, Marty.'

I blinked. Then again. This wasn't in my domain, adventurously speaking. When did augs get it wrong? They didn't, far as I knew. Unless the girl and whoever was roughing her up were NoBodies, Sally's aug must have been malfunced.

Sally pushed forward again. I guess I began to feel a little pathetic, and with my lungs being what they are I was a bit puffered out, but anyhoo I followed her up to the door. She looked back at me, paused for a second or so, then knocked.

It seemed like an aeon before anything happened. And then that door opened. The little girl opened it fully, standing there looking all happy like.

'Hello...?'

Sally looked at me with a curious blend of surpriseness and incredulation. I expect I flashed the same right back.

'Hey, little lady,' I said to her, stepping forwards a touch. 'Everything okay in there?'

She just smiled this delightful smile, keepin' her eyes locked on mine.

'Sure, mister.' Then her face changed a tad. 'Why wooden' it be?'

Me and Sally exchanged those looks again. The air seemed dead around us right there, like the three of us was in some bubble. The sound of the streets had gone too. I think if I'd tried to hear my heart beatin' that moment, I'd've heard nothin'.

Then Sal leaned around a bit, tryin' to see past the girl and into the apartment. She saw somethin' but didn't let on there or then. The girl leaned up closer to meet Sal face-on and that's when my blood proper curdled. Her little mouth opened so wide it looked like her head was gonna split open. This almighty roar came out, fast and hard like a bullet. It hit Sal right in the face, sending her head back with a snap. Her body followed. Me and the girl looked down at her then, and seeing her life was over then right back at each other.

Then she stepped up to me, I guess primed to take another shot. Shit, I dunno how or why really, but I just dropped to my knees. That shot came and flew right over my head, thank the Lord, but I sure felt the force of it. Left this groove in my scalp, as is plain to see. Took all the hair in that strip clean away, carving up a path through a thick head I'd been growing for longer than she'd been alive.

6

Then that girl comes right up to me, puts her hands on my face and readies her next shot. *Shit*, I thought. *Here we go again.* Her mouth opens so wide and I see right inside. There's something solid but slippery and dark red sitting there in the back, a fat lolling tongue like a snake's head, and I see it about to lurch forward. But the girl, lucky as finding a gold nugget in a steamin' turd, well she was just a girl. I pushed back against her with my palms, sending her onto her back. Then I saw that oily red bullet come right out, breaking out like from a shotgun into this wide arc, leaving a trail back to the girl's mouth. It missed me by a foot. Her body spazzed off the walkway, and she just laid there. I dunno... as if she didn't know she was lying down or something. Her head rolled from side to side and then she saw me, kneeling down a yard or so away.

'What the hell, little girl?' I wished then I hadn't asked.

She crawled over to me, menace dripping off her little face, then scrambled up to her feet and faced me head-on again. This low growl came out: the lowest, most devil-dirty sound I ever heard. I felt all the heat leave my body and I froze on the spot. She stooped a little and advanced on me, so slowly, her face contorted into pure evil.

'Now... you... die...'

That voice cut through time and space. I felt it right in my soul. Then out of nowhere, this flash comes. Bright as the sun in a blue sky. For a second or fifteen my eyes were out, and then when I could see again the girl was on her back again, but not moving. This time her body was crumpled. But I could see she was still breathing.

Then I felt these hands on my shoulders.

'Get up, Marty. Come on!'

2

'Hooo-leeee shit, Marty! What the hell was that?' Georgio leaned back against his shop door. He'd just closed the whole shop front with its reinforced titanium security sheet. Not a great surprise considerin' the expensive items inside.

In all the commotion, I'd forgotten to thank the Italian stallion for saving my arse. Lucky for me, the girl, and himself, he'd hit that demonic little bitch with a flashbang at just the right moment. And now, her body breathing but assumedly sans demonic throat shotgun, there she was laid across Georgio's floor.

It wouldn't have occurred to me, I must admit, to pick the demon up and carry her back to his shop, but Georgio took the lead on that. He saw the little girl and his fatherin' instincts kicked in. Besides, once the flash went off, I'd been outblinded but Georgio saw the whole thing: the girl was flung backwards and as she hit the wall next to the door she'd just come out of, something large and long and kinda spiky looking flew straight out of her, letting out some crazy loud scream that I didn't hear as I guess my ears were kinda blinded out too. Or so Georgio explained it to me, anyhoo. I was satisfied enough with his explanation. Apart from losing a streak of hair and a sliver of scalp two inches wide, I'd come out fairly unscathed.

'We better get the girl tied,' I offered. 'Just in case it ain't... that thing... ain't *gone*.'

So we did. Georgio took her arms and I her feet and we took her into the back stock room and workshop. Georgio had about ten miles of cables back there and we made quadraspazzly sure she was fastened to the bottom of a sturdy shelving rack.

Now I should make it clear that I ain't got nor used no augs – well, beyond the mandatory ones – but I've seen most of the shit that's out there. Georgio had some highly specialerised stuff in there. Not out the front for the usual customers, but some black market gear I reckoned was some miles ahead of what his contemporisers were fuddlin'.

No matter. What's more important is we roused that girl. Soon as it seemed not impolite to do so. Georgio loaded another flashbang into his arm-mounted LaunchAug and directed it right at the girl's open jaw.

Now I, being a man of faith, do not fear no death as I walk through its valley, but I'll profess to being some way towards a bowel movement as I opened her up.

I almost verily sharted as my first attempt at rousing the junior bitch got her mouth open and her eyes flying wide. But Georgio fired not. As I scrambled back up he said: 'Look.' So I looked. The girl's face was serene, if a little damaged. But the importantest detail: her mouth was clear as a turd floatin' in clear blue water. And as I opened it further, her mouth gave way to a throat free of anything peculiar.

Relief, we felt – at last. Georgio lowered his arm. We regarded her for a full minute as she came back around. Her eyes opened up a little and then fully, and in that instant she seized up and pushed back against the rack. Hell, all was in her eyes now was fear.

She let out a gasp, then closed her eyes shut. Her fists clenched up too. Then she opened them, looked up at me, then to Georgio, and screamed. Whatever that thing inside her had been, it looked like it'd gone.

Course as one problem resolved itself, another reared its head. The street was by no means empty when we carried that girl into the aug shop, and them that'd seen us close the securi-shutters in all probability fancied us as up to something. But by natural extension, given dear Sally's somewhat conspicuish passing, we might've expected the law to show up. And show up they did.

Now we need to backtrack a bit here, as you may not be so familiared with what happens when someone is killed. Just so happens I am, to a degree. First things first, be they as they be, far as we knew we'd left poor Sally there on the walkway, dead as the dinosaurs. What we didn't know was the little girl's father was dead too, or rather not too, but deader than Sally for a fact. As she wasn't dead at all. See, it all happening so fast kinda made it hard to nail the facts down in the moment.

Here's what happened: when we looked up at that window, and then ran around the back, the girl – her name bein' Jessie, by the way – was running from her father, 'cept it weren't her father as it was his body but kinda *possessed* by that thing, whatever it was. Next thing it tore the poor guy in half, making a switch of sorts as it jumped into her instead, like a parasite finding a new host, just as we got up the stairs. Guess it was looking for an opportunity for a stronger host maybe.

Sally, good old girl, being what she is and all auged up in her line of work, is quite the capablist at dealing with trouble, sometimes in the form of large, angry men – and hell, glad to know it, she activated all her defence augs as we got to that door. When her sensors turned up with nothing, she smelt a fish all right.

Now when Georgio flashbanged that thing out of Jessie, and we got her up and took her round to his shop, Sally got on up and took a look inside at what she'd seen just before. She found Jessie's father, all torn up. Nasty thing to see, by all accountancies. But the plot thickened there and then: Jessie's father didn't show up on Sal's aug, meaning his body shoulda still been warm and so he must've been a NoBody.

So the law didn't show up because someone had died. No – as far as they were concerned, me and my friend Georgio had just kidnapped some little girl and murdered her father, NoBody or not. And you know how NoBodies become NoBodies, taking out their teeth implants and replacing them with old enamels. No chips in them, see, but they still got rights.

When Jessie proper wokered up and we managed to calm her down, she told us what happened. Her father had picked her up from school across the bridge and brought her south to New Wimbledon on the shuttle. Then he'd hopped he and her across to Morden, then down to Kingston. Now for those lucky folks who ain't never been as far south as Kingston, it's gone the way of the sewer: full of everyone's shit. And it ain't no place for little girls, but by her testifications she'd been livin' there almost her whole life. And at ten years old, that was a lot of time to be swimming in everyone's shit. And in that time she'd swam in some good deal of it and seen all the hell spewing forth, but when that parasite ripped her daddy in two and went after her, she was introduced to a new hell all together.

Oh, and it turned out much later the little bitch were a little good at tellin' lies too.

3

Georgio had no transport. There weren't any quick escape. Sally was standing. Bruised but upright. She banged on the shutters and Georgio spotted her on his monitor. He rolled the shutters up halfway and she ducked inside, then explained all the stuff I've just explained. There weren't much option, we decided, than to make a run for it. Couldn't just leave the girl, in case that thing came back for her, and I had my reasons to keep shy of the pigs as long as possible.

We made for the Oubliette, across the street as it was, and once inside – me shepherding our new lost sheep – Sally had us behind a wall of a hundred or so Digied-up dancing dudes.

I got a little shift in perspective there and then: I'd played in the Oub maybe a hundred times over the years – and going back to before north and south London were different *countries* – but there was always a locked door here or there I never tried to unlock. On that night, Sally took us through a few doors I don't recall ever seeing, into a room with literally nothing in it.

Jessie was somewhere between terrified and not. It's tricky as hell to stick a tail on that donkey's arse. She weren't smiling, but she weren't frowning either. Guess it was the adrenaline pumpin', and whatever else. The shit she'd just seen woulda blown anyone's mind.

As we made our way through the club, Sally – who moments ago I thought would never see another day – kept looking back at us, leading us through the throng of junkies, whores and average dudes and dudesses.

A hand fell firm on my left shoulder, startling as fuckery and pulling me out of the task at hand. I turned to see the source. This guy, maybe half my age and with this spacey-fuck look on his face, shouted something. I don't know what he said beyond the salutation of 'fuck on', but he made an air-guitar gesture which I took to mean he glanzed some pleasure from my performance just an hour previous. I get that a lot. And that reminded me my buggerin' guitar case was still out front. Hell, I'd even looked at the case on our way in, but been just too preoccupied with all the ongoings.

Anyhoo, in that room with Sal, she took me at some surprise, pushed Jessie down to her knees and pulled her arm up to face the girl's chest. A light blinked on her wrist. I'd seen it before: military grade fusion pistola.

Now sure I felt for the girl, but I felt more for Sally. She'd almost bit the dust just then and I didn't know this girl any better than the shit on my shoelaces.

Georgio jumped in: 'Leave her, Sal. She's clean.'

Sally kept her augs armed, but glanced over at me for reassurance. I nodded.

'What's got into ya, little girl?' Sally kept her defences tight. 'Been, gone and out, huh?'

Jessie nodded, then looked up at me. Her eyes pleaded. I was surer then, the evil was out. And what evil to change her face, her fabric, and turn her into some kind of weapon. I ran my hand over the groove in my scalp. Then the girl looked Sally in the eye.

'I want to go home.'

That was the first time she'd spoken without a promptation. Us grown-ups conferred that notion via body language. Fact was there weren't no home left for her.

Georgio proffered: 'We'll keep you safe. Just keep it calm.'

'Just a bad dream,' Sally offered.

Now I, being of some cynicalism, considered this some notches quite far up the shitladder, and by no means a dream. Sure, I knew why Sally said that, but my opinionisatory nature led me to irk a bit and a bob.

'Plain speak to the girl,' I said, some of that irk showing through. 'Shit she's just seen deserves a glass of respect.'

Sally backed off. Then we heard the siren. It was muffled by the several walls separating us from the street, but sure clear enough.

Georgio had an idea. Now he was, in respects, a respected businessman, and from time to time he jivvied up augs for the pigs. He reckoned a few reasonablised words along with some names and descriptions of Sally's punters spewed forth would buy us enough time to do a runner. And he promised to look after my guitar, for which as natural as mother's milk I was keenly grateful. I told Sally she had to stay too. As much stalling as possible to help us get out of the city, please. And so it began.

12

4

Out the back of the Oubliette, we found ourselves in another alley, but narrower and darker. There weren't no apartments on top of the club, and a little left-right-left manoeuvre saw us heading for Kingston bridge. Now back in the day before the River Thames had been sealed, I remember it being as pleasant as a pheasant around there, but now it's dirty just like everywhere else south of Waterloo and Westminster. The domain of the uneducated, the lost souls – and me.

Not that I woulda offered it myself, Jessie took my hand as we made through the streets and over the bridge towards the old Bushy Park, which way back in the day was as green and pleasant as England's jewel, but now more like its bumhole. There weren't many people out and about and we managed to sneak far enough to find a secludered spot away from the pigs' search cone. I'd learned my way out of that cone a few times before. Their sensors could reach out maybe a half mile at a push, depending on the terrain. Course if other pigs closed in from other directions, they could triangulise. We were okay for maybe five minutes, I guessed, maybe longer if Georgio and Sally got their ways with the law.

'I ain't chip and pin,' Jessie said, looking up at me. 'They won't know where to find me.'

Hold on... no chip and pin, no school. If Jessie was off the grid – firstly, that must've been shittin' painful for the kid when they pulled her implants out, and secondly, she wouldn't be in no school. Almost on the break of me asking the question, she set the matter straight.

'I got an aunt up there, in Angel. She's legit. She teaches me while dad's...'

Damn, that girl broke herself down right then. I guess I ain't much in the way of comforting, but I drew her into my arms anyhoo. She tucked herself in and sobbed, clinging tight.

'We gotta move,' I said after a while. 'They'll be closing in.'

We made it as far as the old Hampton Court Palace gates when the chopper appeared from over Bushy.

'You run,' Jessie said, pointing me in the direction of Old Esher – a good four miles of open road. But she weren't to know the fallacy of that. 'I'll explain everything.'

'I ain't leavin' yer.' As those words sprang from my dry lips, I felt some sense of fizzy humanity along with the stomach-turning reality of what was coming.

Now it's not like I was a fugitive or somethin' like that, so they weren't scanning for me all over the place on the off-chance, but putting my head in the lion's jaws simply was not going to end well. And indeed it did not.

5

Much as I'd been lookin' forward to my first helicopter ride, the chopper only stayed until the pig cars turned up then zoomered off someplace else. I guess probably in all rightitude the pigs had to put us in separate vehicles given they thought I'd just murdered the girl's father and wanted to do dastardly shit to her too.

Next time I got to see her, she smiled at me and then nodded. Now what the pigs made of that I don't know, and I wasn't sure what I made of it much either, but they marched me quite roughly past the room they had her in – three or four concerned lookin' ladies rallying around her – and down a long corridor, then threw me – and I mean that as literal as you like – into a cell. The door slammed and a large steel bolt clunked into the wall before I even managed to stand up. I've been in a cell before, drunk and disorderised, but not accused of murder. Wasn't quite sure what to expect.

The cell was old school, a relic, I could tell. A barred window, white painted walls and a cement floor; a bed shelf and a toilet. Nothing else.

After some time I was hauled out, led into another white-walled room and cuffed to the large table in the centre. At least the seat was comfortable for the arse I was carrying.

Two men introduced themselves. I forget their names right now and would rather not try to recall them given what became of them shortly after, so let's call them Paul E. Sofficer, One and Two. Or PESO and PEST for short.

We exchanged the usual pleasantry, three ways.

'Mister Martin Molloy?'

'Uh-huh.'

'Fifty years of age?'

'Haven't been counting.' True – this was news to me. I knew it was somewhere around there, but I've never been one for celebrating.

'And you live... says here you're registered at Justice Heights, New Wimbledon.' PEST smirked, I suppose at the irony.

'Ain't lived there for a while,' I said. I smirked back at him.

'You're behind on your sperm payments.' PESO shot me a look of contempt and puzzlement. 'Why?'

'I don't dig dicking in those dirty machines,' I said. And that was the pure truth. As any moderned man knows, and it's one of them several reasons that leads many to become NoBodies, the mandatory annual supply of sperm, like a cow gettin' milked by a robot sitting behind a glory hole, is for most guys as unpleasant as fucking a wall sounds.

'Don't mind it myself,' PESO offered.

'Only place you ever get to stick it,' PEST responded, nudging his colleague's elbow.

PESO cleared his throat. 'Well, seems you're three years out on that so you can expect a triple-whammy today. Now then...' He put his tablet down on the table and leaned back in his chair, then looked at PEST and back at me.

'Why'd you kill Daniel Dickson?'

I tried to lean back too, but the chains hooking the cuffs together pulled tight and brought me to a somewhat deceremonial stop. Felt a touch foolish, I did.

'I didn't.'

PESO sighed, then PEST took over: 'Okay, Molloy. Then why'd you kidnap the girl?'

'I didn't.'

'Did you take her implants out?'

'Nope, not that either.'

PESO linked his fingers together behind his head. 'Listen, Molloy. This all goes a lot smoother if you co-operate.'

'Far as I can tell I'm doing that,' I said. 'You ain't askin' any questions I can answer in the affirmative, see.'

I could see PEST was rather transfixerised by the groove in my head, front to back cutting a little into my skull. I bowed over in response, givin' him a good look.

'How the hell'd that happen?'

At last. I told them how that happened. From start to finish. At points they looked at each other, and me, and laughed with incredulity. I knew they would.

A little girl being a NoBody? No chance, they scoffed. Some kind of demon parasite thing jumping between bodies? Even less likely, they said. So

16

I was suspect number one in a group of no others, despite no evidence tying me to any crime.

I feel it's important, nigh on essential, to state that these guys were nothing of a threat to me. Just doing their jobs. No ill will from me to them. I can't speak for the pigs, but they seemed unconvinced that a fifty-year-old guitar maestro would suddenly turn murdering, kidnapping bandit on a whim.

None of that mattered anyhoo. Right then we heard something, loud and plain unusual. A... a child's scream, again. Oh Lord, I thought. *That scream.* Course by now I knew what that scream was, and it ain't comin' from no kid. PESO stayed in the room with me while PEST went to see what was happening. Then another, even louder scream came, followed by an almighty crash not far away and a whole lotta screaming, human and whatever else.

I found out whatever else when I saw PEST's body thrown past the doorway, his guts trailing right out of his belly, and then less than a second later he snapped back into view as if on elastic or something, stopped in place right in the doorway and dropped in a heap right there with a splash of sorts. PESO – who was armed – got straight up and without looking back at me, sprang himself around the doorway to the right, deftly avoiding his colleague's messy splattery – and started firing off. Now me, being not altogether accustomed to such brutal dismemberment, raised my eyebrows high as they'd go when PESO's arms flew back into the room and skidded across the floor, leaving a crimson swish as they hit the wall behind me. The right arm's hand was still clutching the gun. Not that I had any means of getting to it given my table-cuffed disadvantagements.

I heard more shots ring out and watched flashes bouncing off the corridor wall, heard a bunch of men howling, and then silence. Shit, I assumed they were all in bits.

As was I, emotionally speaking. And I'd let spill in my underpants too. As I glanzed down at the piss dribbling out of my trousers and onto the seat, a single sound increased the flow: a slithering splash. Then another, another, and another, getting louder each time.

I focused my gaze back on PEST, startled to see he was still alive – somehow – with his hands clasped inside his disembowelism, blood spilling over his fingers and onto the shiny floor. Despite having emptied my bladder I felt some relief that the source of said sound was that poor soul rather than anything more sinister in my undercrackers, but then the real shit hit the fan.

17

In a motion I can only describe as fright'ningly swift, in less than the blink of an eye I saw a monster appear in the doorway and then come to face me at the table.

Now when I say monster, you gotta take that in the spirit not of some paedophile or dictator, nor of a man who beats his wife and kids every Friday after supper, but an actual stuff-of-nightmares monstrosity. By vivid recollectionism – and now I've spent some good deal of time in its presence you can take this as reliable testimony – the thing was as a *beast*: four legs, not unhoundlike, and a head with eyes and teeth and what you'd expect, but the turd in the frying pan was its texture and colour and detail. Like tight latex, the skin on the thing was – *is* – shiny and red, as if wrapped around. And its head – just as tight, but an *ingrowing* nose, silly as that sounds, and eyes as black as the darkest night. But the mouth was almost ridiculous, horselike and protruding, with the thinnest red plasticky lips bordering those tiny sharp teeth, maybe two hundred of them. Or more.

I take no pleasure in mistruths, so I state with some pricked-up confidence that there and then I added dessert to the main course in my underpants. Also, I was readied up to die. Far as I could tell, options otherwise were thin on the ground.

The monster's forelegs slammed on the table, splitting it clean in half. The table, that is, not the monster. Fortuitously the cuff-linkers sprang off, freeing my hands. I instinctively raised them to my face. Then it spoke, in a voice I remembered very well.

'Where... is... she.'

There weren't no inflection as to mark that as a question, but given the grimmity of the scene I refrained from pointing out the syntax error.

Peeking through my fingers I watched its face draw nearer to mine, until it was right there – maybe half an inch away. I could have stuck my nose into its ingrowing one, had I the nuts. Obviously, a man sat in the warmth of his own muck lacks the nuts to a degree.

Anyhoo, just as I lowered my hands, its forelegs raised up then gently came to rest on my knees, one at a time. Our eyes were locked, me staring into an eternal darkness. There was real depth in those sockets, like swirling tempests, an abyss like the deepest and darkest ocean on Earth.

'I'll take you to her.'

Now we need to be clear here. I don't know why I said that for sure. Perhaps just the desire to live a few moments longer, maybe an urge just to stand up and get that thing out of my face, but I know it occurred to me that this thing wanted Jessie, and it thought I could help it reach that conclusion.

So I was happy as hell to go along with that for as long as I might. And by the very act of being able to relate this tale, it's clear that it worked out for me.

The beast backed away, just an inch, and then after a pause, another, until it came to stand upright on its hind legs. The thing looked quite astonishing. All shiny and red. Then I noticed its limbical protrusions, like a bastarded mishymash of hands and claws and hooves. It stood over seven feet tall there, its shiny head almost scraping the ceiling.

I stood up, the shit in my pants taking a little tumble down between the cheeks there and resting just under my balls. Ordinarily it'd be something of an embarrassment, but I housed that turd there for a good deal of time onwards like an incubating shit-egg.

I turned to eye that gun in PESO's severed arm, but there weren't any way old Red were gonna let me have that.

Then, sharp and painful, the beast's right foreleg rose up and slapped me across the chops, knocking me clean down. I fell face-first and put out my hands to break the fall. Which they did, just a bit. Almost broke my jaw, that slap – and the tooth I spat out on impact looked, I'm happy to say, lonely. Facing the doorway, now I saw PEST *properly* dead, his face contorted into an expression properly befitting his predicament.

Then right away the beast was on top of me, those forelegs at my shoulders and its head drooped over so its mouth prodded at my ear.

'Take me... to the girl...' Jumpin' jerkins, that growl was chilling.

I edged myself up, the beast backing off just enough to let me do so. I stepped carefully over PEST's mess to find PESO's legs, head and torso all lying separated in the corridor. There was more blood than I'd ever seen, sprayed up the walls, on the ceiling, pooled around the body parts. The beast prodded at my back. I moved.

Before we rounded the corner at the end of the corridor I counted six bodies, some of them lacking any kind of discernible feature – just flesh, as if eaten and shat into wet piles. Crucialist, the room I'd seen Jessie in before was empty. No sign of any ladies. I felt a little relief then, for her. The security gate at the end of the L-shaped corridor was smashed in and the wall around it crumbled and crumpled. I stepped over the rubble and into the reception. Three bodies on the floor and one on the desk.

That short journey concluded my working knowledge of Kingston copshop. I didn't have a plan. The place had gone to hell but I figured – *hoped* – Jessie'd got away and the reinforcers were on the way. So bold as a gorilla's arse, I turned to face the beast. 'How come you ain't killed me yet?'

Astonishising every inch of me, right down to the shit in my pants, the answer came back not growling but in my own voice, weird as hell seeing that mouth forming those words as if I'd said 'em.

'Yet be the right word, sunshine.' The horsey, plasticky-tight mouth almost seemed to smile. 'But if you get me to the girl, I'll make it a quick deal at the closing.'

I felt I had to keep the convo going. 'What's so important about her?'

Red came right up close again. 'That ain't none of your fuckin' business, shitfly. Get moving.'

It was the end for me. I knew it. Figured the only chance I had was to lead the beast outside and hope the reinforcers were waiting for us. So I did. The entrance doors were busted out. I stepped over more debris and at the exact moment we reached the open air I felt it: the freaksiest feelin' I ever felt for sure.

I can't even musterise the explanation for how it came to be, but I felt every bit of it as the beast – in a flash – leapt into my face, bits of it peeling away into strands like snakes – red and shiny like licorice sticks – and in through my eyes, nose, mouth and ears. And then it was just hanging there, like just suspended inside me, filling my throat and belly and every inch below the skin, but at the same time leaving me in control... or so it seemed.

Out of the darkness came light, and then appeared seven or eight guys in heavy armour and with big guns, striding towards me with those weapons levelled right at my face. I put my hands up. A spotlight happened upon me at that moment, and then another, from front and behind. Having come from the relative quiet inside, out there it was suddenly noisy as hell.

'On your knees,' one called through a loudspeaker. I did as requestened.

Then the voice in my head: 'The girl.'

I thought back to it: 'Even if I knew where she is, I ain't giving it up.'

'I'll tear you to pieces.'

20

'OK then. Tear me to pieces.'

Figured fifty years had been a fair stretch.

'The girl!'

I had to try hard there and then to not think about her or where she might be as it woulda helped that beast. Sure, in hindsight it might've seemed obvious to anyone that she was back in that station someplace, but it wasn't obvious to old Red and I wasn't about to make it so. Red could read my thinkings.

Now being of not considerable intelligence but able to think laterally like, as some people call it, I had a quick idea and acted on it before – hopefully – Red would get wind. Maths being as far from my strong point as the Earth from the Sun, I began to swirl numbers around my brain in a bid to distract my new internal organ.

One hundred and ninety-nine thousand, nine-hundred-and-ninety-nine-point-nine-nine-nine...

'What are you doing?'

...plus ninety-nine-point-nine-million-billion-and-five-fifty-six-seven...

Red started twitching inside me, causing me to shake somewhat. Those guys and their guns had stopped and were staring. 'Stop it!'

...and four-five-seven-billion-billion-thousand-billion...

The twitching got violent really quickly and then I felt it rising up, joining together in my throat. Then my neck snapped back, my mouth opened wide and it shot up and out, straight ahead and into the only dude who wasn't wearing an armoured helmet.

I fell backwards with the force, knocked out as my head hit the ground.

6

Some time had passed when I came around in Kingston Hospital, not that I knew it right away of course. Hospitals tend to look much the same I guess, even south of the river.

Now I know two things about Kingston Hospital:

1. It's in Kingston.
2. It's a hospital.

No, make that three: this Kingston Hospital ain't the *right* Kingston Hospital. It's like a hundred years out. The tech's all wrong. The docs ain't auged. No one's auged. I'm out of time and place, freaky as that can be. But we'll get to that when the time is right.

Meanwhile, let me perspectivate a little. I was born in Hackney in 2071, fifty years or so after the world's collective shit hit the universal fan. We learned all about it in school, not straight away but as soon as we could fathomise that stuff. I guess I was about twelve, thereabouts. Anyhoo, in 2018 the third world war kicked off proper. Nuclear weapons had all been deactivised but see, some sneaky bastards held some back. Russia fired on America; then Korea, north or south I forget, fired at America too, and then Japan.

Japan was the first to go under, I mean literal like, shot to pieces and sunk into the ocean. America somehow fired on itself – their second civil war was a kinda catalyser for the world war in the first place, and it ended real bad for them. Effectively the civil war led to President Johnson and the Republican leader – I don't recall the name exactly now, but it was something like Donald Duck – having a fisticuff in the war room, and as they both wanted to launch nukes but at different targets, they got their maths all bust up and ended up firing on themselves. No one knew which of them pulled the trigger. Maybe both. But we know now.

Anyhoo, the United *State* of America was left in the middle after the fallout, down in Texas somewhere. South America took a beating too. They didn't have no nukes, but there was nowhere for them to go. Europe put up a front and managed to stay true with its anti-nuke programme, but the fighting between nations there became too much to bear and much of Europe mainland just never recovered. Trade routes were shut off and the fallout from here and there swept serious radiation across the continent.

Ah, I forgot about China. The Middle Eastern states shot first to the east. China was sneaky though. Somewhere along the line the Chinese'd been messing with subterranean shit, on the pretensism of frackin' for oil. Really it'd figured out how to cause shifts in the geography of a place. It fuck near ripped Iran and Iraq apart. Fair to say Saudi and Israel and all the promised land ruptured and fell to pieces. Now Britain was luckier than most, relatively speaking. Some places were only touched by the fallout, like Australia and New Zealand. And here in England, there was a clear focus on looking after London. The banks, the powerful eliters, you know. That was always the way. London's first in the lifeboat and if there's any room left, they'll fill it with money and anything that ain't poor people.

Just so happened the second English civil war was waiting in the wings. Once they put up the fallout fences, and just in time, there was no way in or out for the likes of me and everyone else. They kept Heathrow Airport alive, but really for domesticised use only as there weren't many holiday destinations left by then. The boundary – and let's be clear it was Chinese tech, a sorta semi-matter anti-rad film that joined organically between posts erected – snaked around the peaceful countryside to just south of Guildford and Godalming, north of Borehamwood and just outside Stevenage, eastwards to Romford and down a bit via Gravesend – where the Thames cut in – and westwards to Slough and parts of Reading. Now the US's New England was blown to hell, but we got our very own after that. And it ain't a large enough size all told to coop up all them people. Once that freedom to move was gone, people got a little shitty. Well, more shitty anyhoo. Not that I was alive, but I've seen the images. People were sad. The world was *gone*.

The army manned those fences real good and eventually engineers pushed out a little further and started erecting more of them posts. Soon enough, by 2035 I guess, they'd covered down to the south coast, with this extra safety net. Everyone caught in it was dead though. Literally a dead zone. Same for the regions out north, east and west. The army just rolled all those bodies up together and let them burn.

Then that second civil war broke out, and although there weren't no north and south factions so to speak, the Thames became the divider, being the only real geography left of strategic worth. But no one won that war, see, and it came to something of a frustrationed impasse. You've got those north of the Thames and those south. It's civil again, mostly, but the fighting kicked the shit out of the infrastructure.

Rebuilding was slow, slow, slow, and with us bein' cut off and all, industry went the way of the toilet. You gotta think of the effect on all the rest of the outside just not bein' there anymore. Education and medicine nearly all gone; imports and exports... *all* gone. But in the midst of that came the surge in private tech.

Before the internet went offline – although now we've got our own intranet – the growth in augs was slow but once they had nothing else to do, the techy brains got to focus. And focus they did. And those augers ended up creating these teeth implants that keep track of everyone, see.

Our government was over. Some saw that as a good thing, but I never mustered much of a shit about that. I never saw anything good or bad enough to form an opinion. I grew up watchin' the only TV that was left, the old American westerns and such. Our archives and studios had mostly been blown to bits in the in-fightin', but the US stuff had held its own in some bunker under the US Embassy and been retrievered. Apparently some President Reagan back in the day had decreed that an archive be kept alive down there, even after he weren't. And so it was.

Over a year or so after the civil war, once the guys were bein' civil again, The Council formed up. Now The Council had good intentions, better than those who'd been in charge before, anyhoo, and they took an altogether more sensibled approach by putting people who knew shit in charge of the shit they knew about. And New England began to rebuild itself, but focusing first on the north. Without the manpower from Europe we'd had previous, and only a small pool of skilled guys and gals left, that took years... and years... Meanwhile, the south bein' neglectered never changed. While the north got richer, they put more and more into that, and the south slipped further into the drain.

But I'm happy, mostly, operating down there. I've always been able to fly under the radar. See, I ain't in a position of contribution or otherwise, I just merely *am*. That's mostly 'cause I operate purely in the sphere of entertainment, so I ain't worth tracking. Sure, I'm clicked through checkpoints just like anyone else, but I ain't been through one since I last had to, and that's goin' back a'ways. That's why I ain't shot my load into those wall-mounted dicksuckers that are supposed to ensure the future of humankind. You work in a school, a hospital, an office or anywhere else that deems you a critical part of society and you're part of a programme, nothing else. Me, I prefer to sow my oats the natural, God-given way.

So that's why it is how it is. But not how it is here and now, in the *wrong* Kingston Hospital.

7

Anyhoo, the Kingston Hospital I woke up in that morning was the *right* one. For me, there and then. I was glad for the sunlight streaming through the ward windows, having had a fair few shots of darkness the night before. I thought back to having that thing inside me, crouching within my frame, then pouncing out. The numbers – I didn't know why I'd thought of doing that at the time, but then it occurred to me: that thing was sharing my mind, so I was sharing its mind too. Somehow I'd *known* doing that would force the beast out. Maybe. I supposed it was the parasite mentality, seeking survival first and foremost, and the reason it didn't rip me in half was one of two things: it either needs me to find the girl, not that I knew why at the time, or it felt trapped and just had to escape. I sure felt trapped too, having all those guns and spotlights trained on my head.

How wrong I was! Course I had no idea what'd transpired over the small hours or how I'd ended up in hospital. Then a pretty nurse comes over and says, 'Hi Marty.' Naturally I assumed she's seen me play, and me being something of a talent in that regard my name stuck. 'How are you feeling?'

I mustered a smile. 'Okay,' I said. 'Head's a bit wonky.' She chuckled. Then a doc comes over, his MediAug clamped around his neck with a bunch of cables and cameras and shit hangin' off it.

'Mr Molloy? How are you feeling?'

I responded the same way as to the nurse. 'Seems you had a lucky escape last night.' He didn't know the half of it. 'Ambulance brought you in. You'd fallen into a ditch and banged your head. You almost drowned.'

Drowned? Huh? 'What about the police station?' I guess I looked all quizzicalled.

The doctor shook his head and shrugged, then went back to his business the other side of the ward. I began then to feel somewhat wonkier. Looking around, I saw a few guys and gals in beds. Some were clearly out of their heads, others not so much, but they were all clearly Southerns. You can tell easily enough, most of the time. The class divide may have been turned on its head, but the symptoms of it were clear as shit on the shoe.

Not much happened for a while there. After maybe two or three hours the doctor came back, told me to take it easy for a few days, and then a nurse offered to call someone for me. I said I'd be okay. Mostly all I'd been thinking about was how I'd come to be in the hospital. I replayed the night's events and there wasn't any water to drown in, not that I recalled anyhoo.

That thing had showed no mercy in the pig station yesterday, so why hadn't it run amok in the hospital too? Best I could come up with was it didn't need to. Jessie wasn't there – hell, I had no idea where Jessie was either – so killin' however many folks were in the hospital was a waste of time and effort. And me personally, well, as I said at the start I ain't special, so it had no further business with me anyhoo. Maybe.

Sheesh... I just didn't have any answers. I didn't really fancy having them either. Sure, I felt some loyalty of sorts to seeing that girl come good, but I also had a gig to play in Barnes. So my first thoughts were to go pick up my guitar from Georgio, pop in on Sally to say hi, then make my way over to the Half Moon. Man's gotta make a living. Besides, I had no idea where Jessie was. No idea at all. I wasn't equipped to go scouring several hundred square miles looking for her either.

8

I never made it to Barnes, not even back to Georgio's place. Soon as stepping outside of the hospital, I walked two minutes up to the main road at Kingsnympton and in the broadest of daylight, this van pulled up. Three heavy-looking guys appeared out of it, stuck something clothlike over my head and bundled me in.

Got my second blow to the head there and then. I didn't know how far or where they took me, but it was out of the district for sure. When they 'ventually took the hood off, I was surprised as a goose born from a pig to see myself in the countryside. Now I ain't usually got much need to be out of town, seeing as that's where I ply my trade, eat and shit and sleep, but there's something just beautiful about it. England used to have so much green and now we've got a tiny slice of it all told, in the grand scheme, but what's left still takes the breath away.

Once I'd taken the view in, I suddenly remembered my head was hurtin' some. And it was – throbbing, from two blows I thought I didn't much deserve. Anyhoo, I looked around at the men standing at the back of the van. They weren't that heavy-set, as it happened, but I guess the shock of it'd blown them up a little in my view.

One of the guys stepped up to me and put his hand on my shoulder.

'Sorry about that, old bean.'

I ain't ever been called a bean before, old or otherwise. I kept my face straight.

'I suppose you'll want to know why we've brought you here.'

Nothing from me, still. He sighed, turned back to his chums, and moved his hand down to my elbow, pulling me towards the van again. Course I instinctedly put some effort toward preventing that, but the man's strength far outshone my own. We walked around the van and came to a wall, one of those old-style wonky-bricked things about a metre high. A gap in the wall led to a dirty trail which then took us down into a forest – and that was pretty as a tit too, I must say, with the sun streamin' down through the canopy. Out the other side of that, we came to a clearing. In the middle of that was some kind of door – in the ground, that is. A trap door, you could say, except at that point I didn't know if it was a trap at all.

One of the other guys lifted it up, and we all went in. We walked down a short, dark passage. A camera above a sturdy looking metal door made a whirring noise, bleeped and then the door swung open.

My Lord, what I saw next took the wind out of my stomach and balls and stuck it back up my arse. My mouth dropped open as the door clunked behind me.

'Faaaarrrrrrrk.' I heard that come out of my mouth although I'm not sure I'd intended it.

There was I, stood at the entrance to some pristine technicology facility. A giant fuckin' place it was, all glass and muted colours and fancy tech. Then I understood where I'd been taken. The fabled underground city – the New Republic. I say fabled because it was fabled, but not in the old fairy tale sense. Funcational rather than mystical, over the last eighty years or so it had grown from a small bunker into what I saw for myself right then.

But let's be clear: this ain't magic. And it wasn't called the New Republic either, as I soon found out. This was the hard work of men, women and children who went underground and never came up again. The place, I came to learn, had its own water treatment facility, food production, medical and maternity centre, and a school. Oh, and an armoury.

But so much more than that. See, those clever folks had escaped down there during the civil war – they used to do animal testing and shit, and now it'd become a home away from the overground authorities. They'd grown it too, digging tunnels out and then even up a bit, taking into its fold a large mansion which itself was then reinforced to keep the outside world out. It was a fortress, no less.

So what the hell was I doing there? Good question. But first, I ain't saying *where* it was, because the kindness those guys showed me – apart from that knock on the head, which I guess was kinda crucialised for them keeping their secrets secret – was real.

Two of the guys stayed back while the other led me down. Took about ten minutes to walk through the length of the place and into that mansion at the far end. Frankily I couldn't quite believe how well they'd done down there, but I guess over most of a century they'd bled their hearts into their home. Old labs and common areas were now family apartments, with all those facilities dotted around.

The mansion, not that it appeared so on goin' in, was indeed mansionable. It was like stepping into one of those old dramas the Yanks liked so much, all butlers and shaggin' servants; except here it was offices, and people working in them, and a canteen serving hot food and cold drinks.

Blown back and away, I was. Truly. Sure, I'd heard stories tellin' of this place, and most folks seemed to think it either didn't exist or it did in some degree, but not like this. Seeing it for myself was something of a high point in my otherwise fairly mediocal existence.

The guy, his name being Sean it turned out, led me up two flights of elegant staircasings and then knocked on a door so large and heavy I couldn't imagine it opening. With a loud clunk it did, but real slow.

And there she was. Little Jessie. In the centre of the room, smiling at me like a long-lost friend reunited. Hell, I smiled right back at her. She didn't come at a gallop like you see in those old movies, but she strode over with a confidence I ain't seen before in such a young thing.

She put out her hand to shake mine. Bit formal, I thought, but what the hell. I shook it. Then I looked around the room a bit. Screens on one wall showing all kinds of stuff, mostly static images it seemed to me, and computers on desks.

'I'm so sorry,' the little girl said, 'to get you involved in this. So sorry.'

Involved in what? I thought. She musta heard the cogs in my brain as she answered soon as right away.

'You must be confused. Let me explain.' She took my hand, not as firm as she had the night before, and led me over to the wall of screens.

'These,' she said, 'are our eyes on the outside. We've got cameras all over, hidden mostly. Some are The Council's, which we tap into.'

I nodded some.

'You're in what we call Eden. It's a fairly closely guarded secret, as you probably know.'

I nodded some more, happy as I was to learn stuff rather than bein' bashed in the head.

She continued: 'What happened last night... well, that wasn't really what it seemed. I guess you're seeing that now.'

I wasn't seeing that. Dunno really what I was seeing beyond the big hole in the ground with a load of people making a home. That much I got. I think she noticed my lack of understandment.

'Marty, you're the most important man left in the world, and you're not safe out there now, and time is short, which is why I had you brought here.' She said that with a look of sympathy, kinda condescending like. Got my back up a little. Who's this kid to tell me I'm not safe, and not allowed to go outside? And the most important man in the world?

'I'll take my chances,' I interrupted.

'There's more of them out there, and more coming,' she said.

'More of who?'

'Come with me,' she said. 'I need to show you something.'

9

The girl, she weren't called Jessie at all. That was the first shock, albeit fairly minorly. She was called Angie. And she weren't ten years old either, but we'll come to that later.

Angie took me down the stairs I'd just come up and then down another set into a cellar. There were more computers and screens down there, but she led me past them into a dark room and stood me still. 'Wait there,' she said, and then she called out 'lights'. The room weren't dark no more.

I almost sharted myself for the second time – oh, and in case you were wonderin', my previously sharted and pissed undercrocks had gone the way of the hospital's waste collection; I'd been flying commando since, although my trousers still faintly smelled of the mellow yellow: the little bitch'd stuck me standing in a room full of glass cabinets or cages or somethin', each with one of those red damned beasts in it. The sound coming out was muffled, but those demons were gnashing and thumping against the glass.

Their eyes, still dark as the bottom of the ocean, focused on me, all at once. Then one of them did that snaky thing, which is mighty hard to describe in my limitised vocab. Imagine you see a seven-foot-tall plastic red demon horse just suddenly break away into misty shoots, but so quickly you hardly see it at all. Then those shoots start flyin' about, like fireflies or something leaving thick trails behind them. That's not even close.

I gotta admit to having a touch of the trembles watchin' those things. I didn't like being in there one bit.

'See?' Angie said. 'These are our heavenly familiars, or attack dogs.'

That revelation fair jolted me in the bananas. 'Attack dogs? You mean, that thing… is *yours*?'

I'd had enough. 'Listen, girl, whatever your name is. I've got a gig to get to. I've gotta pick my guitar up and get over to Barnes. Now all this shit's fascinating as a fanny fart, but it ain't none of my business or where I particular want myself to be right now.'

That was the truth, and I hope it's understood that I don't consider my language in that instant pardonable. I don't usually talk like that to anyone.

Angie, well… she smiled at me again, all sympathised.

'I'm sorry, Marty,' she said. 'But I can't let you go. Not yet.'

'Goddamn it!' I clenched my fists a bit, real tight, then exhaled long and slow.

'Come back to the ops room,' Angie said. 'I'll explain everything.'

10

Turns out that sometimes what you think you seen ain't what you seen at all. Now I've lived some decades and witnessed a whole lot of stuff, some crazy and some not so, but I've always trusted the eyeballs in my head.

Angie sat me down in a comfy leather armchair in a room off the main ops centre. She told me to close my eyes while she walked me through some shit.

When I'd looked up at that window, having heard the scream – not a child's, but that red demon's – I saw the back of the girl's head and assumed she was in trouble. Not so. In fact she and the demon were up against that Daniel Dickson feller for a damned good reason: he weren't just a NoBody, he was – and I make no apology for strugglin' a bit to believe this part – *from another place*.

Course then I enquired what she meant by *another place*. Angie explained further: she took me and Sally to be with Dickson, which is why she and that beast attacked us. But when Georgio forcibly ejectered it from her, and we carried her back to the aug shop and shuttered ourselves in, she had to create the act. Yes, she and the thing had murdered Dickson, but he wasn't a NoBody at all. He wasn't even human.

I was dizzyin' right up with all this weird information, but I stayed sat in that comfy leather and listened intently.

The beast woulda caught up with Angie and me earlier, had it not been for the fact that Georgio's flashbang was flashy and bangy enough to knock the thing out of sorts for a while. When we'd got as far as Hampton Court, with Angie keeping up her act, and then when we were taken to the police station, it sniffed her out.

Now coincidental like, some other of those guys *from another place* had sniffed us out too. It wasn't that red beast that'd torn PEST and PESO apart, and the other bodies I saw when I got out into that corridor were those who'd come to kill her, and me.

Angie said she felt superly bad for PESO and PEST, and the other policey folk who died there, but she assured me it wasn't the beasts that did it – they'd come to protect her, pure and simple, and protect her they did. I'd made me some wrong assumptives.

Thing is, she explained, those beasts aren't the sharpest tools in the box, despite bein' adorned with somewhat sharp tools of their own for the purpose of tearin' and shreddin'. The beast could smell the girl on me as earlier she'd held my hand and *pretended* to cry into my chest, which is why it came after me.

At that very moment her task force – that's what she called it – turned up and secured her outside. So those heavy guys with big guns were with her all along. When we got out there and the beast saw the lights, it did what it had to do – jumping inside me as a hiding place. Then when it saw she was safe and sound it jumped back out. It had nothin' to do with me spoutin' those numbers after all. *Apparently.*

'Bullshit,' I said, but I couldn't rightly disprove any of the detail given I'd just lived through some version of it.

Naturally it took some time for this to sink in. A crazy story had just got much, much crazier. But what really naggled at me was why they'd bundled me into a van and taken me to Eden.

Because, she said, I'd become a marked man. Far as the police were concerned, I'd still killed that feller and kidnapped that girl. I'd been taken to a station which had been damn near smashed to pieces and they'd eventually find my body not there.

I'd been lucky in the hospital that my name hadn't flashed up in any alarms, but Angie's guys had had to finish the job on the station once we were clear. While one of her men took me along to the hospital and told them he'd found me about to drown in a ditch – he'd stopped by the river at Kingston Bridge to make sure I *looked* wet – the others set about torching the station.

Course the doc in the hospital knew nothing about that because there weren't no bodies to tend. They were all dead and torched to shit. The police who turned up later woulda assumed I'd burned too, along with the girl. Tragic atrocity number one, that was.

It was beginning to make sense... a kinda twisted, unbe-fuckin'-lievable sense anyhoo. But I sure didn't like the idea of livin' underground.

'So where's this *other place*?' I asked the girl.

She smiled at me, her face all bright and her eyes sparklered.

'You heard of Heaven?'

Course I nodded.

'And Hell?'

Angie was called away to the ops room. I followed her in, my brain fizzing with stuff I had no business knowing or thinking. Sean was there, standing with his hands on his hips and chinwaggin' with a handsome looking woman. By handsome I mean she looked enough like a man. Certainly not a cup of tea I'd stir with my trouser spoon.

He saw me gazing at the monitors and came over, then put his hand on my shoulder.

'We're nearly ready, one-thousand-and-seven,' he said.

'Huh? Ready for what?' I asked, bamboozlerised.

'She didn't tell you?'

Course I said no, she hadn't, rudely interrupted as we were. Angie overheard us speaking and called over: 'It's okay, Sean. Tell him.'

So this is as close as I can recall of what he said, and believe me, I was payin' attention. He started, he said, from as near the beginning as was necessary.

'World War Three started a chain of events. It put something in motion.'

He referred to the Book of Revelation in the *Bible*, something I've never read beyond the front cover.

'Revelation speaks of a hundred-year event, leading to the 'pocalypse. That's where we are now, you might think, a hundred years after.'

'The 'pocalypse, now? That's it?'

He nodded. 'Well, not exactly.'

I shrugged and he nodded again, then smiled.

'Pardon me,' I said, 'but I think we already had the 'pocalypse. That's why they call our situation post-pocalyptic.'

'Well,' he went on, 'there's that and then there's *this*.'

Sean led me over to the wall of monitors and pointed at the one on the top-right. 'That's ground zero.'

My stomach made for a triple somersault. What the hell was I seeing? Hell, it looked like Hell. The camera wasn't moving but everything else was, like a big swarm of wasps all writhing around each other. But these wasps were flesh-coloured, slimy and disgusting to look at. The camera had some distance from the scene, blurred a little by the radiation fence, but those beasts had fire and chaos in their eyes. I could see that. I turned away from the horror.

'That's where one of the rips appeared,' Sean said. 'And there's more opening up every week now. They open and close quickly, but stuff nearly always pours in.'

'Rips in what?' I enquired of the gentleman. I was still tryin' somewhat to figure out why he'd called me one-thousand-and-seven.

He put his hand on my shoulder again. 'Marty, that's a rip in everything we have. That's the Earth, the galaxy, the universe… the whole thing collapsing like a punctured lung. And those things, those beasts you can see that've come through it, they're only held back by the radiation fence. This fence is one of the outer ones, back up north of the second fence outside of Birmingham. But that's only 100 or so miles away, and once they get through there they'll get through another, and then another, and then it's game over.'

Game over? And what's this got to do with me? That's what I asked him.

'Well, as usual you got yourself stuck right in the middle of it,' he told me, all matter of fuckin' fact. Apparently, he went on, I'd bumped into the right people at the wrong time. Literally.

'Hold on,' I said. 'Just grab your dick for a second, pal. What do you mean "as usual"?'

He said I'd have to ask Angie about that, but he told me that Dickson feller came through another of the rips, with some others too. And they were still out there.

'The demons can take many forms,' he said. 'Our friends help us spot them. That rip was inside the perimeter though, which is rare but still happens. Best we can figure is it's random, like the very fabric of the universe is splitting at the seams. It started two years ago, with just the one rip, right outside Eden here. Now we have another opportunity to stop it.'

My stomach was still acrobaticising. So the 'pocalypse, right here and now? And we could *stop* it? Coloured me a shade of curious, that did.

I asked him, 'So how come you got a ten-year-old girl in the hot seat?'

Sean laughed. 'Marty… Angie's not ten years old, and she's not a girl. Angie's an angel. Straight from Heaven.'

12

Angie came back into the room. Dogs, she called them. Those giant red horsey-lizardy-plastic-fuckin' demon beasts. Barely had my stomach stopped throwing shapes on the anatomical dancefloor than it got going again with the thought of having one of them back inside me. More were coming at some point, she said, but Heaven was a little light on manpower given everything that'd been going on. Course I'd assumed something again – that it was just us there in little England bein' besieged by those fleshy bastards, but Angie put me right straight on the matter. They were hitting the world with the hammer of Hell, all of it that was left. It was the clean-up operation; the real ends of the Earth.

It was just me and her in that room then, the one off the main ops room.

She told me I weren't gonna believe what she had to say next, but it'd be easier to show me.

Out of nowhere she suddenly sprouted up, her body and arms and legs – well, *all* of her really – to about three times the little girl's size, and then bigger, and bigger still, until she were towering over me. Her face changed, twisting up and back is the best description I can manage, and then she put her arms out straight level with her shoulders, from which sprouted these giant flaps. Man, she looked like a giant *bat*.

Her voice came even bigger the next time, but it wasn't just in the room. It was *in* me. It shook through my whole body.

'This hurts,' she said. 'My true form... revealing it... takes... tremendous effort. As will this, but you need to see.' Then she moved right up to me, her big arms and those bat-wings coming down around me. I was plunged into darkness. Then I no longer felt her around me. My eyes were closed, but I could see – and what I saw stuck my balls back inside my body.

It was a bird's eye view – hey, an angel's eye view, I s'pose – of the Earth, looking down from space at the beautiful planet. Then I started to see small red blotches on the surface, like droplets of blood. Then my view got closer, and closer still as it rushed down through the stratmosphere and through the clouds. Those red blotches weren't blood – they were fires. I didn't feel anything then – I was just there, watching, weightless and disbodimented.

One of those flying hell beasts appeared, then another, and after a few seconds I guess there were hundreds and then thousands. We followed them down to the surface. I saw London being torn to shreds. St Paul's Cathedral, the Shard, the Gherkin, the old Houses of Parliament... *everything* was on fire. Further down still, I saw those beasts devouring all around them. My gaze fixed on a poor soul, a lady getting on in years. The beast had her held up by the throat and just squeezed. Damn, her head popped off, her body just falling to the ground. Then it spiked through her head with a claw sharp as a samurai sword, mushing it to shit.

My view turned around then whizzed real quick down at the street level like a hawk going for a mouse. Few seconds later we were in an area without fire, in a quiet road up somewhere nice in the North. Coulda been someplace like Finchley or Camden. This guy in a suit walked along the road, then crossed up to the town houses and knocked on a door marked '9'. The door opened but before I could see inside the view drew back into the air again, looking down. Lord, there was one of them suited guys outside every house down that street. At the same time they all raised up their arms and started changing, just like Angie did before, into these giant creatures. 'Cept not like her... they'd twisted into the same hell beasts I'd just seen filling the sky and popping people's heads off like fuckin' watermelons. We stayed hoverin' up there and didn't see them tearing the people apart, but their screams told me all I needed to know.

And then there was this bright light. Angie shuffled away, shrinking back to her human form. Her voice was back to normal. Well, still with that gravity to it, but not like the one that went right through me before.

'You have seen what I have seen. This vision... is going to come to pass.'

Course I, being somewhat a champion of lateral thinking, fell back on the bed of logic.

'If it's going to happen, what's the point of trying to stop it?'

Angie regarded me with her deep eyes. 'Now is not the time.' She thought for a while. I just stood there, the image of that woman's head turning to slush. Then she said: 'The 'pocalypse is not for now. It is not for your lifetime, nor that of your descendants, nor theirs. When humans die, their souls pass on into other living matter or, if they are finished here, into Heaven or Hell.'

'Finished here?' I asked. 'What do you mean?'

'A soul's Earthly lifecycle, just like on the other humanoid planets, is not finite or infinite. There are achievements to…'

She trailed off. 'Achieve?' I offered.

'Yes, to achieve. Most humans sit in the middle, neither achieving nor not achieving. Those conditions do not earn one a place in Heaven or in Hell. But those who achieve in the right measures are granted their places.'

That ain't how anyone taught me things in my fifty years. Far as I knew, there weren't any Heaven or Hell but as the religerisers said it, you lived like a saint and you'd go be with the creator – everyone else was gonna sit in some eternal fire, burning their arse cheeks off.

The girl read my mind. 'No, that's not right.'

'So this…' I said. 'This 'pocalypse brings it all forward?'

Angie sighed. 'No. Not exactly. See, what has happened was not foreseen and it was foreseen. And you and I, we have met many times before. Many times.'

My bullshit radar started bleeping.

'I think I'd remember that,' I said, I guess a little on the side of sarcasm.

'You wouldn't,' she said. Damn, her eyes turned cold and she fixed me hard, turning my smug smile downwards. She said, 'This is the day – the single day when a difference can be made. There's a tear, and we need you to go through it.'

Course I had no idea what she was on about. So she told me: those tears that the demons come galloping through… well, there's one that's different. And every time this time comes around someone gets sent into that tear, back to the time before. Before those nukes went flying a hundred years ago. Yep, into the past.

My mouth was dry. I swallowed hard involunteerily and it hurt. She carried on: every time this time comes around, on this day, something changes. Every time someone goes back, that someone is the someone who was different that time around. The events of the last couple days, she said, she'd lived through many times. Before that, the events were different.

My head was spinning with this hoo-hah. I was the guy. The different guy. She'd met me before many times, but I'd always done the same thing – Angie and her pet dog-demon kill that Dickson feller and me and Sally and Georgio get involved. Then it all happened the same up to the point where we got to escaping together. See, in all them times before when she'd gone to take my hand, I'd refused it and we'd parted ways soon after when I took the road to Esher. Angie had always had to play along, over and over.

If it had gone the same way as before, she'd have gone on to play the events as they progressed and waited for the change – *any* change at all. And she said there *always* was a change. She was sure sorry for what happened in the police station, but she'd always had her grunts following the action just in case. And none of that mattered anyhoo – they'd all be dead, along with everyone else, soon enough.

So me changing my action there for whatever reason, well it comes down to what Angie calls some butterfly effect. So whoever went back last time, they did something that ended up with me doing what I did.

Now in the presence of a bona fide angel I made to watch my language a little. 'No fudgin' way.' I had of course with religious intenderment initially pegged to say the big F. 'I ain't up for this.'

'Yes, you are.' She said those words with some power I ain't ever felt before. 'You *are* up for this. It's too important not to happen. Heaven is not ready for this and God is absent. The real apocalypse must come to pass, which means this false one has to be stopped. There's no getting around it. Even if you don't go willingly, you're going through that tear. Today.' Angie looked over at the clock on the wall, then she said: 'In about an hour.'

13

Hot damned biscuits in a brown beer barrel. Willingly or unwillingly, I was going. I set about putting my mind to the quandary while Angie regarded me with those cold eyes. Hell, I could go make a difference, but what difference would that be?

She uncoupled my carriage from the train of thinking: 'Every time we send someone back, they take this book.' She handed it to me. 'As far as they make it down the road, what they do or don't do goes in here. And there's some general guidelines about what you have to do, what you absolutely cannot do, and what you should do. There is a singular point at which the false 'pocalypse can be averted. You will read about the monster John Thump. He must be stopped. We recover the book and use it to help future sorties, as no one yet has managed to get to that point.'

I had to ask her what sorties were. She looked annoyed, but gave me the definition. Those sorties – zooks, I like the word, okay? – were detailed in that book. I flicked the pages. Hundreds of them. Some very short. I read one page that simply said 'fuck this, and fuck the future'; another read 'I've come back to before my grandparents were born. I never met them.' There weren't anything after that. Who knows what fate became of these people? I supposed I could track them down when I went back on my sortie.

She was in my head again. 'There's no time for that. They probably died too. We know some of them did. You have to follow the path.'

I never did much in the way of reading, but for the next half an hour or so I read as much of those longer reports as I could. The lengthiest went on for thirty pages or more. I read that one all the way. Holy shit. That girl did a lot, or so she claimed, and some of it not even related to the stopocalypse. That's my word, by the way. Mine, all mine. My mission: Stopocalypse. I started feeling aroused, you know. Not down in the penis, but of my whole self. I was about to get a shot at something. I wasn't getting to that gig anyway.

'So I do this,' I asked her, 'and we never come to this point again? That what you're saying?'

'That's right,' she said. 'You have to stay away from your life as much as possible, to ensure you remain here. It seems you did anyway, or you probably wouldn't be here now.'

I nodded, as if I had any fuckin' clue anyhoo. Angie carried on: 'Use the book. Follow the path. There is no easy way to ascertain the variables that will lead to salvation. But you have to try. It's your turn.'

She led me out of the mansion and back into that labyrinth of laboratories, and as we went more people came up behind and joined us. Once outside again, which came as something of a sweet relief to get some air again, Angie walked me a good distance away and we turned back to face the wall of people.

'We always do this. They need to say goodbye. It helps,' she told me. 'It's on you now. God bless you to succeed.' That wall of people, though, weren't looking at me. They were looking off past me and Angie. I followed their gaze. Then it happened. The tear – it just came from nowhere, sitting like a window with no frame in time and space. We were all transfixed on it.

'It is time,' Angie said. She put her hands on mine. I expected her to go back to that bat-like form, but she didn't. I was gladdened a bit at that. I told her I needed to know something before I went.

'What did you mean when you said Heaven isn't ready for this and God is absent?'

She regarded me closely. Her eyes warmed up a little. Then she did sprout up, her head levelling with mine. She pressed her forehead against mine, and in that instant I saw it: the universe laid before me, a billion-quintillion-wazillion stars as bright as each other, and then one much brighter than all. We zoomed to it. When I say zoomed, that's no understatement. And I should say I ain't good with numbers, so my approximation of illions ain't necessarily accurate.

I digress. It's hard to describe these moments with visual claritiseness. Once Angie did that shit, it was like being in the film, not just close up on the characters but seeing through their eyes. It was the last time that ever happened, so I make sure to remember it often as I can.

So we zoomed in, and there it was. Some kind of planet much like the Earth, but not the Earth. That was where He was, though I didn't understand why He couldn't come back.

Her voice was in my head too. She spoke, soft as the breeze over Eden: 'We are one of many, but there is only one Heaven. What is happening here must be stopped for all.'

Angie let go of me then. I smiled at her, face to face, and her warm eyes went warmer still. She'd done this so many times before. She pointed to the book under my arm. 'It's all in there. The path. Follow it to the point, then write your own story.'

I looked down at that book, shrugged, said 'OK' then put my other hand up to the crowd. A bunch of them looked over. Then one started clapping. Another joined him and whistled. Then after a few seconds they were all doing it, cheering me.

I only looked back once, at Angie. She smiled. I walked into the tear.

PART 2

1

Supercalifuckerylisticexpialidoughnuts!

I was there. I'd made it. Me. A relic from the future, bounced back to before I was even a little jizzpole jostling for position in my father's nuts. For such a miraculous event, it's not something that lends itself to grand terms, so I'll put it as simple as day turning to night: I stepped through that tear, with that angel and all those people waving, and came out the other side. Just an empty clearing, same as before, that trapdoor entrance down to that underground lab. A hundred years earlier. I was somewhere in the region of minus fifty years old.

Hell's bells, I was in a pickle. All of a sudden the shit hit me, right on the nose. Figuratively that is. There weren't no actual flying turd. That kid had force-fed me a bunch of religerised claptrap and I'd swallowed it all with hardly a murmur. I mean, really, telling someone they're about to sail across the sea of time and prevent the end of the world is kinda a big deal.

But an angel? It was the convenient icing on a cake of confusement – I'd been there, in the right place at the right time, and it was, she said: *my turn*. Zooks and cheesy balls, I didn't have a choice anyway, but now it was a rankle on my wankle: if angels have big bat wings, and hang around with scary plastic red attack horsedogs, all them religerised stories from my childhood were wrong. And every Christmas tree top with an angel on it? They need to swap those for gargoyles and werewolves.

I'd been raised by parents of a faith, and to their minds there was a narrow path to Heaven. God made everything and chucked his boy down to sort stuff out when it went bad. After that, there's not a lot. The Muslims – well, they have their own God, and far as I know there's other religers with theirs. Always seemed to me they were one and the same, just in different languages. I didn't pay much attention to all that, but I did prick my ears up at school.

All the fighting I'd been taught about always came down to religers. Except the last war, the one that kicked a nuclear foot into the balls of humanity. That one was, so we learned from our esteemed educators, down to one single thing: the mad Republican leader, one John Thump, pissed all over the Russians' breakfast in some giant diplomatic incident gone tits-up.

Meanwhile the US President, Joseph Johnson, couldn't do anything about it. The second American civil war had left the country fragmented. Now only a handful of States involved themselves in that civil shit, but it was enough to make a split and wave goodbye to that crazy constitution they always harped on about. A constitution that said it was everyone's legal right to carry a gun, for fuck's sake. Well, that civil war would've been a lot less warry if they weren't all shootin' and shit.

Anyhoo, Thump had made a deal with Johnson to job share; well, kinda like that. I don't recall the specifics. Johnson got to keep his title and Thump got a wing of The White House. None of that mattered anyway. Once Thump got his leg over on Mother Russia, the nukes flew. It had been a long time coming. Russia was under increased world scrotumy 'cause they'd been the wrong side of audacious in other people's considered 'pinions. The hostility between North Korea, Russia and the US, and a lot more besides, was boiling over.

And it all came down to immigration, so we were told. Now back in my version of London, all that's left on the Earth far as I know, we're a rainbow of all the colours of man, woman and child. And I like living under that rainbow. There's no immigration or exports there anyhoo. We're stuck like shit to a shoe.

And there I was, the only man of my time to experience time travel itself, about to stop that prick. That was the least of my worries, it turned out.

2

Save the world. Stop the false 'pocalypse. Course it had occurred to me just then that I didn't know *where* I was at all. Was it a hundred years back, more or less? And geographically speaking, I was as good as lost. Hell, not just geographically: I was lost in all respects. A fish not just out of water, but floating in a cosmic toilet. First things first, I had to get out of that clearing – I didn't want to run into any scientists or security, or anyone for that matter just yet – and find somewhere safe to get my bearings.

So that's what I did. I walked back up that track to where those men had brought me the day before – my approximisement of it anyhoo – and carried on for a bit. It wasn't long before I came to a road. Zooks, those cars! Now in my time there are cars and vans and electric cycles, but they don't look like these. Well, some of them were kinda similar looking, but there were so *many*.

Then it hit me: the air. Clean and crisp, not sheltered under radiation domes. This was real, from one end of the Earth to the other – the eternal breeze. I stood watching those cars for a while, then wondered what to do next. Guess I stood there like a lemon for a while before I remembered the book in my pocket. I took it out, flicked it open and read the first page. At the top it said 'IMPORTANT'. Then the rest said:

'Thank you for going back in time to save the world.' *Yep, fine. Happy to assist.*

'This book is your best weapon. Guard it with your life and do not ever lose it. Do not tell anyone about it. Record your experiences.'

Yeah, keep a diary in this magic book. Right.

The next page had 'START HERE' stuck at the top. Under that, just this: 'There's an envelope of money in your pocket. Use this for whatever is necessary. Do not waste time.'

An envelope in my pocket, huh? I checked. Sure enough, that bat-baby must've slipped it in there. I thumbed it open and there was a wad of paper money. I'd never held any of that before. In my time we paid for everything with our creds. Paper was dead too – we needed all our trees just to survive. Although I'd learned to write as a boy, it was never on paper.

I did a quick count to see what was what. Man, I had no idea what it was worth at that point, but in my time ten grand was a lot of money. I guessed it had to be enough to get me to America anyhoo. That's where Thump was, so I s'posed that's where I needed to be.

Soon as I put the envelope back in my pocket and started perusing the book, a car pulled over to the roadside just in front of me. I looked up to see two guys smiling at me. One of them started chittering.

'Hey, old dude. You lost?' I kinda felt I was, so I nodded.

'Love the hair, dude!' He grinned at me. I grinned back, then remembered what he was talkin' about. That groove in my hair, two inches wide and smooth as the moon. I reached up and felt it.

'So you wanna lift mate?' he called. Yeah, I guessed I did. It was either that or a long walk, in no certain direction. And I had money. I could pay them something in return.

I got in the back. 'Fuck on, guys' I said. They giggled at that.

'Fuck on?'

I'd not heard it as a question before. 'Yeah,' I said. 'Fuck on!'

We introduced ourselves. Now what happened next I s'pose was a bit on the silly side. The guy in the passenger seat was called Dave. He lit up a joint – first real, non-digital one I'd seen since I was a teenage prick – and after the driver, who called himself Frosty, had taken a blast on it, it was offered to me. Having never been much into the smoko, I dunno why I took it, but take it I did. My pipe from back home, still there in my top pocket, was strictly for synthetic tobacco. This joint though: it was smooth, silky smooth. A few minutes later, my cheeks were red and my face hurt from laughing. Clearly those guys had been smokin' for a while. I reckon I caught them up too, with my first jay in twenty-five years.

Course they'd asked me where I was headed. Turned out they were headed up to Epsom. They'd picked me up just outside Dorking. Back in my time, both those places were dives – the real shittiest of holes; slums. Here, they were beautiful.

Course they also asked me where I was from and what I was doing at the roadside. Then Frosty asked me what part of America I was from. America? Shit, I told him, I was as English as he was. My accent was odd to him, I realised, so I came up with some bullshit answer: my parents were American and I'd spent a lot of time out there but never lost the accent. That settled his curiosity, it seemed.

We rolled into town about forty minutes later I guess, baked like Alaska.

I told them I had to get the train to Wimbledon. I wanted to see my old place. Well, my new place. My place that one day might still be mine. Not that it was mine anyhoo. Everything was rented from The Council in my time; no more property ladder, as I recall it was known. Sure, one or two people still owned their places, but there weren't hardly any houses or flats that ever went up for sale.

Dave piped up. 'No, not yet, man. Let's get into the pub. I'm gasping.'

All told, I thought there and then I deserved a drink. So I agreed. Big mistake.

3

Dorking. That word went round and round in my head as I tried to focus on the room. Twelve hours I'd been asleep. Guess my body needed it. Twelve hours since 3am and crashing in this squat with these fuckin' stoners.

'Fuck on,' one of them said from across the room. 'Yeah,' I said, getting up to my elbows, 'fuck on.' My eyes adjusted and I saw Dave there, sitting cross-legged and rollin' another joint. 'I fuckin' love fuck on,' he said. 'Fuck on is genius. Man, *you*... are a... *genius*.'

Now followin' my story closely enough will lead one to conclude that I ain't no genius in the traditional sense. I've got my talents, sure, and maybe they're on the expert side and possibly even world-class, but I can't take credit for 'fuck on' in any respect apart from introducing it back to a couple of stoners a hundred years ago. I guess it didn't catch on anyhoo, given it became a part of acceptable parlance well into my lifetime and not before.

There'd been a Council-led campaign to manufacture an atmosphere of positivity in New England. That involved, amusingly, changing 'fuck off' to 'fuck on'. And you know what? It worked! Simple as that, 'fuck on' became the standard greeting. Now if you didn't venture forth a 'fuck on' you'd be considered as riding in the rudemobile, but I guessed back a hundred years ago they'd yet to enjoy that eureka moment.

Still, these boys went for it. They liked me and I liked them. That night had been wild. Hell, in the space of six hours or so I'd been exposed to the full force of 2016 pub culture and much more besides. We took a table at the Setting Sun pub, where we'd had what I would call *quite enough* – and we're talking beer here, beer like I'd never tasted before. Beer. Shit, let's not dally around this one: beer is beautiful. I tried about seven or eight of those. Then it was back to the squat, about half a mile up the road, in a quiet dead end. There were houses boarded up – a whole bunch of them. We went in there, fizzin' and hungry. More joints, more beer. Sleep.

So there I was, staring across at Dave. I told him I was most grateful for his hospitalism and made to make my farewells. He said: 'Come back and see us when you're done.'

'Done what?' I enquired, confuzzically.

'Killed that Thump twat!' he laughed. Then he put the joint in his mouth and sparked it up.

Frosty appeared in the doorway, looking as rough as I felt. His eyes drooped like a grandmother's cuckoos. He joined the conversation: 'Did you find the book?'

Damn, that felt like a boot in the arse. The book. What about the frickin' book? Oh shit – it became clear as the snowdrop on the end of an eskimo's bell. Last night, in the pub, I'd left the book. As some vague recollection sprang back into my sore mind, I saw all the pieces of the puzzle I needed to follow the story: we'd left just as the pub closed, and then when I realised I'd left the book we went back and there was no one there; it was all locked up. Now it was 3pm the following day and I had to get back there. Dorking. No, not Dorking. Dorking. No! I had to shout it internally. 'No, not fuckin' Dorking. Stop banging on about Dorking!'

I got up to my feet and then, thinkin' it'd best be checked, patted my other pocket. I'd been keeping the book in the left and the money in the right, 'cept now the book was gone the money mighta been too. Thank all the forces of the universe, it was there.

Dave noticed. 'Thought we would steal your money?' He looked all kinda fakey-upset. 'You need that for your big mission!' He and Frosty laughed. Then I remembered again: oh shit, I'd been reading them bits of that book in the pub, and they were laughing so hard that I just kept going. As I didn't have my guitar to entertain, I s'pose I fell back on my supreme ability to tell a story. Then the weirdest part of it, I recalled – it was only me who could see the words. Like a bolt of bambuzzlement ejaculated from the dick of surprise, I was showing them it as I was readin' it, but man they were laughing so hard and said they couldn't see shit. To them, the pages were blank.

That's how I came to leave the book. We took it up to the bar and were showing the barman, to see if he could see the words like I could and they couldn't. Turns out he couldn't, or wouldn't. He was busy, see, and served us a bunch of shots. That was the end for us, between then and getting told it was time to leave. I guess I could barely see by the end of that session.

Now I had to get back to the Setting Sun. I delivered my thank-yous and farewells and passed a bunch more squatters on the way out. I'd spent a fair few hours in squats myself. Happy days, mostly. But I shoulda known, as I found out once I made it back to the pub, they'd have at least some of that money. And so they had. Just five of the hundred notes. I vaguely remembered giving it to them. They were good guys, I s'pose.

Once I got up to the bar and asked about it, the barman did something that strangered me out – he made this gesture over my shoulder. Next thing I knew, I was flanked by these two guys in suits. They'd each got hold of one of my arms and led me out through some doors into an outdoors bit. I think we'd smoked a joint out there the night before. I hadn't been this darkened about the events of an evening in a long time. Not that it mattered much, given what was coming.

There was a guy sat at a table in the middle of the little courtyard. The heavies dumped me into the seat opposite him and stayed standing at my side.

'Hello, Marty,' he said. 'Fuck on. Lost something?'

Over the course of some two or three minutes we danced around it. The guy asked me questions and I awkwarded around them. Then he slapped his palms down on the table and leaned forward. Up until that point he hadn't seemed so angry. Then he most certainly was irked up to the balls. I flinched. Those heavies' hands settled on my shoulders.

'Where's the book?' Plainly, he wanted to know where the book was. As did I. I told him I didn't know. Gave me a shock to the socks when he pulled it out from under his jacket and chucked it onto the table in front of me. Course my eyes widened and met his expression of unhidden contempt.

'What does it say on page three of this book?'

Damn, I felt foolish. 'Um... I think it says something about keeping a hold of it,' I told him. He nodded, then smiled, then frowned. 'It's your bible. You know how important the bible is?' I chuckled. Couldn't help it, given his accent made it sound like 'bibble'.

'The bible as in *The Bible*?' I enquired.

'Yes, *The Bibble*,' he said. 'That's *your* bibble. It's not *The Bibble*, but it's your bibble.'

I fixed him with an odd stare. 'How do you know about the book? It's...'

He interrupted me: 'You don't think we'd go to all this trouble to bring you back here and just leave you to it?'

He told me his name was Gabe. I spoke up in defension of myself.

'Well, Gabe,' I told him, firm as a dead man's cock, 'I'm a little out of my depth here. Yesterday I was a hundred years away and now I'm here and I guess kinda superwhelmed by it all.' He looked at me blankly, as if waiting for me to continue. So I did, but damn strange as anything I'd seen in the last few days, his voice said it at the same time as mine: 'And what's with the bat wings?'

Then he laughed hard. While I was busy processering the bizzare event, he stood up and sprouted. Like out of nowhere, they flew out of his side like big meaty curtains. 'So we're not white and fluffy,' he said, before receding them back into his body. 'So what?'

I shrugged, not feeling any other kind of response appropriate at that point. Then he said: 'Anyhoo, as you are so fond of saying – which, by the way, is irritating as hell.'

I winced a bit at that. Irritating, moi?

Then all of a sudden the situation changed, big time. I almost made another stinky deposit in the Bank of Pants, but managed somehow to hold it in. See, this is another of those things that defies easy explanation. I'll attempt it anyhoo. Yeah, anyhoo. Suck it.

The air got sucked out of the place and even though we were outside, it was like the walls closed in on us. Yeah, there weren't any walls, but it was as if the sky and the ground and everything around just started focusing in on us there. A second or two later Gabe faded from view and it was just black. I tried to draw breath, but there was nothing, as if I didn't *need* to breathe.

Then his voice came out of the blackness, and instantly I felt myself lift off the seat, just floating above it, but I couldn't see nothin' so I guess I just assumed it was still under me.

His voice was loud, clear, as if right inside my head: 'This is what is coming...'

Faaaaaaaaaaaaaaaaaaaaaaaaaaaaaaaaaaaaaaaaaaaaaaaaaaaaaaaark.

If I had to describe the feeling, which I kinda do now, I'd say it's like a screwdriver plunged right into the centre of the brain, twisting around and mushing the shit out of it. And then that stopped and all the colours came into view. Just like back before with Angie, I was seeing through another pair of eyes. We started up above the clouds, watching some grim display of giant rockets filling the sky all at once, some of them hit by other, smaller ones and blowing up right there, but others made it through.

My vicarious view latched on to one of those showers, following it closely in the mess of burning fuel and everything around it warping in its wake. Followed it right down to the Earth. I don't know where it was, but at the point of impact everything slowed down to a crawl. The cluster of missiles tore right through rooves and walls and right into the ground beneath, going down a good distance before releasing their payload. Then my view zoomed back out and there I hovered above that town, seeing it all.

Some kid, he can't have been older than seven or eight, was ripped apart like foam in a bubble bath – just vaporised in a flash; then I realised it was in a park and got the full force of the horror of it: mothers and fathers and their

58

sons and daughters all gone the same way as the fire of hell rained upon them, their heads popping open and their brains turned to mist. All of them gone.

I couldn't breathe – there was no atmosphere in this ringside seat, nothing to suck in or dispense – but I wanted to scream, or just to get down there with them and have it all be over and done, but in an instant I was ripped away from it and put somewhere else.

Those eyes showed me a city. Skyscrapers, bridges and a wide river. I guessed it was somewhere in Europe, or America. That wasn't relevant anyhoo. They wanted me to see the carnage, and see it I did. Blood, a whole lot of blood. People's faces melting away, the skin just falling off into their hands and then their eyeballs, stuck in full surprise and horror, popping out and splatting on the ground with this muffled squelch. Cars smashing into each other, alarms and sirens wailing, and screaming at a volume no one could ever be comfortable with building to a crescendo where I thought my own eyes were about to eject. That sound filled *all* of me.

I saw it all – my host taking me from death to death, watching the sickening final moments of thousands of these people who had no idea it was coming, pawns in a game played by a handful of people who weren't playing by the rules.

Through the red mist, all that was left was the buildings, and the bridges, and the river, with all signs of the souls that made those things meaningful lying in pools of themselves. Then everything went black again. Pitch black. Suddenly I felt like I was rushing somewhere, propelled through that darkness and going faster every second. And then it all stopped again, and I was left there in that state for what seemed like hours. Genuinely, hours. That whole time those images filled my brain. I wanted to scream, to react in some way, any way… but all I could do was hang there in the darkness seeing in my mind's eye those people being torn apart and melting into themselves.

Wham! Just like that, out of nowhere, I was back in that seat, with those two hench-holes at my side and Gabe leaning across the table.

'So if you thought for a second you could come back here and just hang around and get stoned, if you just want to wait around and watch the fireworks, I'll kill you right here and right now. I've done it many times before and judging by your performance so far, I'll be doing it again and again. But I get a sense that you might see things a little differently now. Hmm?'

Man, it all came at once then – that terrificating assault on my senses, some kind of spiritual motion sickness and the fact I could suddenly breathe again… I chucked last night's shenanigans all down myself. It came out like a bucket from a first floor window, just one huge sloshing mess sploshed down onto my clothes. It was still dripping from my chin when I looked up at Gabe.

'Don't mess this up again.' He clicked his fingers – everything turning to black once more, the click sharp and snappy like a branch breaking in my brain.

5

Rewind, fast-forward or whatever else: I was back in that clearing, thankfully back in my clothes before I'd chucked up all over them. For a minute I just stood there, numb from the assault on my senses and sensibilities. Then I realised I was holding something.

I clasped that book tight. Tight as I'd hold my own schlong during some happy alone time or precision pissing. Then I opened it up to page three. My mission; the rules of the game. Don't lose the book. Gabe'd given me a second chance.

I made it up to the roadside and stood waiting for Frosty and Dave to turn up, assuming they would. Instead of watching the cars, I flicked through until I found an entry that gave me something to do – something better than getting baked with a couple of feckless dudes.

There it was, some advice of the sage variety: get to America. I'd need a passport. To go anywhere you needed a passport, just like in my time to cross from South to North London you needed enough creds in your account and a chipped tooth.

To get hold of a passport, I'd need to take someone's identity. To do that, I'd need to be a little bit cunning, and maybe – according to the contributor of this wisdom – a little murderous.

Zooks, I hadn't been feeling particularly murderous, being raised somewhat in the pacifistic frame. I was also lacking in any self-encouragement to kill Thump in the first place. What I didn't know was why I had to kill the guy. If there were so many players in this game of 'pocalyptic pissantery, why him? I didn't even have the first idea about how to do that. I vaguely recalled Dave and Frosty laughing at me when I told them what I had to do. Dave said he knew someone who had a bat and could mess people up for a price. That wasn't my style, and it was hardly the solution to this problem.

And I'd read a lot of entries in this cosmically incredible book, but was still not particularly wisened by them. Indeed, some were all for killing people and others weren't. I was the type to seek a peacefulled resolution. But no one had gone so far as to get close to Thump, or anyone else for that matter.

Before despair could set in, those guys turned up right on time. But this time it was different; it had to be. I'd spent a wild night with them, but they'd not met me before. I steered the conversation my way.

Neither of those guys had left England, ever. I guess it didn't come as any surprise and hey, I couldn't stand to make a judgement on that as up to that point, I hadn't ever left my environs either.

So how, I enquired, could I get hold of a passport? Dave told me straight: 'You need a National Insurance number, a registered address, and proof you are who you say you are.'

Course, I wasn't in possession of any of those things. Then Frosty jumped in: 'How come you haven't got a passport? You must've used one to come here in the first place.'

Ah, course he'd assumed again that I was an American. This time I told him a half-truth: 'Nah. I just watch a load of American TV.'

He looked at me in the rear-view mirror, a look of mild suspicion, then his face lit up. 'You can be me!'

Dave had taken something of a big hit on the reefer. Natch, I declined this time around. Last thing I wanted was another front row seat at The Last Film Ever. Anyhoo, he spat that smoke right out, his body convulsing in a spasm of unexpected laughter.

'Frosty, ya fuckin' idiot. You can't even manage being you.'

I chuckled at that too. Frosty took the joint from Dave, took a massive drag and held it down for a while. Then he coolly exhaled, passed the spliff back to his friend and fixed his eyes back on me in the mirror.

'Seriously,' he said. 'Abso-fuckin-eriously. A grand. You got a grand, you can be me.'

Well, that was easy.

6

In my future, not everyone has a job. There aren't quite enough things to do, see. Once the world outside was gone, everything in it was too. All those self-justifying industries had gone up in flames. None of that was good. You remove one cog from the machine and the whole thing stops working.

Still, Epsom had a Job Centre. Now on the basis of being offered a slam-dunk piece-of-piss identity swap, I'd committed to jumping onto a bit of a runaway train. Things were about to get super interesting.

I hadn't realised quite what a knee in the nutsack my exposure to this brave old world could be, having been in a state of warm inebriation before. Now, sober as a baby, I drank it in.

The whelming hit me real proper: people, loads of them. Cars, noise... people.

As I walked up Epsom High Street with Frosty, people looked at me kinda funny but I did the same to them. I didn't even feel it like it was real yet. Subreal, I call it. All these guys were staring at devices in their hands. I mean, most of them were. It was creepy. Then occasionally they'd look up to see where they were going and flash me a weird look, then back to their hand-computers. We got those back in my time too, just not quite the same. They're old school to us, super old school. Our stuff's mostly neural, all brain-fired and shit.

Looked like I was one of the only guys not doing that. Frosty, too. Occurred to me the down-and-outs might be the only sane people left, those untouched by this fuckin' soul-draining tech. I walked past a bunch of screens in a shop window, some of them showing a news broadcast about rioters going crazy in some other country. I watched it for a while but couldn't hear what they were saying. Didn't matter. As I knew, what I learned at school all those years ago, this was all part of the problem. And I was there to stop it. The butt plug of humanity. Sent to grab that poop as it comes down the chute and ram it right back in there. Divinely.

Then as if those screens knew I was watching, Thump appeared with the headline: 'Thump clear in polls – Johnson camp could concede.' There he was, just his photo to one side, with the presenter – a woman – looking like she was grimacing through it. Clear in the polls? I felt a jump in my chest –

the shit was happening right there and then. Clearly the guy had believers, despite his problems.

When we got to the Job Centre, Frosty got in a line. Well, he put himself at the back of that line. At the front was some obese guy hanging out of his clothes, sat across a small table from some bored looking fat woman in equally shitty attire. I'm not the kind to remark on a lady's less appealing physical whereabouts, but also I'm not accustomed to seeing people the size of two. I s'pose one silver lining to the 'pocalypse is that all that shit that made people fat back here was gone. We had no sugar, no huge food processing plants producing refined carbohydrisers. Once the dust had settled, we focused back on what started it all off in the first place: fruit and veg, eggs and whatever meat could be vat-grown without those fuckin' vegans going mental.

I looked around. The place was full of no-hopers. S'posed I was one of them now, jobless and – in my case at least – homeless. No prospects, 'cept for saving the world. Me and my army of weird bat-angels and their silent henchmen. Yay for us.

Just then it hit me, a sudden realisationism that maybe this whole thing was a shitcake. Angels, 'pocalypses, time travel... I was trusting what I'd seen less and less when this lovely young kid stepped up to me.

'Can I help you?' She was shorter than me, pretty in the face and with bumps that wouldn't look out of place stuck to my palms. Far too young for me though. Hold on... I was feeling – well, I guess randy is the only word for it. Perhaps the whelming of this buzzing world a hundred years before mine was somehow arousing my loinal apparatus.

Anyhoo, enough of that. There was a job to do, and bein' as I was in the centre of operations dedicated to making people do jobs, I was getting straight to it. Course I told the young lady I was just fine, waiting for my friend. She patted my hand and smiled, then asked if I had anywhere to go. Caught me a bit strangely, that did. Then I looked beyond her and noticed other people were giving me shitty looks. Might it have been my cool, unusual hairstyle with its parting-of-the-Red-Sea vibe, or just the fact that, well, I s'pose I looked a little on the dishevelled side? No matter.

I almost jumped out of my skin when a hand slapped down on my shoulder. Guess I'd become a bit jittered after recent events. 'Dude, we're done.' Frosty grinned at me, his browning teeth lined up like old weathered

64

fenceposts. It was a smile worth a million turds. It was a reminder of his stinky-as-shit breath too, something I'd had the displeasure of many times over that wild night – a night that, as far as he knew, had never occurred. Anyhoo, that winning smile – in terms of being able to win a shitty teeth competition – sent that pretty girl packing for good.

Once we made it back outside, that smell really hit me. I guess we'd been in an air-conned building, so back out on the high street the fumes crawled up my nose and started nailing a pain into the brain. Petrol, I realised. Gas. Pollution. Course in my time there's none of that. Our cars are electric. Pretty much everything is. There's no oil left for us. Well, maybe there is outside our radiation protection, but it's not oil we can get at. Electricity does us just fine anyway. There's no long distance anyone can travel anyhoo. Yeah, anyhoo.

7

Frosty suggested we celebrate our arrangement with a drink in the Setting Sun. Happy as I woulda been any other time, I knew it couldn't happen so I put an excuse in: I don't drink. He looked a touch disappointered, but after a little thought he said it'd be better to complete the transaction in his house. Now, having been to his 'house', I was cautious not to give away that I'd been there before and likewise not to pass comment on the fact that although it looked like a house, on the inside it was more like a waste hole – debris covering every surface, a toilet that looked like it needed its own toilet, and the not so sweet odour of what I can only describe as 'arse biscuits'.

Still, we rocked up there a few minutes later and headed inside. I remained as interested as I could be as he gave me another brief tour of the place, or at least the tour from the front door into his and Dave's little shitpit. Dave was there, unsurprisingly midway in the act of rolling a reefer. We exchanged a little small talk before Frosty gave me the low-down.

He'd gone to the Job Centre to get his info, the info I needed to become him. He'd showed them two pieces of ID from a couple of years previous, when he still lived at home with his parents. One of them was photo ID, so they were happy at the Job Centre on that basis to give him that info. Course, being I looked nothing like him, the need for my own photo ID was kinda pressing. Course, Frosty knew 'a guy'. He'd take me there after I handed over the money.

'It's all I got,' I lied. The way Frosty's eyes lit up – I couldn't see Dave's, obscured as they were by a mushroom cloud of smoke – I could tell he'd never handled that kind of money before. Truth was I hadn't either, but to him it had value. To me, it was sheets of paper I needed to save the world. I s'posed I'd already started.

The warm feeling didn't last long. There was a loud crash, then a scream from downstairs. We all froze in the room. Frosty shrugged at Dave, then they both shrugged at me. I offered my own in return. Gabe? Had I cocked up again?

Another loud bang, another scream, and then sobbing. We heard it clear: 'Please, please, no!' Then silence again.

Our eyes went wide. We looked like three statues competing to win 'best surprised shrug' in the 'oh-fuck-what-do-we-do-now' award. Frosty stuffed the money into his trouser pocket. Dave took another big drag on his spliff before stubbing it out on the floor. Then it was over.

Two guys dressed in tight black suits and kinda ninja-style hoods strode into the room and within probably half a second dropped those two stoners out of existence with some kind of sonic boom – it came out of their *hands*. For a moment they stared at me, motionless as I was, minding maybe I could pull off the statue thing a little longer. Then one of them advanced on me, grabbed me by the arm and slammed his palm into the side of my head.

8

Shit on a brick, my head hurt – approaching double figures for head injuries over the last seventy-two hours. Here again, I was waiting for my eyes to adjust to the room. At first I assumed it was Gabe again, but holy moley it was worse. Much worse.

As my vision began to creep back in, all I could see in my mind was those two hapless stoners crumpled on the floor. Now, thinking more about it, I'm not sure what having hap would mean, but considerin' they were lacking in the hap department I've made my peace with that expression. Maybe the opposite could be hapful. I certainly felt I'd lost a whole load of hap there and then.

There they were, casualties of my crusade. I replayed it in my head: those ninja-like guys, throwing these kind of warping blasts from their hands.

I imagined those blasts entering Dave and Frosty's heads and becoming all confused in the haze of prolonged stonership, their brains effectively mushy and soft like pillows. Like, 'Hey dude, I'm here to kill ya, but let's just chill for a bit first, huh?'

See, somethin' else I'd read about in my bibble was the notion of teaming up. I couldn't do it alone, it said. Just as in the Book of Revelation there was reference to these Four Horsemen of the 'Pocalypse, it was suggested I should find my own. I guessed I was the first Horseman then. Never been much into horses, anyhoo.

A hand grabbed me by my shirt and yanked me up. There was strength in that hand, and the arm attached to it. It righted me to stand, then pushed me forward into the dissipating darkness. I stopped just to let my eyes adjust a bit more and another shove came. I fell down to my hands and knees. The hand yanked me up again.

'Hey!' I shouted. 'Go easy!'

That strong bastard stayed silent as a sneaky fart and just pushed me forward again. Then the lights came on.

We were in a long corridor, dimly lit but with lights that came on overhead as I was frogmarched along it. At one point I went to turn to look at whoever this guy was, but all I got was a glimpse that turned my stomach: a white mask, just blank and expressionless, with this hooked nose coming out of it a few inches. The mouth was straight across and those eye holes – suck-a-million-dicks, they were as black and empty as all of space itself.

He shoved me forward again. I held back an urge to puke. Something about those eyes, almost drinking me in and drowning me in the well. Holy shit.

I kept my eyes forward. 'OK, OK,' I told him. 'You don't need to keep pushing. I'll walk.'

Damn near did puke right then as his hands grabbed my shoulders and twisted me round to face him. I got a better look then. Dressed in a red and black robe, with a hood over the head... just that mask showing. It froze me to the core. He took me by the shirt collar and pulled my face up to his. Those eyes bore into mine like drill bits. I could feel my brain burning behind my eyes, drawn towards the endless black holes of his. Then he pushed me away slightly and lifted his head up, as if aiming something at me.

Second I saw it, out came a wet one from the cack canyon, like a shotgun – or, I s'pose more accurated we can call it a shitgun – blast... a single blast in an unwarranted attack on my trousers. See, I was still somewhat lacking in the underwear department.

I might've paid more attention to the brown river running down my legs if I hadn't seen that long tongue come out of the mask's mouth. At first I thought it was like a snake's forked tongue, but it wasn't: it was thick and red and dry and then, on the end, sharp as any knife I'd ever seen. He had a firm grip on me and leaned in a little closer. Then that sharp end flicked at my nose, cutting it open across the bridge. A spray of my blood shot out onto his tongue and across the mask.

I gasped, shat myself again and dropped to my knees. That guy just stood there for a moment while I sobbed like a kid with a grazed knee, then knelt down right in front of me. I looked up just enough and saw through my tears that tongue coming out again, my blood speckled over it. It curled back as if primed to deliver a killing blow.

Course I couldn't tell this story if I was dead. I was about to find out some very encouraging information about my lifespan, but first I did all I could think of.

'Please, please... please... no, just no, please.' All that shit. Pleading for my life. And it didn't work because no sooner had I finished this pathetic ploy than I was yanked up by someone else. As I was put back on my feet, I realised where I'd seen that tongue before, and those eyes…

'He was only playing,' came the voice from behind me. It was a jolly tone, yanking me up psychologically as well. I turned to face this second man. He continued: 'He could sense that… you've *had* one of his kind. He could smell it on you.'

A droplet of blood dripped from the tip of my nose and landed on my bottom lip. 'Don't worry,' he said. 'It's just a scratch. It won't scar. Much.' His face lit up at that.

I managed to regain some level of composure. 'Where am I?' I demanded.

The man smacked his lips together and smiled at me. 'Nowhere. Literally. That's what we call the place. It's neither here nor there. Nowhere, really.'

9

'Everywhere's somewhere,' I said. The man, still smiling, was obviously keening to put me straight on that. We'd left the corridor and emerged into what I'd call a cavern, but one of stark ornateship. That bastard creature had followed us down the corridor, this time bizarrely on all fours, its robe crumpled around its legs and that eerie fuckin' mask bobbing up and down.

The cavern was huge, more like a dome I s'pose, with a ceiling so high it was mostly cloaked in shadow up there. Light came from what I thought at first were candles but I soon saw were not anything at all – just orbs of light, hanging in the air. The walls of this cavern were ribbed, stretching, and the thing that reminded me I was still poised to puke, moving. Those ribs were veins, I realised. We were inside something *living*.

'No, not here,' he said. 'Not *this* place. In the truest sense, it's not even a place. No, not like that. As I said, neither here nor there. So come on, out with it. You have questions.'

I looked around for somewhere to sit and almost immediately an armchair sprang from thin air. Then another. The man motioned for me to sit in the one closest to me. He was dressed very nicely, I must say. A neat burgundy suit, quite obviously tailored, with a crisp white shirt under a bright red tie. His shoes were darker red, but for want of a better description, just stylish.

Once he'd sat down, barely had I registered the thought that it looked odd without a table than one appeared between us. He smiled at me again.

Then he chuckled. 'Look, I already know what you're going to ask me, so I'll leave it up to you – we can have a conversation or I can just get cracking, so to speak. Thing is though, I don't get much in the way of company down here, apart from Giggles there, so if it's up to me I'd say let's go with the dialogue option. It's more fun that way, isn't it? Hmm?'

'Giggles? That's what you call that thing?' Naturally, I found that a little at odds with its embezzlement of my nasal account.

'Really? No,' he said. 'I said that for your benefit really. Trying to defuse the situation a little. It's, erm, no skin off my nose!'

That set him off laughing and it shook him all over. He was clearly in a state of enjoyment some distance from my own. I looked past him to those throbbing veins, then let my gaze follow them up to the darkness above. Then I could see there was something up there, fleshy and pulsating.

'Don't worry about that,' he said. 'So as you've started us off down the dialogue route, firstly you'll be wanting to assign me a moniker.'

'A moni-what now? You want me to call you Monica?'

He laughed his arse off again. Once he stopped, he fixed me cleanly: 'Of course I knew that was coming, but it was still *funny*.' That set him to another bout of chuckles. Gotta admit, I was kinda liking the guy. He was, all things considered – and by that I mean the fact he'd just murdered my new friends, abductered me to some fleshy prison and let his puppy have a go at sucking my face off – a pretty amiable kind of guy. A bit like me, I guess.

'Well, that's very good to know,' he said. 'I like you too, if that helps. So... ask me about whatever you like.'

First things first: who was he? He said I could call him Monica if I liked. I said no, not really. After a little dilly-dallying, we settled on Roger. That was his idea. Next up: where were we? He said it again – *nowhere*. It wasn't on any map. In terms of how humans always had to peg things in terms they understood, he said it didn't exist. Not in human terms. So I asked him what it was in his terms.

'Now that,' he said, 'is something I've already explained. You can't understand these things in my terms – just like I have trouble sometimes understanding things in yours. But that's by the by. Believe it or not, I'm here to assist.'

'Assist how?' I asked. 'What do you know about my mission?'

Well that just set him off again. He got me laughing too. Truth is I didn't know what I was laughing at. Giggles, who was sat a few feet away, let out a low growl.

'There's nothing I don't know about anything,' he said, wiping his eyes. 'Look, I'll make this easy for you.'

He stood up from the table, which vanished as soon as he did. Then he put his arms straight up and in an instant – quite literally, I must stress here – just went up in flames. A moment later his physical form was all gone, replaced by this pillar of fire towering above me. A face began to emerge from the flames, shaped from the licking, lapping fiery chaos.

His voice this time was deep, crackly and seemed to fill the fleshy cavern. 'No, I'm not a man, nor am I fire, nor am I anything you might want me to be. I simply am. No, I am not God either. God does not come here. The reason you are here is because I need you to be. I have an offer for you.'

Roger – geez, I wasn't entirely comfortable calling a terrifying pillar of fire Roger, or anything for that matter – paused for a moment, then continued: 'They would have died anyway. Did you know they were both called Dave?'

I shrugged. He continued: 'The world is in a perilous state, and you are here to save it. I need that to happen too, but there are some things I must insist remain off-limits, so I've slightly altered a few bits here and there. The corridor back there, those doors – you wondered what is behind them. Quite simply, my sustenance. What I need to survive. When the world destroys itself, I lose my sustenance. The act does not destroy me or my slice of nowhere, but it would see me starved out of existence. And Giggles here, he would go hungry too.'

I couldn't be sure if I'd blinked or not, but then as suddenly as he'd set himself ablaze he was back in his seat in human form, smiling at me.

He fixed me with that clean stare again, right into and almost through my eyes.

'Crucially, Martin, there's something you need to know. By your very act of coming back here you've become immortal. That should give you some heart to go forward. Well, to a point. But for now at least you're safe. No one can harm you except yourself. By which I mean, you can hurt anyone, yourself included, but no one can harm you. Not physically, at least. If the angels have blessed you this far, then you have nothing to fear. But yet, I wouldn't trust them at all. And yes, you're wondering: can you trust *me*? Maybe. What you have is free will – as does every man, woman and child. The information I'm giving you is yours to do with as you will. My life, apparently, rests in your hands.'

I sat there with my slack jaw, locked into Roger's gaze. I couldn't break it at all.

'Before we part company, let me be clear: there's war in the Middle East. The US is in flux with the chance of either a liar or an idiot for their President. The Russians are seething. The North Koreans are firing warning shots at China. Racism is spreading like a virus and there really isn't a solution to that. Your options are limited and the window will close sooner than you think. I can offer one more piece of advice: find your first Horsewoman. You'll meet her anyway, very soon. Recruit her. That is vital.'

He stood up again and walked over to me, then put his hand out to shake mine.

'That help at all?'

I stood and shook his hand. 'One more thing,' I said. 'Can I borrow some clean trousers?'

10

Time travel. Blacking out and waking up somewhere else. I was becoming good at this, although it's true I had no part in making either happen. Unfortunately by the time I'd re-appeared this time, thankfully decked out in a fetching new set of rags, I took another bang to the head. Cosmic sense of humour these guys had. Hilarious.

See, Roger effectively and quite literally threw me under a bus. He'd simply clicked his fingers and the world went black, as usual. Then when the light came flooding back, I heard shouting, managed to turn around just in time to see the bus coming at me and jumped out of the way. But the bus clipped my leg and sent me flying into the kerb, knocking – yep, surprise – my head and blacking out again.

Why that fiery, amiable, smartly dressed bastard did that became clear pretty soon, but at the time – all seven or so seconds of the situation – I guess I was mighty pissed.

So it was that I found myself back in Kingston Hospital, this time with a thick bandage wrapped about my bonce. Painkillers must've been strong as I couldn't feel it at all. Looking down, my leg was in a brace too. At least I didn't smell of shit anymore. They'd given me a bath.

I went back to sleep for some time, dunno how long. It was dark outside when I woke up though. A pretty young nurse saw I had my eyes open and left the ward, then came back with another, older and even prettier lady who stopped at the foot of my bed. She didn't look at me once, just stared at my notes. Now I'd never seen notes like those before. In my Kingston Hospital, it's all digital. There's no paper anywhere. It was kinda interesting to hear the rustling of it as she flicked the sheet over and back again. Not a lot to see, I thought.

Then finally she looked up at me. 'Dave Frost?'

For a moment I forgot who I was supposed to be. 'Uh, yeah. That's me. Frosty.' I nodded, probably too much.

She eyed me suspiciously. 'Twenty-four years old?'

OK, I was rumbled. I stopped nodding.

'I'm the senior psychiatric consultant here,' she said. 'Dr Susan Poynter. If it's all right with you, I'd like to ask some questions.'

I nodded again. I could manage that.

First she asked me my name. I told her: Marty Molloy. Then she asked why I had Dave Frost's ID. I told her I'd found it. She tutted, then came closer and pulled a seat up so she could sit next to me.

'What part of America are you from?' Course I told her I wasn't from America.

'Listen, sack the bullshit,' she said. 'My job is to tick one of two boxes. The first says you're OK to leave. The other says you're not. If you answer truthfully, I'm more likely to tick the first one.'

'Which one's that?' I asked.

She snarled, transforming her pretty features. 'I just told you that.'

'No, you didn't ma'am,' I said. 'You said there were two boxes, but not which one was the first.'

A few moments I'd put in the drawer marked 'awkward' passed. I don't think I made a good first impression.

'The truth? You want the truth? It's a long story,' I said. 'A very long story.'

Susan was irked, clearly. 'Well I don't have long, so make it the quick version.'

I made it as quick as I could.

'Religious claptrap!' That's what she said, the pompous tart. Now I'd been making an effort to keep my story succincted, while entertaining, but also quite hushy-hush given the ward was kinda busy. But I also knew on the advice of that crazy bastard Roger that I was supposed to recruit a Horsewoman, and for all I knew she could be the one. So I tried to make it compelling.

She leaned in close to me. 'So the result of all this nonsensical babbling, Mr Molloy, is you've been sent to me by some fiery demon who wants me to help you save the world?'

'Yep, that's pretty much it,' I said, unable not to grin.

'Well, there are two problems with that. First, stopping John Thump is rather off the table.'

I shook my head. I didn't know why.

'The President was assassinised last week. So it looks like you can relax.'

Relax? Whaaaaaaat? My pulse started racing. I felt my tongue swelling and my chest got tight all of a sudden. Susan looked down at me quizzically.

'Are you all right, Mr Molloy?' she said, lookin' all semi-un-pitiful.

I looked frantically around, then managed to croak at her: 'The book. Where's the book?'

She reached down, picked it up off the bedside table and handed it to me.

I grabbed it and started fanning the pages. They were all blank.

11

It took me a long while to get settled after that, but once the kindly nurse whacked another shot of morphine into my arm I cracked off to sleep pretty quick.

She'd said Thump was the President – but… hey, Thump was *never* President. And assassinised? These thoughts were rolling around my head as I woke up. How long had I been in there? I barely registered the nurse topping me up again and I missed entirely what she said to me.

Time passed. Then an orderly came by and got me out of bed, put me in a wheelchair and took me for a ride. We went in two lifts, along some long corridors, and ended up in the reception of a psychiatric clinic.

A few minutes later I was wheeled in. The orderly left the room and closed the door behind him. Susan sat there deftly twirling a writing stick between her fingers. Then she got up and came round her desk to sit on it, facing me. 'Mr Molloy,' she said. 'What year is it?'

'Twenty-sixteen, miss,' I said, confident as I was.

She didn't move, not even a hair on her lip. 'You sure about that?'

I nodded. 'Yep. Are you saying it isn't?'

Then she got up and walked over to the wall behind her desk. 'This' – she pointed to the calendar on the wall – 'tells me, and you, that it isn't.'

Being I was half-cut to the painkillers, I couldn't rightly focus on that calendar. Susan noticed I was struggling. She took it off the wall and calmly walked back to me, then dumped it on my lap.

It read: 'October 2019'. I felt my hands and feet tingling, then my head the same, and seconds later I passed out. I guess she brought me round pretty quickly. It was one of the rare occasions I hadn't shat myself. Once I'd regained my composure, she sat back behind her desk.

'You puzzle me, Mr Molloy. Very much so. We ran blood tests and found no chemicals whatsoever in your system. Well, apart from nicotine. So you're not on any drugs, apparently. We've also run a brain scan and found nothing out of the ordinary in there. But your story – well, as unbelievable as it so obviously is, you tell it with conviction. And you seem, I'd say, genuinely surprised to hear that Thump was killed and that it's three years later than you think it is.'

She was twirling that writing stick again. She cocked her head a little and stared off into space, before carrying on: 'But what's really bugging me is your association with David Frost. See, he was a patient of mine, up until he died three years ago in circumstances that you couldn't have known about unless you'd been there.'

My pulse started quickening again. 'The idea that you've travelled back in time, sent by an angel to prevent US President John Thump from destroying the planet...' She paused. 'Well, he did nothing of the sort. In fact, in his two years he did quite a lot of good in foreign relations, got America back on the road to a stable economy, and heralded a crackdown on domestic and international terrorism. All in all, I'd say, I'm struggling to see why you'd want to prevent that.'

I managed a shrug. Truth was, right there and then I was well and truly stuffed. Had I ever been in a comfort zone, it'd been folded up and shoved into my back passage with a broom handle.

'You told me about a civil war in the US, and another one here. Well, by your reckoning they would have occurred last year, and I can tell you they most certainly did not.'

I ventured a deeper shrug. Through the morphine haze I tried to latch on to something, anything, that could explain what was happening.

'So,' Susan went on, 'I'm left with a decision to make. I can refer you on to the inpatient mental health clinic, where you'll be monitored and treated for as long as it takes until you come right again, or I can let you back out into the world. Which would you suggest?'

12

Back in bed, yet more morphine coursing through my veins, I felt strangely flaccid. The drug was strong and foggy. I could feel thoughts just out of reach, unable to focus on just one and reel it in. Had I genuinely lost my marbles? Was any of this real – the time travel or the mission from God or those monsters or Roger and Giggles? Hell, course they were.

I picked up the book again, my bibble. Then it struck me. The blank pages seemed irrelevant – why would I even have this book if it wasn't real? If the book was real, surely everything else could be. I suddenly felt less flaccid. Like the penis of potential rising between the balls of hope, my mind sprang to attention.

I opened the book to page three. Zooks, as accustomed as I'd become to skiddin' my pants to that point, this time I could have done it in celebration. The words were back, but this time different.

It read: 'Get up and get out of there. Now.'

Then, right before my eyes, more words just appeared on the page: 'They're coming for you. Move.'

I guess the adrenaline rush cleared enough of the morphine fog as I found myself kicking off the sheets, unhooking the drip from my arm, and getting upright off the bed. I looked around the ward – one of the nurses saw what I was doing and hurried out of the room. I grabbed the bag with my clothes in, dropped the book in there and hopped it fast as I could with my leg braced up. Out in the corridor, I headed straight for the lift I'd been taken in before. Just as I got in, I heard commotion in the corridor and as the lift doors closed, I caught a glimpse of two armed men striding into the ward. By the sound of it, there were more of them on the way.

I stared at the numbers on the panel, having no idea which to press. I desperately needed to get to Susan. Then I don't know what drew me to it, but I flicked the book open again. As soon as I did, 'Hit 1' appeared. So I hit 1. The lift started down, but as it descended I heard more commotion outside. They knew I was in there. I looked down at the book again, and sure enough, my next move: 'Run right, to the end of the passage. Then look left for another lift. Get in it and press 4.'

I did exactly as I was told, hobbling rather than running. But I guess the book didn't know I was wearing a leg brace. It didn't tell me to take my bag with me either, but considerin' it had all my worldly possessions in it, I considered that common sense. Besides, Roger or whatever his name was had given me some pretty swish rags. I at least fancied the chance to wear them for more than one run-in with a bus.

Course I passed a whole bunch of people in various states of chaos on my travels up to Susan's office. I was huffin' and puffin' and donking my leg up and down on the shiny floor, dragging my bag and moving as fast as I could. They were running and screaming, and some were just sat there watching all this unfold.

When I got there, I dodged past the receptionist station and barged right in. She looked at me with a mix of surprise, anger and, well, may I say arousal... probably a little bit of that anyway, although it could've been the morphine clouding my otherwise spot-on judgement.

As an aside, which I reckon is worth pointing out at this junction, I found Susan something sexy. I guessed she was a little younger than me, maybe mid-forties, but she was slim and had good contours to her cheeks – both sets.

It's not like I had the time to stand and admire her then though. Not particularly sure of how to explain my intrusion, I went straight back to the book.

Sure enough: 'Tell her men have come to kill you.'

I did. She added a layer of surprise to her already many-layers-of-surprise. More words appeared. 'She knows. She told someone who made her call the police.'

My heart sank right then, down as far as my nuts. How could she? I'd been honest with her, and this is what I got in return.

I told her I knew. She stood up quickly, then said: 'What do you mean, come to kill you?'

'I got no idea, miss,' I said, venturing forth all the truth. 'That's what it says in my book here.' I held it up so she could see.

'They're blank,' she said. 'Come on... you expect me to believe that...'

The commotion outside interrupted her. I looked at the book again.

'Open the window and crouch behind the sofa.'

Susan watched me. 'Please, don't give me up,' I said. '*Please.*'

The door flew open, and far as I know – given I didn't want to stick my head out for a duck shoot – a bunch of guys came in pointing guns around.

'Where is he?' The guy's voice was urgent like the onset of diarrhoea.

I could just see Susan's left side and she put her hands up. Then one of those guys came around in front of her. He leaned over behind her. 'Out the window!' he shouted. Then all the guys rushed out again. Susan waited until it was all clear and motioned for me to get up.

'I'm sorry,' she said. 'But was it you?'

'Was what me?' I asked.

'Did you kill Thump? Did you assassinise the President? And David Frost?'

I understood. She'd taken my story and slept on it, maybe even shared it with a confidunte. But arriving at the conclusion that it was me; well, that just hurt.

'No,' I told her. 'Everything I told you before is true. All of it.'

I felt the book call to me again. Now 'call' probably doesn't cut it, but I'm in the zone here so I'm not stopping to explain it yet. I flicked it open. 'You have to take her with you,' it said. 'Get dressed first.'

I did as I was told. Susan turned to look out of the window. We could hear the commotion had moved outside. Then she turned back to face me, in a snap. Now that was either fortunate or not given I was stark bollock naked at that moment, my carrot and potatoes swinging in the wind.

'Gosh,' she gasped. Then she looked back outside, then back at me. 'OK. I'm coming with you.'

Once I was fully garbed in that swish suit, it was the first time Susan had visually acknowledged my sexual appeal. She looked me up and down and smiled, then said: 'So what does your book say?'

13

It didn't take us long to get up to the roof. Susan went out in the corridor first to check all was clear. I heard her shush some patients. Then she came back for me and we went out together, along to the lift and straight up as far as it would go. Then it was just two flights of steps, which she generously helped me up, and through a single door out onto the roof.

'Now what?' she called.

Man, it was noisy up there, and we only realised why when a helicopter suddenly appeared over the cusp of the building. A cusp? Yeah, we'll go with that. I dunno actually what a cusp is, but it'll do for now.

The chopper was facing away from us, pointing a bright spotlight down at the ground. 'They think they've got *you*,' Susan said. 'I saw you... down there!'

Huh? Two places at once. I had to see for myself. Once the chopper descended out of view again, I hobbled over and peered down. Sure enough, there I was. Or he was. Although it was down a fair way, I could see myself, so it seemed, cuffed and under guard by about twenty guys with rifles.

'I don't understand any of this,' Susan said. 'How can there be two of you?'

'That,' I said, 'is at the other end of my knowledge tunnel. Way down the end of it. I'm here and I'm there. A hundred and five years back, three years forward, two of me and one of you. Which, by the way, is enough.' I got myself tangled up a bit emotionally there, so I explained to her: 'I don't mean one is enough as in more than enough. I mean you're a mighty fine companion right now, and that's good enough for me.'

The morphine was wearing off, which meant the pain was coming back – hard. I looked down at the book again. For a moment the pages stayed blank and I stayed staring blankly at them. Next thing, we heard gunfire coming from the street below. We peered over together and saw a whole lot of those armed guys shot up, the helicopter swooping down close to the action, and then – buy me a new arse for Christmas – inexplicablated, me waving up at us. Then he – that is to mean *I* – scarpered around the next building and out of sight.

The book called to me again. 'That bought you some time.' The words shimmered on the page. Then some more came up under those: 'It's time to get wet. Jump!'

I told Susan. 'Wet? Jump?' She looked mighty peeved. 'I'm not jumping anywhere!'

'Where is there even to jump *to*?' I shouted. The helicopter was coming closer. Susan pointed – apt, what with her being a Poynter and all – and I followed. Over the other side of the building was a straight drop down but with an open-topped water tank – just a narrow gap about a metre wide stood between us and it. And it was a long way down. Destiny took over.

'I'm on God's mission!' I cried. Just then the roof door flew open and banged against the wall beside it. Armed men started to appear behind us. 'It's now or never!' I called.

Susan grabbed my hand, then leaned in and kissed me. My heart skipped a beat. Then she shook her head, pulled me with her and we legged it for that jump. I forgot about my leg brace and just let the universe take over. I felt like we were flying, the rush of adrenaline surging through my every fibre.

Just as the helicopter let off its first shots at us, immediately followed by a spray from the rifle-wielding goons coming up behind us, we leapt, right off the edge.

We soared through the air, hand in hand, as if in some kind of slow motion. A bullet tore through my right shoulder. I barely felt it. Barely had time to. Another hit me straight in the back, narrowly missing my spine, and out the other side. As I went to look at Susan, I saw one tear right through her cheekbone and take a couple of teeth with it. She shot me an expression of 'huuuuuhhhh?' Our faces smashed into the side of the water tank. About two seconds later we hit the fucking ground. Splat. Dead as droopy dicks.

14

Being dead is an unusual feeling. I can recall exactly how we looked there on the ground, just lying there next to the water tank. We'd missed the jump by a good two feet. Odd that we were right outside the hospital yet didn't stand any chance of recussiterising.

Anyhoo, it felt like a camera pulling away slowly from the scene, some kind of dramaticisation of the end of our lives. Our brief time together, going from mild contempt to a blossoming love in less than a day. Starring us, playing ourselves. It was perfect.

Apart that is from the fact it looked like someone had emptied a tin of plum tomatoes where Susan's head should've been, and my legs had bent all the way in the wrong direction and I was there, my spine spazzed and what was left of my head buried in my groin. What a picture.

Regardless, onwards and upwards. As my camera view drew back, I realised I was still holding Susan's hand. I looked at her and she at me. We were in some kind of spectral form, and it was that same feeling of when I'd been hanging in the darkness, only this time I actually felt kind of happy – relieved. Obviously I still looked fuckin' cool in my garb too, even as a ghost.

Was I a ghost? No. The camera faded. I felt like it was coming – the end. No journey into the light, but one into the blackest hole. Black as a baby's first turd.

And then there we were, hanging together in that darkness. Floating in the eternal nothingness. I should say it's not exactly floating, not like it'd be on or in water but more like just hanging there, just not attached to anything. A feeling of weightlyness but no externalised forces tugging elsewhere.

That wasn't meant to sound rude. Anyhoo, then it happened: THE BIG ONE. The darkness seemed to stretch in front of us, tiny specks of light appearing slowly; at first maybe two or three a second, and then suddenly as many as twenty and then just multiplying and going and going... it was a sky full of stars, in all directions, some brighter than others. The whole time, there was no sound at all. Absolute silence. We hung there as these stars filled the space with light, and then as if they were all exploding like suns or something they completely obliterated the darkness. And then everything was just light.

Then, with a feeling like a hand at my back, we were propelled forward – pure light, brighter than anything I'd seen in my minus-forty-two years rushed all around us, as if it was somehow there physically. Light we could *touch*.

We looked at each other again and held eye contact, our mouths turning up into broad, joy-filled smiles. It was both overwhelming and yet entirely welcome. And then, that guiding hand slowed us up and set us down. At last, something beneath our feet – a reminder of our physicality and yet also a bit of a fuckin' downer to be honest.

Our smiles faded as we waited for something, anything to happen. Footsteps sounded very distant but grew closer. Out of the white stepped a man. He must've been dressed in white. Seriously, all I could see were his head and his hands. It looked seriously weird.

Then it spoke to us: 'For goodness sake, guys! Way to cock everything up!'

S'pose he was right. I had kinda fallen at the first hurdle on my holy mission. I tried to speak, but nothing came. I mean my mouth moved, but did nothing else.

'I've got you on mute,' the disemboderised head said. He had a sort of South American accent. I'd seen enough Westerns in my time. 'Now listen. Fortunately for you there's a binding agreement of guaranteed immortality at the hand of others. I say fortunately as it's a bit of a stretch to say that wasn't your fault, considering you ended up blowing yourself to death.'

I wondered if he meant blowing ourselves up or the fact I'd ended up with my splatted mouth having a romantic dinner with Mr Penis.

'Yes, that one,' said the head. 'Embarrassing, I'd think. So the terms of the agreement are being honoured this time, given that apparently you are an important individual and because someone else shot you before you hit the ground it could be argued in a court of reasonable justice that the bullet is the thing that killed you. And hey, if it was up to me, I'd say big bollocks to that and let you take your demise gracefully.'

I looked over at Susan.

'Yes,' said the head. 'You were holding on to her at the time, and she was shot just after you, so she's been let off as well. I mean, come on, there's someone rooting for you guys here. Bending the rules. I'm just in middle management. No one tells me *anything*.'

Yeah, OK, can we go back to the heavenly light flight now?

'No, that's enough of that. I have been instructed to reveal some things to you. So pay attention.'

He started waving his armless hands out across his face, then as if flicking paint off his fingers he created an image that formed across the light, hanging like we'd been before. The image began to transform and morphise until the diagram became clear. It was like one of those technical diagrams in mechanical manuals, with three lines of three green and blue orbs.

'I present the information not exactly as it is, but in a way the feeble human mind can understand,' the head said. 'Now listen…' He pointed at the first line of orbs. 'These, if you're not entirely thick, are clearly mini representations of the planet Earth. Now this one at the top left represents your Earth, Martin. This one over here at the centre right represents Susan's.'

He paused, looked over at each of us, and said: 'Follow me? No, I see not. Martin, you've obviously not got a clue. I suppose that's to be expected given your level of intelligence, but haven't you figured any of this out yet?'

I shook my head.

'I'll elaborate then. These three Earths on the top line are the actual Earths. Those on the second are the ones you've been to, Martin. And the third is a selection of your possible futures. That line could in theory have an infinite number in it, but that would spoil the diagram, don't you think?'

My shrug turned into a nod. Yes, I s'pose it would have.

'So what you've done, somehow – remember I am not in receipt of all the pertinent information here – is go from your Earth down to this one, centre left, then across one by one until you got here, where you just blew yourself to death. Now that happens one of two ways: either we put you there or one of the Tremendous did. Have you communicated with a Tremendous?'

I didn't know. The head focused on me. I could feel it registerising my ignoranusness as it looked intently at the top of my head. Then it pulled away.

'Ah… now all is clear. That explains it. The Tremendous you met plucked you up, then fucked you up. He told you he was helping and made out he just needed a little something in return. What he was doing was quite the opposite. He stuck you back, but out of time and on the wrong Earth.'

His left, disembodied hand reached up to his floating face, then settled on his forehead. 'That was an interesting move. And you didn't do too much damage, but I see you encountered yourself too. These are things that usually are not allowed. Well, realistically they are all but impossible. Perhaps this is why you are a special case.'

I nodded, looked over at Susan, who nodded too, then turned my attention back to Head'n'Hands.

'Now you want to know what happens next. Well, it's rather the simplest way to sort this out, although rather a massive event to that end. Highly irregular. Now brace yourselves. Fuck on.'

Yet again, just as any mind that has reasonable ability to predict where a story's headed would surmise, everything went black.

15

'Where are we?'

Susan was the first to speak. We'd come out of the darkness, got re-accustomised to breathing again and after a half-minute of that, she broke the silence.

I replied, 'Dorking. Just outside Dorking.'

Course she enquired: 'How do you know that?'

I loved her plummy voice. I guessed she'd had one of those privilised upbringings, somewhere in rural Berkshire or the Surrey Hills.

'Because this is my third time here,' I said. 'Three times in three days I make it, give or take a handful of massive fuckin' re-adjustments.'

Susan laughed. Man, I needed to hear that. I really did, and I joined in too. We stood there, holding each other's hands and just laughing into each other.

OK, let me qualify that. Now some might say I'm not the most reliable storyteller, but I got no reason to tell lies here. Maybe there's a little exaggerisement here and there, but with this lady if it wasn't exactly as I say it, it's exactly as I felt it at least.

Anyhoo, I didn't bother taking the book out of my pocket. I knew what we had to do and where we had to go, except now I had my first Horsewoman. One down and two to go, it'd been a rough ride but hey, wasn't that always the idea? A mission from God isn't supposed to be easy.

We walked hand in hand up that pathway, then up to the road. I told her: 'In about two minutes Dave and Frosty are gonna pull over, offer us a lift, then get high on the way to Epsom.'

We waited. And waited. Susan directed her eyes at mine. We shrugged together. Eventually, I came out with it: 'OK, this is weird. This isn't right.'

'Maybe we should head back?' she suggested.

'Back where?' I genuinely wondered what she meant.

'To that place, the one you were telling me about. Eden. Back there.'

That moment, lasting upwards of far too long, I spent dilemmered. Finally I decided that yes, that would make sense. Let's go have a look at Eden.

As we retraced our steps and came back down the hill towards the break in the trees, we heard a vehicle. 'Get down,' I said, instincterively following my new action-hero mentality.

We got down. A van trundled up the shingled track and stopped just ahead of the tree break, then the guys in the front got out. We watched as they went to the back, swung the rear doors open and yanked a passenger out. He was wearing a hood. One of the men yanked it up and off.

I felt like I'd just shat in my own mouth, swallowed it and shat it again, into my own mouth again. OK, that's not how I felt at all; I just fancied making that statement. Vulgar yet intellectual, no?

Bang! Susan elbowed me in the ribs. She flashed me a look that simply asked 'What the effing eff?' and all I could do was respond with a groan of pain.

'What was that?' One of the men looked over in our direction, reached down to his side and unholsterised a gun. We ducked down behind the cusp – yep, there it is again – of the incline we were hiding on, which was maybe just thirty feet from them.

'No,' I heard the other man say. 'It's nothing. Just a rabbit. Let's move.'

As we waited for them to head off, I tapped Susan on the shoulder. 'This is when they brought me here in the first place, before I ever came back in time. So this is my time.'

She flashed me a look of 'OK… but…'

Turned out that wasn't the case at all. Two men stood over us, pointing their guns at our heads. Or so I thought. In actual fact they weren't holding any kind of weaponry, just extending their hands to help us up.

Get up we did. 'This way,' one of them said. He had a moustache. The other had a silly little beard. 'Quickly.'

We didn't argue. I hung back a couple of paces deliberately to get a good look at Susan's rump. It was good steak, but it wasn't dinner time.

We made it to the entrance to Eden and then the guys stopped. 'OK,' said the one with the goatee. 'You've been here before, but this time we're going somewhere different. Bear with us.'

We beared with them. The route I'd been taken along originally to meet Angie started the same but then took a detour. We were led through a series of dark corridors with armed guards at every corner into a room with nothing in it but a lightbulb hanging from the ceiling and a door on the opposite wall.

Moustache Man spoke: 'Thank you. Apologies for any inconvenience.' He took the door handle firmly, then twisted it open. As he led Susan and I through into the next room, our jaws almost hit the floor.

Supercalifuckerylisticexpialispazzballs.

There at the far end of a big rectangular table in the centre of the room was Angie. Everyone else was me.

'Fuck on,' they said.

I raised my hand to salute.

'Fuck on.'

PART 3

1

'Sorry I'm late,' I said. Cock-on-the-cob, I was feeling cheeky. It had the required effect though. The seven other *me*s sat around that table chuckled right on cue. I'd always been good at making myself laugh – now I could do it literally.

I realised how weird this scene was: eight of me in total, all dressed the same, with seven of me looking up at me as if waiting for me to say something.

Course it's kinda obvious what I was going to say: 'Frick, Angie girl! What the hell's going on?'

I fixed her with a hard stare. She pushed her seat away and stood up, stretching herself by a foot or so until she was level with me. Weirdly, I'd gotten used to this girl being of no fixed physicality. She could grow and shrink at will – a useful skill to have.

'Marty, sit down,' she said. 'I'll explain everything.'

Seeing as there was one spare seat at the table and it was conveniently right in front of me, I went ahead. Just as I did, a minor scuffle erupted behind me as Susan was bundled out of the room, apparently not altogether happily.

'Hey!' Naturally I found such a curt expunging of my woman at odds with my genteel manner. 'Where are you taking her?' Turns out, I guess, I'd become quite attached to SP and her two sets of anatomically competing cheeks.

Angie made for me to settle down while the rest of me swang their necks left and right as if watching us play ping-pong. Which, by the way, I'm amazing at.

She told me: 'There's not enough room in here for everyone, I'm afraid. She'll join the other Susans.'

Ha! The *other* Susans. Of course! 'There eight of them too?' I enquired. Angie nodded. Made sense, I guessed.

Anyhoo, she carried on: 'Well, now we're all here, I suppose it's time I gave you an explanation.'

We looked around at each other and made our appreciation of that supposition clear as a tear.

'You've all been on the same journey, which most of you realise. And you've all arrived back here at different times, just a few minutes apart mostly. So far, that's quite normal.'

Yeah, I thought. Or we *all* thought. That makes perfect sense and it's entirely as might be expected. Straight up, no problem with that so far. Immortal time-traveller on a mission to save the universe. Easy.

She registered our collective sarcasm and continued: 'Well it's normal in this context. So allow me to give you some of that context. This has never happened before. The reason why it's happened now is because you messed things up in a way no one's ever managed before.'

I chipped in, seeing as none of the other *me*s seemed like they were gonna. 'So which one of us helped me at the hospital?'

The *me*s all looked over at me, puzzled-lookin'. Angie explained it. She said no, none of them had helped me. That'd been another me from another time and place. Me *later*. Huh? Course then I was even more confused than before.

'All of you did the exact same thing up until a certain point,' she said, 'so you all had identical experiences up to then. These are other versions of you that were created when you crossed over between Earths.'

I came right out with it: 'Bullshiiiiiiitttttttt.' The other *me*s burst out laughing. Inserting a little levity into proceedings seemed a healthy idea.

Angie looked like I'd just shat on her grand piano. 'This is not bullshit, Marty. It isn't. We have a situation here, a bad one. But fortunately we also have a plan.'

One of the other *me*s started telling me what it was: 'Because of what happened to you, we – the other *you*s, that is – all went off in different directions.'

A me on the other side of the table piped up: 'It's true. It ain't bullshiiiiiiittttttt. At the point of our – your, that is – being abducted by the Tremendous, everything got messier than a budgie's nappy.'

'And who the fuck is the Tremendous?' I enquired, chuckling at my other *me*'s amusing quippery. Holy-hoobies, what can I say? I'm a funny guy! I was pleased to see my sense of humour was still intact in the other *me*s. I'd always been into my own jokes, but seeing some other version of me tellin' them was even better.

Anyhoo, jeepers-frickin'-creepers, this game of me-tennis was getting interesting. The next one of me to speak finally got to the point: 'But we didn't get abducted because one of you – *us* – came back here and warned Angie, who put it in the book, which got the next bunch of us out of it. Just not *you*, because you have the *original* book.'

It'd just become a toilet full of runny brown confusement. My head ain't really wired for time travel. How we could all be there at the same time but in different times was bothering me.

Angie heard my thoughts. I'd forgotten she could do that, the nosey bint. 'They all arrived at different times, and we've been waiting for you to arrive. It's always today though, when you come. You probably saw yourself being led in here, after the van arrived. That's not the original you. *You* are the original you. These other yous, if you need an easy term, are echoes, or clones. And those echoes don't just go forward, they go back too, so in effect everything you've done to any point keeps echoing back on itself to consolidate it in time. That's just the way the universe works.'

My expression of pure bepuzzlement was clear.

She continued: 'In human terms you've drawn a line under it. You see, we have practised this moment a great many times, except now we have caught up with *you*. And this, right now, is helpfully a point where you get to choose a fulcrum.'

'Choose a what now?' I wasn't up with stupid words no one uses.

Then another one of me started yapping. I think he'd been one who'd already talked. It was hard to tell. He said: 'Fulcrum. Dude, it's just a word for something important, something that can turn a bad situation good. Or the other way around.'

Angie got back on topic: '*Choose* is the operative word here, Marty.'

For the next, I don't know... two hours these other versions of me all gave their accounts of what they'd done and where they'd been.

Maybe it's a sign of advancing years that I can't recall all of those *mes*' stories, but I'd heard the only one I needed to hear. I'll get to that in a minute. See, some of the other *mes* had done some crazy shit. *Absolutely off-the-chart crazy*.

One had positioned things so I'd be high up in government. That being the UK one, which is worth stating given some of those guys had done shit in Mexico, Poland, Russia... damnit, anyhoo, he'd got in bed with some cheeseball called Neil Garage or something and started a ridiculous 'movement' they called Britout. He reckoned taking the country away from Europe would help get it on the right footing for after the war – the same nuclear war which ended up with just us – or *part* of us – left on the planet.

Dick move, I thought. Although I didn't get the full understanding of it all, we were supposed to be stopping it, not making the best of it. I wondered how come he hadn't thought it was a dick move too, being as he was me? Guess it came down to a couple of things. One, I'd made my fair share of dick moves too, and two – well, refer to point number one.

OK, so that was one of the less attractive choices. Another had gone on a killing spree in London, Jack the Ripper-style. There was no indication why. Guess he'd just lost his marbles. I could see how that might happen.

At least he wasn't one of the *me*s in the room. He'd been killed too, and *we* all agreed he'd deserved it. Justice for a bad man, but what had made me then become a psycho? It didn't matter. All those other accounts weren't mine. I'd had choices of my own to make and a jury made up entirely of myself to give a verdict on those choices.

That book of tales had all this stuff written in it. Guessed maybe I should've spent more time readin' it than fuckin' things up. But hey, it didn't matter. Seems like it'd all turned out not too shabby in the end. Once every *me* had finished telling all their stories, I had to make that choice.

Angie answered a question I hadn't asked yet. Howlin' hooters, she was smart. She said: 'No, it has to be you. These other *you*s have positioned themselves and left you with a fairly binary decision: there are clearly two scenarios here which make the most sense. Which one do you favour?'

I didn't know what binary meant, but as it sounded a little like library I decided it must've meant something intelligent. So the option I went for, well... turns out to be the one that worked. To a point, anyhoo.

'What happens next then?' I said.

Angie looked at me, kinda sympathied like: 'You just have to say it. Say what it is out loud. And then it shall be so. It's not the be all and end all, because whatever you do will create other waves of echoes, but the fact we're still here means you can right this wrong, right now. The fact is, Marty... nothing anyone else has tried has led to what we need to achieve. But this... this is a point where you can change it for the best. Do it and all else stops. This – it *all* stops, and I'm sure we all want this to stop, right? You're the original. Remember that.'

All the other *me*s looked over at me, waiting to hear what I intended to do. I stood proud as a puppy's penis there and then and delivered my decision.

'Fuck on,' I said, sticking my thumbs up to signify my confidence in the decision.

All the *me*s stood up and stuck both their thumbs up too, then smiled at me as they said: 'Good luck. And fuck on.'

Then everything went black.

2

It was the easiest way to get to America. That's why I chose the scenario. Frankly all those stories about this and that and what worked and what didn't and these hundreds of versions of me doing all this shit all over the place... well, I wasn't feeling they had many positive contributions. Seemed like all I'd been doing was pissing in the toilet of time, running around in circles and getting nothing done.

The way I saw it, my mission remained: stop Thump at all costs. Seeing as getting to America seemed to stick up the biggest obstacle so far, taking the short cut made a hell of a lot of sense. I was now six-thousand miles closer to my target. Cheesy peas. But I was also further into the future this time, at what the 'me' and Angie had described as a 'crunch point'. The other attractive scenario Angie alluded to was pretty similar – but I'd still have to get to America. Stuff that.

Hot damn, I was pleased to see Susan had come with me. The way she described it, she'd been put in a room with a bunch of *hers* too. They'd chatted about all sorts of stuff, things she'd encountered and would encounter on different paths – and too many variables for her to remember. Now I'm not saying she's thick or nothing. I couldn't remember most of the shit I'd been told either.

But on that note, a word about the woman: in the past I've had many a divvy lady's company of a night, but that ain't what's true about Susan. No, she's got this light in her – something so bright and fizzy. It gives me the physical and psychologic horn. Gets my brain erect as well as my lovesick lovestick.

Anyhoo, it took us a little while to realise where we were. Susan was from a time where the United States still existed. Back then people had gone wherever they liked in the world on planes and boats. Furthest I'd been was St Albans. I'd never even seen the sea up close. Nice town, don't get me wrong, but I'd grown up watching all those American shows. America had everything I never did and St Albans had nothing of either. Lordy, I'd always wanted to experience the American dream and now I could. Sorta, except it weren't no dream as much as I wished it was.

The hotel room was nice. A classy place in New York, the scene for all those movies I'd grown up watching. Susan threw the curtains open and there we were, about thirty or forty floors up in the downtown area. I'd never been up so high. Susan knew the place because she'd been there before, in that very hotel, when she attended some seminar or something. I guessed that's why we'd decided to go there in the first place.

Although I felt we were growing closer, I guess you could say we weren't quite at the comfortable stage. She was getting used to shit as much as I was.

'I was told to tell you to open the book to page five,' Susan said. She'd been given that message from one of the other *her*s. I flashed her a look with cocked head for effect.

I did as instructerised, minding that this kind of book just keeps on giving. The perfect gift. A different story every time. Sure, the story might be hard to follow sometimes, but at least it's got some variety. Except this time I realised all the other pages were blank – all those tall tales of time-travelling tittery, just wiped out. That realisation made me feel a little queasy.

Then I got to thinking about what had gone down back at the base: suspifically what about the tear in time? Back when this had all started, I'd stepped into some universal rip in time and space. This time it'd all just gone dark and I'd appeared a moment later in New York. Why not the rip this time? And what about all those other *mes*? Something wasn't right. I felt I was being manipulerised. Did I even trust Angie?

Anyhoo… I turned to page five and squinted down at my instructions: I was to go out of the hotel with Susan, get in a car that was waiting for us, then travel across town to another hotel where I was gonna meet Thump himself.

Holy hell! Seemed like I was almost done. The way the other me had told me about this, I'd been positioned in a good spot. I was known – something of a celebrity. Thump had become President-elect – not how it was in the history books I'd read. The future had been altered already, but the reason those pages were all blank now was it had all been reset. Kinda. I think.

But still, fizzin' farts, this was the milk from the nipple: I was about to complete my mission. I'd already got my time travel wings; now I was cutting out all the boring travelling shit in-between and jumping from one essential moment to the next, across hemispears and time zones. One of those other *mes*, whatever became of him, had set this scenario up. I s'posed Angie was a sort of editor, sticking the scenes together, editing them into the movie to end all movies.

Anyhoo, Susan and me had some shit to take care of and I needed to find out more about these Tremendous fellers. Guessed I would in good time. But Thump came first.

3

Susan and me talked some small talk for a bit, not much of note. Before we'd leapt forward in time, I could tell she wasn't too keened on me looking at her as a sexual being, but it was hard not to. Yeah, fine, she wasn't the most beautiful woman on the planet, but she had bumps and curves that made my nuts twitch. Now, though, as sudden as all that other shit, we looked at each other with those eyes. Those eyes of knowing, of liking and maybe even loving.

Just as I was admiring those lumps 'n bumps, there was a loud rap-rap-rap on the door. We s'posed this was our cue: time to get up and get on. So up I got, walked across the fluffy carpet and opened the door. Normally, I guess you might expect I would've checked out the peephole first, to see who was there. Truth is, I didn't give half a turd who it was. I felt confident. Slippery skidmarks, I was immortal. Certainly confers an air of arrogance, that does. Still, I ain't judged no one, so don't expect to be myself. I'll allow myself a little arrogance once in a while.

Three goons, whoever they were, were stood in the corridor. For a moment they looked like the strangers they were, but then almost as if I blinked they suddenly became known to me. *Angie*, hey... she must've done some magic or something, fusing my memories with those of the other me who'd already done this shit, or part of it, or whatever.

'Sir,' said Tim Gibbons, 'it's time. The car's waiting.' Right away I knew Tim – he was my campaign manager. Hold on... I had *a campaign*? All of a sudden my head was filled with this weird sensation of hundreds and thousands of feelings and memories rushing in. It didn't hurt or nothing, but it was something I felt, like water going down the throat – knowledge pouring in.

I instantly realised I knew so much about the guy: he was married to a fit blonde bint called Kirsty, with a young son named Kyle, and they lived out in the Hamptons part of Long Island. It wasn't like new information: I knew this guy. I trusted this guy.

All of a sudden I 'remembered' what my meeting with Thump was about. Yeah, he'd just been elected the next President of the United States of America, but following his campaign he'd asked to meet with me.

Me? Turns out I had found myself unwittingly leading some group of disillusionised malcontents who called themselves The Fist. Seriously – The Fist? It was a weird feeling realising I'd landed in the shoes of some other version of me who'd started some rebellious organ of dissidenters. But at the same time, I kinda fancied it wasn't as cheesy as my old self thought it was.

After all, what's a fist? Just a bunch of fingers clenched together, clenched for action. Clenched for change. Holy greasy fingers, clenched to save the freakin' world!

The other two guys with Tim, Klein and Hugo, were bodyguards – part of my security detail. Hugo was black; Klein was a whitey. He wasn't as white as Tim though. Tim was one of those pale-faced weasly-looking dudes, with narrow slopey shoulders and a kinda wet handshake. Klein was a solid man, but Hugo was a real side of beef. I felt safe next to these guys. I felt like they belonged with me.

Weirdly, or I guess not so weirdly after all, Susan recognised them too. We went down in the lift and walked out into this huge lobby, all marble and shiny and cool-as-shit glass furniture. Course I recognised this stuff straight away too. This hotel was expensive – and classy. I'd spent a week or so there, my new memories told me.

The stuff back in London was different. North of the Thames was where all the nicer places were. Most of the hotels in South London had become converted or makeshift apartments or squats. I'd spent some good times in a few of them, but all that seemed so long ago even though it was just a matter of days to me.

How could I afford all this? How had I got to this point? I took a moment to 'recall': protest songs! I'd written a few tunes – maybe not my best work, I guess, but good enough – and published them on UniTube. That had been about a year ago, just as the presidential race got going and Thump started making waves in the political pisspot. Amazingly, the first song I uploadered got about a million 'hits' in a week. By the time I put my third song up, I had close to fifty million views and people were talking about me on SocialStage. I was 'trending'. Having spent so much time hearing about the old internet, now I was seeing its power for myself. Too much power, if I'm honest, and its size just plain simple scared me, but it did the job.

I needed to get noticed. I needed to get close to Thump. And I needed support. Now I had it, and I had Thump's attention. Tim had contacted me through my UniTube account and offered to represent me. Originally it was just going to be to manage my music, but soon enough people saw me as a political force. I wrote more songs, played some gigs, appeared on some news programmes and positioned myself as someone Thump needed to know about. The Fist was Tim's idea. He said it represented a determination to stand up and be counted. Soon other people were doing just that – wearing the T-shirts and caps, plastering posters on walls.

Susan was a busy bint too. Soon as I became 'a personality', she stood in the spotlight alongside me, and took it over on occasions too. As a psychologist, she'd made waves of her own, commenting on this and that and getting her own following.

We headed out onto the sidewalk. A few people were staring at us, excited looking. Back home I'd occasionally get recognised from my gigs here and there, but that was small time. Then this guy bounded up to us and thrust his fist towards the sky. Klein and Hugo went straight up to him, ready to tackle him. I stopped them.

'Hang back there guys,' I said, sounding even to myself a little calmer than I'd expect to be among all this new-but-familiar shit. 'Let's hear what he has to say.'

They stepped aside and he strode right up to me, keeping his fist kinda half-aloft. 'Marty – I just wanted to say how much we admire you. My wife and I. We're so stoked about what you're doing. So stoked.'

I shook his hand. 'I'm stoked too,' I said. 'Stoked to stoke the fire I'm about to light under Thump's ass.'

On the way to the hotel to meet the President-elect, Susan kissed me and held my hand. We were so close to changing the future of mankind; to stopping the false 'pocalypse.

4

Although Susan's passionate kiss left me wanting to squeeze the lemon of love, I had a job to do. A man can't be pleasing his woman every second of every minute. It's unrealistic. Maybe every other second.

When we arrived outside the New York Grand Hotel, a wave of camera flashes washed over us. Klein opened my door and I stepped out into a cacophony of cheers, boos and a barrage of questions flung from what seemed like all directions.

Tim appeared by my left side and Susan took my hand on the right. We walked up the steps and past a bunch of Thump's large security detail, then into the hotel. As the doors closed behind us, the sounds outside lessened to a low hum, then disappeared altogether. See, I'm good with sound. When a man plucks a guitar string, he hears it all – attuned to every vibration. My ears were my most trusted allies.

Thump's manager, Kelly Casey, greeted us and led us through into a giant room: high ceiling, loads of seats arranged in rows and a stage at the front. Thump was nowhere to be seen.

'The President-elect will be with you shortly,' Kelly said. 'Please, have a seat at the front.' She left the room.

We walked up the long central aisle and sat either side of it: me and Susan and Tim on the left and Hugo and Klein on the right. For a minute we just looked around at each other, waiting and wondering. Then a sound startled us – a microphone coming on and feeding back with a screech.

Thump came out onto the stage in front of us, carrying a guitar. He was wearing a cowboy hat.

Now none of us was expecting this shit. Thump started twanging the guitar – badly, like an infant might I guess – and singing badly too. Still, I recognised it was one of my melodies, a chorus that would've gone: *People of the world, our history unfurled, we gotta stand up together, and fight for our future.*

Now I'm not saying they were my best lyrics, but that was just one part of a song that had a lot to say. Geez, it had a few million plays on UniTube.

Anyhoo, Thump had changed the words: *People of the world, Molloy's a fuckin' chump, sit down and shut up, it's time to bow to Thump!*

He dropped the guitar on the stage, hopped down off it and strode over to me, offering his hand to shake. I stood up to face him and kept my hands well away from his.

He fixed me with his icy-cool, kinda creepy stare. 'Much better than yours, wasn't it? And that was my first go! Seriously, my first go!'

I chuckled. 'That much was obvious,' I told him. 'Don't give up the day job. Actually, scratch that – *do* give up the day job.'

He chuckled too, then turned on his heels to face my bodyguards. 'You guys, you can leave. And you, Tom or whatever your name is…' Then he turned to Susan. 'And Susie… heck, you can stay. Nice to have something to look at. And you should hear this too. I have a proposition.'

I wondered for a moment about the sense in giving up my security, then decided it was OK. Hey, I was immortal, right? Thump was on his own anyhoo. If he'd got it in mind to stick his dukes up, I'd be ready to put my foot in his poop chute.

'Hey, don't worry,' Thump said, slapping his hand down on my shoulder. 'I just wanna talk. I called you here because…' He grabbed a chair and swivelled it around, then sat down facing us and motioned for me to sit down too. Much as I didn't like being bossed by this tit, it seemed like the right thing to do so I did.

'Because what?' Susan asked, her tone irritated and impatient.

Thump flashed her his best smile – she seemed to recoil from it a little.

'Because we got some major shit to discuss!' he grinned.

I shrugged. 'We do?'

'Sure we do,' he said, still grinning. 'See, I know who you are. I know what you want, and I know why you're doing it. Only thing I don't know is how or when, not that any of that matters.'

'That's two things,' Susan said, smiling. 'How is one. When is another.'

Thump looked at her blankly, then got back to me.

'Let me tell you a story,' he said, fixing me all serious. I nodded disinterestised.

This is what he said: 'I'm a businessman. A supremely successful one. I can businessise anything I like, because I'm great at it. Just fucking great at all that stuff. Let me give you an example. Behind this hotel let's say there's some girl who gives handjobs for five bucks. I can go round there, in that dirty alley, and get a handjob. That's a business transaction, for a service, and

107

I attach a value to it. But let's say there's another whore back there who gives a better handjob. So I go to her to try out the competition. Turns out it's a better experience for the same money. That's so easy. It's a no-brainer, right? Really easy. Then the first girl comes back to me and offers her lower quality handjob for four bucks. Fuck that, I say. I'll give you two-fifty, and you gotta chuck in a bit of a blower if you want the full five. The second girl comes over to see what's going on. She can't believe this shit, being undercut by some other shanky whore on her patch. So she offers me the full blowy and a thumb up the ass for the five bucks. I give it a try. Except once we're done with that, I'm dulled to the experience. I'm not even sure of the quality anymore. It's just all the same shit, all at the same price. So I'm feeling like maybe I want my money back, if I pay for something that doesn't hit the spot. What do I do? I'm gonna introduce some handjob insurance, and all these girls gotta provide premium prostitution or I get my money back. The customer's always right, even when it's all about emptying his balls onto some junkie bitch.'

Susan snapped her fingers to get Thump's attention. She did not look happy. 'What the fuck are you on about?' she cried. 'You misogynistic prick. Seriously, what is the point of this?'

He leaned over at her menacingly. 'Supply and demand, price and value. That's all. I kinda liked the metaphor. You see, we're all whores here. I'm doing what I'm doing because at the end of it all, I get a seat at the table. You think I want to be President? I'm giving out the mother of all handjobs in exchange for the big prize at the end. You guys, meanwhile, are giving out substandard, budget handjobs and it's just not cutting it for the customer. These guys just voted me in as the most powerful man on the planet. The American people have spoken. You can't beat me now. I won. So I'm just gonna be kind here. I'm a kind kind of guy. I'm gonna offer you some handjob insurance.'

I was bepuzzled. 'What do you mean you get a seat at the table? What table? If you know what we're here for, what we're trying to stop…'

He interrupted me, grinning his sickly condesensered grin: 'Heck, I'm already tremendous, but to really become one of *The Tremendous*? I'll suck a million dicks if I have to. It's all a means to an end.'

Man overboard, I could feel anger rising in my stomach. 'You fuckin' what?'

Thump stood up, walked over to the stage and hopped up on it, dangling his legs over the side. The anger reached my throat.

'You heard me, chump,' he said. 'And it's a one-time offer. You and your pretty little lady girl there can join me. You'll write your songs for me from now on. Songs about how fuckin' tremendous I'm becoming. And when the nukes fly and I'm watching the show from the top of The Tremendous Tower, you can watch too. We'll hold hands and drink expensive Champagne, and once all the ash has settled we'll all sit at that table together.'

'You're mad!' Susan shouted. 'Absolutely fucking bonkers!'

I couldn't disagree. The anger was bubbling up to my tongue now, ready to let rip. I managed one last refrain: 'You can't kill me, Thump. You surely know that. But I can kill you.'

As I leapt out of my chair and started running towards him, Thump burst out laughing. I was going to wring his neck and watch his eyes fill with blood. I got about a metre from him when he just clapped his hands together.

5

I was getting properly tired of this shit: whipped out of whatever I was doing, transplanted into some other time and place and forced to listen to these celestialised pricks.

So there I was, back in that giant gonad or whatever it was. And there he stood, in that lovely suit, with that stupid hell-hound sitting next to him. My patience had all but worn out.

First things first, where was my lady friend? While she, hot damn lucky for her, was spared the pleasure of sitting in this fleshy bulb, I was concerned as one would expect.

'She's fine. Don't you worry about her,' the demon who called himself Roger said. 'You'll be reunited soon. I promise.'

Man, I was angry with this streak of piss. Course I knew who he was now, something he'd conveniently forgotten to tell me the first time. But still, it had been botherin' me a tad that those other *me*s hadn't answered my question about the Tremendous. It was a barmy name the first time I heard it and still occupising that realm of thought. But then I remembered how *tremendous* the weird fiery guy had been. Shit on a shuttlecock, I was still wearing one of his suits. He'd made it for me. And yeah, that suit was *tremendous*. Along all of this crazy roller coaster, he'd been one of the real highlights, getting all weird on me in some giant pulsating testicle or whatever it was. I guessed in some respects I didn't mind him that much. He was a kinda cool guy, despite being... whatever. *On fire and a total bastard.*

'Yes, that's right,' he said, grinning like some overly demented clown. 'I'm a Tremendous. No point trying to tell you otherwise. I suppose it was somewhat inevitable.'

I stepped right up to him. I was too irked to be frightened of this bastard. 'Ain't nothing tremendous about you,' I told him. 'Nothing at all. You're a lying shit.'

He looked like he was trying to look offended, then laughed that really irritating laugh. It bounced around the bollock.

'Okay!' he cried, with a little too much glee for my liking. 'You've got me! I did tell you a little lie, or two, or possibly as many as ten, but you have to understand I was doing what was in our best interests.'

Bullshit, that was. 'In your best interests, not mine,' I said, with a snarl. Now it's worth pointing out here that in all my life I'd not been particularly snarlworthy, but stirred in the bowl with all the last few days' milk and eggs I was feeling not exactly the pancake I considered myself to be.

'Not exactly,' the bastard retorted. 'See, your viewpoint may not reveal what's in your best interests at all, whereas I see it all. The whole, as you say, sheeeeee-bang!'

Now clearly, I wasn't happy being back in the Testicular Prison, the Bollock of Deception, but I have to give this bastard some credit: the next few minutes became the most enlightenised of my entire existence thus far. And that's saying something, given the shit I'd been showering in of late.

First things first, I asked him why he'd stopped me doing Thump over. 'Isn't that obvious?' he said. 'I need Thump. The *world* needs Thump.'

Then Roger the Tremendous clicked his fingers just like the last time, and there again those chairs and that table popped up between us. But this time, he changed it. 'No, no, that's not right,' he said. He clicked them again: the table vanished and the separate chairs were replaced with a couple of bound reclining armchairs, red leather. Hell, they looked comfy.

We sat down together, a single wide armrest separating us. They gently began to recline, until we were looking up – up at that weird pulsating fleshy shit.

Roger reached over and patted my hand on the armrest. Then he wrapped his fingers around mine. 'What we're about to see, well… it's probably the greatest show on Earth,' he said. 'And it's a highly private viewing. Just me and you. Oh, and my doggy friend. But he's not interested in this really. He likes watching horror. Loves the gore, he does. Not so much into secrets-of-the-universe documentaries.'

I looked over at Roger. He was smiling back at me, his wavy silver hair framing his handsome face. I realised all my anger was gone, as if he was drawing it out of me while he gripped my hand. I felt peaceful; damn, I felt OK. Better than OK, I guess. I felt happy.

'Just lie back, look up and enjoy,' he said. So I did.

A darkness crept across my vision until all that fleshy shit was gone. Then everything was gone – apart from a sheet of blackness. The grip of Roger's hand faded away too. Then the show started.

111

Roger's voice floated around the space, narrating the visual feast in front of me. At the start it was just stars, filling my vision. Some twinkled and others exploded, creating more stars, and then more until they were just everywhere; a starry blanket. Then the voice-over came.

There are precisely seventeen trillion stars in the universe. Multiply that by seventeen trillion universes. That's seventeen trillion times seventeen trillion, which is... erm... let's move on. I'm not great at maths. But these numbers do matter, just as everything matters.

Except nothing matters. Everything matters and nothing matters. At the same time. You humans, see, you only understand things in human terms.

I heard a finger click. Then the camera zoomed in on one of the stars. I'd kinda predicted it was going to be Earth. Even celestial cinema delivered in giant metaphysical pulsating testicles was predictable.

This is the first day. The day when the Earth was created.

The view zoomed further in, settling on a beautiful vista of a jungle with a river running through it. There were strange metallic, reflective structures rising out of the ground and large, stranger shapes – creatures of some kind, it seemed – flapping and splashing around in the water. They were majestic, beautiful yet otherworldly; rising out and weaving around the metallic pillars, like manta rays with feathered wings and long tails ending in colourful, luminescent fan shapes.

Then Roger appeared in the foreground, grinning like a fuckin' cheeseball.

I wanted to tell him he'd ruined the movie, but he started speaking direct to camera. Direct to me. Standing there between two trees, the water glistening behind him.

This, all this, is what was created, and this is where I took my first steps. It is precisely the centre of the universe. Your Earth, this Earth, is the beginning of all creation, and this point here is the precise centre of your Earth. To add a shot of perspective into this delicious cocktail of privileged knowledge, this was just over one million years ago, give or take. The way your scientists have it figured is entirely wrong. You see, science changes. If you assume that you are writing a book and can change the story at any time, it's the same principle.

There was no evolution, at least not how you humans are supposed to think of it. Evolution is an extremely simple concept applied to an extremely complicated truth. Let me explain further.

Another finger click later that beautiful vision was gone, replaced by nothing but pure darkness again.

'What can you see?' His voice was coming from next to me again.

'Nothing,' I said. 'Just… well, nothing.'

'Exactly,' Roger said. 'But that's not what is really there. It's just what *is* there, you cannot *see*. I'll tell you what is there. There is an entire civilisation going about its business. Well, *you'd* call it a civilisation because that's how humans view things. Everything's about societies and communities and faith and hope and all this meaningless human drivel.'

I looked over at him. I couldn't see any light source, but his face was lit up like a candle. No need to question how; I was done with trying to understand that kinda stuff.

As I watched him, the end of his finger lit up too. He pointed it out into the darkness, and I followed. It all went dark again, and his voice came then from all around. The Big Bollock of Deception apparently had surround sound. The light from his finger floated away and burst in front of us, a supernova exploding and returning colour to the scene. We were back on Earth, overlooking a massive body of water, with thousands of those creatures coming in and out of view.

When your world was created – the first world – it was for us, the Tremendous. We, all seventeen of us, had the run of the place, so to speak. We loved it; our souls given bodies at last and feet to walk with, hands to touch, eyes to see and ears to hear.

He forgot the nose. Nothing to smell then? I didn't say anything.

But it wasn't to last. You see, the problem was that we were too Tremendous. Too Tremendous to be there. We revelled in the beauty at first, but it wasn't enough for us. So we started warping the creation; we wreaked havoc upon this beauty. We wreaked havoc upon each other and the beautiful Earth. Imagine a tyrannosaur battling a stegosaur. Now imagine the tyrannosaur fucking the stegosaur. Now imagine them laughing and fucking and killing and ruining each other over and over again… that's what we did. And so we were banished. For bad behaviour, really. We were given freedom and we squandered it for our pleasure.

113

A finger clicked. The scene morphed before my eyes: a huge rock sprouted from under the water, then another and another. Land began to replace the sea. The creatures were dying, all around, their shrieks and screams louder than thunderclaps. Bodies floated on the surface. Then out of those mountains came huge eruptions, spewing lava forth. Gotta say, it was a pretty cool movie.

Then suddenly the camera whooshed out once again to the original view of the stars: infinite space. Well, not infinite, was it? Seventeen trillion times seventeen trillion. You may recall I'm not great at *illions*. I have no idea what a trillion is. The show went on:

So you see, the Earth was ours. A gift. It belonged to the Tremendous. It was created for us. But we failed to respect it, or its creator, and we have forever been banished since. We were altered, exiled. We became reavers of souls to atone for our misdeeds. While the souls that worship feed the creator and go to Him, the others come through us – the Tremendous. Except we're hardly Tremendous now, are we? Banished to our, as you say, bollocks. A fraction of our former Tremension. Or Tremendousness. I'm not sure which is the right word. Let's go with Tremension.

You've heard, no doubt, the concept that humans were created in God's image? Well, that's true to a point, except it's not the whole truth. We, the Tremendous, are created in God's image too. Except that image is something you cannot comprehend. Our feet and our hands and our eyes and our ears – and yes, our noses – are ethereal; yours are not. Our brains are those of gods; yours are – most definitely – not.

You've probably also heard mention of how your brains are only working at ten per cent or thereabouts of their capacity. Well, that's absolutely correct. Yet for us Tremendous, we're at closer to ninety per cent. God, or whatever you wish to call our benefactor, is the full whack. One-hundred-point-zero. All of it. The original brain. Now do you understand?

I understood some of it. The bastard was telling me clear as day: humans are the shitstain in the Earth's underpants.

No, that's not it at all. Humans are beautiful creatures, as intended. But they are also made in the image just as we are, and therefore capable of awful things. You guys are wreaking just as much damage on the Earth as we did, but it's become something of a factory line for us – your souls are our food.

114

This is the lesson though: you have free will. Your decisions mean everything, and yet they also mean nothing.

'I don't get it,' I said. 'How come you were such an asshole before, and now you're telling me all this?'

He clicked his fingers. The show ended and the fleshy gonad arena returned. He let go of my hand and motioned for me to stand, so I did. Another click later and the red leather armchair was gone too. Then he put his hands on my shoulders and leaned right in to my face. His breath was warm on my cheeks and sweet up my nose.

'You don't have any friends now, back here. And the one you know as Angie, well she isn't your friend either. An angel, really? No. She's no angel. But you'll find that out for yourself soon enough. Anyhoo, I was punished for what I did to you. Some of my… *toys* were taken away.'

Damn, I wondered what kind of toys this guy played with, then stopped myself thinking about it as soon as I realised. Toys of eternal torture.

'By way of explanation, in terms you can understand, it was in my interest to put you somewhere else. This prison I've been given… this prison I'm in… it is my job to take the high-value targets. I've had many of the big names in here, but my duplicitous behaviour led to me losing some of those too. What you need to know is this: the decisions *you* make will change everything. Those decisions ultimately determine who comes here.'

'Thump, you mean?'

'No, my dear boy,' he said, staring deep into my eyes, his hands still resting on my shoulders. 'I assure you, he's not the problem. Now I'm going to help *you*. I'm not putting you back where you *were*, but where you really do *need* to be. Trust me.'

I don't know why he did it, but then he planted a wet kiss right on my lips. I tried to pull away from it as the colour faded from my vision. The last thing I saw were his eyes twinkling in the darkness.

6

I was wiping the wetness off my lips when an explosion went off just overhead. The air was filled with smoke. I couldn't see anything through it. Now ordinarily I might've shat myself at such a shock, but it seemed my previous 'me' had overcome that little leaky bowel problem.

Still reeling from that kiss, the world came back into view as the smoke cleared. I was relieved to see Susan sitting opposite me in what appeared to be some kind of trench. To the left of me and right of her lay bodies. Shots rang out overhead.

This was where I needed to be? I felt another turn in my bowel at the next explosion. Susan looked terrified. Guessed I did too.

'What the hell are you wearing?' Susan shouted. I looked her up and down – I hadn't noticed before she was dressed funny too. There we were, sitting on opposite sides of this narrow ditch, explosions going off all around us and gunfire ringing out overhead. Some guys were shouting and screaming, then a bunch of them leapt over the ditch and carried on running.

One of the guys to my left raised his head as if to utter a final word, then made this funny expression before collapsing back to the ground.

Shit... first world war, second maybe – from what I remembered of my history lessons this looked just like that. One of them anyway. Old-style uniforms, foreign accents – then it clicked. Nazis. Fuckin' Nazis. That's what those uniforms were, Swastikisses and all. Then the worst of it hit me: we were wearing Nazi uniforms too!

I shook my head vigorous like at Susan. She shook hers back, then shrugged and mouthed something at me. I couldn't hear her, so I put my hand up to my ear so as to insinuise I hadn't tuned in to her broadcast.

This time she shouted it: 'Where have you been?'

I scrambled across the trench to her, getting in as close as I could. 'I've been with Roger,' I cried, trying to be heard over the gunfire.

'The creepy guy in the testicle?' she shouted back.

'Yeah!' I grabbed her hand and clasped it tight. 'I think he's fucked with me again. He did this last time – sent me to another world and...' I stopped myself talking as, in fact, if he hadn't done that to me in the first place I never would have met Susan.

She jumped in anyhoo: 'And now he's chucked us into the middle of the first world war!'

Spicy haemorrhoids with blue cheese, he only fuckin' had, the bastard. But he said he was helping me. He seemed so genuine, but now I felt betrayed and foolish. Not that I'd ever had any choice in the matter; just that I'd come to trust him just a little. Seemed like he'd revealed to me the secrets of the universe, or some of them at least. Now I was sitting in a ditch wearing Hitler's pyjamas.

For a few seconds the gunfire stopped. Then seemingly out of nowhere a man also dressed in Nazi gear dropped into the trench right next to Susan. 'Second world war, actually,' he said, calm as anything. He didn't sound like a German, not like they sounded in the old films I'd seen.

'You look lost,' he said. 'You're supposed to be up there with us. Is this your first time?'

'First time?' I let loose a noise somewhere between an incredulised snort and a mouth fart. 'Yes, this is our first time! What's going on?'

The man looked annoyed. 'I can't believe they didn't tell you this in the battle briefing. Did you miss the briefing?'

Susan shrugged at him. Gunfire began rattling overhead again. 'Yes, we missed the...' She waited while an explosion interrupted her. "...battle briefing!"

'OK,' he said, 'it's quite simple. We're Germans. Panzergrenadier Division, to be exact. Up there, four-hundred metres to the west, the Russian 2nd Rifles are making a stand against our light motorised patrol. They're chucking grenades at us and they've got mortars covering them. Fact is we're in a pinch. We need to get their position so we can hit them with artillery. That's what we're all doing next!'

Next? I was struggling with the present, never mind the future. This guy didn't sound like a German at all, but here we all were in the Nazi uniform. Maybe he was a spy. A double agent. Then he stood up, peered over the apex of the trench and shouted down at us. 'Come on! It's time. This is the best bit!'

Me and Susan exchanged looks of pure horror. War has a best bit? The man climbed out of the trench, looked back down at us and shook his head. 'Fuckin' farbs,' he said. 'Might as well be mops.' Then he disappeared from view.

I put my hands on Susan's shoulders. 'We can't stay here,' I said. 'It's not safe.'

She made a face at me. 'You're bloody well immortal, aren't you?'

Amid all the shouting, screaming and earth-shaking explosions, I'd lost sight of that fact. Yeah, I was immortal. Well, I had been last time I checked. I felt a surge of confidence in my chest and strength in my legs.

'OK!' I said, excitedly. 'Let's do this. Maybe the reason Roger sent us here was to make a difference. Maybe I can turn the tide of battle. Maybe there's a fulcrum here!'

Susan still looked horrified and probably a little surprised to hear me say 'fulcrum'. We stood up together. An explosion went off mere yards away from us.

'Bring it on!' I cried. 'This is the best bit!'

We scrambled out of the trench and were met instantly with mortar fire. A line of bushes and trees ahead of us shielded the damn Soviet scum, hiding like cowards. Another rattle of gunfire sounded close by. Between us and the tree line were four or five armoured vehicles. Kinda like tanks, but smaller than the ones I'd seen in history lessons. The guy who'd been talking to us was crouched at the back of one, occasionally leaning out and letting a few shots off.

I grabbed Susan's hand and we ran as fast as we could to join him. He instantly thrust a pair of binoculars into my hand and shouted: 'About time! If we don't pinpoint their position, we're done for!'

I didn't need telling twice. The adrenaline pumping through me was electric. I moved to the other side of the vehicle and peered out, binocs at the ready. I looked back at our comrade. 'I can't see it from here. I'm going to get closer.'

'I'll cover you!' he cried.

I winked at Susan. 'I'll be back,' I said. 'Stay here with...' The man heard me and turned to face us. He held out his hand to shake. I reciprocatered.

'Shirley,' he said. 'Shirley M. Bottom. Good to meet you.'

Huh? 'Your name's Shirley Bottom?' I guess I looked at him a little weirdly.

'Everyone says that,' he smiled. 'Now are we gonna push the commies into the fires of hell or what?'

That was it. Shirley had me pumped. Keeping low, I ran over to a corpse and grabbed his gun off the ground, prising it out of his cold, dead hand. Made me jump as he tried to grab it back. 'Hey!' he said. 'That's mine.'

I didn't have time for that. So he wasn't dead – good for him. Big deal. I had a job to do. Making my way through the mortar fire, I got ahead of our front line. I think I heard someone call to me: 'Where are you going?' I was going to end those commies, that's where. For Susan. For Shirley Bottom. For the world.

I felt it then – this was my moment. Thump had been a dead end. A human cul-de-sock. Roger had put me back here to change the future, maybe to stop Thump ever getting anywhere, or even to stop the bastard being born.

I ran further up still, getting closer to the tree line, and then heard the rumble of engines behind me. I was leading the charge!

A few more paces and I'd made it. I pushed my way through a thicket and came out the other side. There, right in front of me, was the mortar installation, with armoured vehicles and motorcycles at either side and maybe about forty Soviet soldiers. Shit! Behind them was a column of three huge tanks, flanked by yet more soldiers. I may have been immortal, but could I really take all these guys out by myself?

No, I couldn't, but I could complete my mission. I ducked back through the thicket and legged it back to our front line. Another German grabbed me by the arm, stopping me in my tracks.

'What the hell are you doing?' He pointed down to a large radio unit on the ground behind him. 'You're supposed to radio in the position!'

Geez, I didn't know how to do that. 'You do it!' I shouted as another explosion went off just ahead of us. I pointed to where I'd just been. 'It's just over there.'

He said something like 'are you serious?' but I was already on my way back to Susan and Shirley. They were still crouched behind the vehicle; it was moving slowly forward and they were moving along with it.

I fixed Shirley sternly and told him what I'd seen. He shrugged, made a weird face at me, then pointed at my gun. 'You're a German officer. Why are you carrying a Russian rifle?'

Man, I'd been confuzzled a hell of a lot recently, but this was getting weirder by the second. No one sounded German, or Russian for that matter. Shirley seemed to be pissed off with me. I guessed I was just disorientised in the fog of war, or we'd been sent back to some other version of the conflict.

Suddenly Susan let out a cry of delight. 'Look!' she called. 'Over there. We've got back-up!' Then there was another almighty explosion, louder than the others, as our artillery fired.

Shirley got up and disappeared around the side of the armoured vehicle. Me and Susan watched as our own column of tanks rumbled closer. They were still some distance away. Then we heard a shout of victory from ahead. I peered around. I'd done it! I'd given them the location of the mortars and they'd taken them out with the artillery.

But it wasn't over. The German front line gave a rally cry as the Russian scum started pushing through the trees. I ran out to join my brothers, dived down into a prone position and started letting off rounds. Damn, turns out I was a great shot. I took five of those bastards down, their death screams muffled in the chaos as our tanks advanced behind us and fired on theirs.

Next thing I knew, Shirley appeared alongside me. 'Dude!' he cried. 'Seriously, what are you doing? You're not supposed to be doing this bit!'

Dude? Some Nazi double agent just called me a dude?

8

OK. So I felt like the dick swinging from my own forehead, but Susan was right there next to me. She hadn't realised either. How could we?

Shirley was talking to a bunch of previously dead guys, all now stood up and shaking each other's hands. Some guy walked right up to us, got in my face and almost spat at me: 'Dick mops.' Most of the guys there were laughing at us. Women were noticeably absent.

Then Shirley came back over to us. 'You could've invalidated our liability insurance. Luckily for you, we're OK. No one saw what you were doing. You were way off track there. But you go running off on your own like that and people can get hurt. All those explosions are very precisely placed. How'd you mops get in anyway?'

We knew then that we'd been dumped not in the middle of the second world war, but in a re-enactment of a key battle. Why? We had no idea at that point, but something else was playing on my mind.

'What's all this shit about mops?'

Shirley let out this major sigh, as if he couldn't wait to rid his body of air. 'Members of the public. M-O-Ps. You're supposed to be over there.' He pointed beyond the staging area, where a long metal fence ran the length of the field. Now the smoke had cleared, we could see it all clearly. There were a couple of hundred people, some dressed in uniforms but most just in regular attire.

'Fortunately, no one really saw what you did, so we kept the scene mostly authentic.'

Susan asked: 'Where are we?'

Shirley looked bepuzzled. 'You mean where are we really or where are we pretending to be?'

Susan bit her lip. 'Um... the first one.'

'Seriously?' he said. 'We're in Odessa.'

'Odessa?' It was my turn to ask a silly question. 'Where's Odessa?'

Shirley was beyond the point of patience. 'Texas, for fuck's sake! Odessa in Texas. How can you not know that?'

Susan stepped up to him. 'There's no need to be rude, Shirley. We just... found ourselves here.'

He said nothing more, then turned and walked back to his group, shaking his head. I put my mouth to Susan's ear. 'We can't give ourselves away. We need to blend in or something.'

Susan was great at surprising me. 'We *are* blending in,' she said. 'Haven't you noticed? No one's recognised us yet.'

It hadn't crossed my mind. Course, being a little famous in some places didn't mean we were famous everywhere. Seemed like these folks down in Texas were more into outdoor pursuits than political power struggles. Modern ones, anyhoo.

But it was still bugging me – why did Roger send us here? He said he was helping us. Another lie from a master deceiver?

We didn't notice Shirley coming back, this time with someone else in tow. The other guy wasn't in a uniform but wore a bright yellow vest and carried a radio. He tugged at my jacket. 'Your behaviour out there was pure farby. How'd you get in here? You from another group upstate?'

I didn't like my clothes being tugged by no one. I pushed his hand away. 'Yeah, that's right,' I said. 'Guess we took a wrong turn somewhere. But what's this farb stuff? Shirley called me a farb too. I don't like being called shit I don't understand.'

The guy snarled at me. 'You're a farb for sure. If you don't even know what a farb is, you're a farb. No doubt, ya fuckin' farb.' He turned on his heels and made to walk away. Then he said: 'Shirley, see they get off the field. We have to set up for the next one tomorrow.'

Shirley still looked pissed off. 'Seriously, what are you guys doing here? You're clearly up to something.'

I took my helmet off. Susan did the same. 'You don't recognise us? You ever watch the news? Read the papers? Look at UniTube?'

He looked deep in thought for a moment, then shook his head. Then all of a sudden his eyes widened and he blurted out: 'Yeah, I know you! Your hair. You're the... er... the Fist guy, right?'

'That's me,' I grinned. 'Marty Molloy's the name. This here is Susan Poynter.'

'So you really are farbs,' he said. 'What brings you to Odessa? Some kinda publicity stunt?'

I thought for a moment. Had to answer this one carefully. Then I decided we were already in a wacky position – there weren't any point beating around

123

the bush. Time was running out. Perhaps fate and Roger had conspired to put me where I really did need to be.

'We're on a mission to prevent John Thump bringing about the false 'pocalypse. I'm an immortal agent of the absent God, sent from a hundred years in the future to recruit three horsepeople to save humanity. I've got one so far. Need two more. Guess that's why I'm here.'

Shirley's face cracked into an uneasy smile, then a wide grin. He burst out laughing.

'Holy shit, Marty,' he said, still chuckling. 'This is really happening?' He paused, then continued: 'OK, I'll be your horseman. Count me in. Shirley M. Bottom at your service. What do you need?'

9

Shirley led us off the field, past a row of tents where all the 'actors' were taking a break with various refresherments, then beyond the MOP area to a fenced-off car park.

'You're not gonna believe this,' he said. 'Well, actually I guess you just might.'

We walked over to his car. He opened the boot – well, I guess to him it was a trunk – and started rifling through a large bag. Then he pulled out a sheet of paper folded over, unfolded it and showed it to us.

In big lettering, a style that looked mighty familiar, it read:

'*Congratulations. You've been selected to save mankind! I'll be there soon. Take care. MM.*'

If surprise was a turd, someone had just shat it into my mouth. 'When did you get this?' I asked him.

Shirley laughed again. 'I got this about a week ago. Found it on my doorstep. I showed it to my sister. She said it was obviously from some nutjob. Seemed to me like it was, but I held onto it anyway.'

That was good enough for us. Clearly one of my other *mes* had set this shit up. So I told him everything, right from the very beginning. We sat there on the grass drinking his coffee and eating his food. At points he stopped me to ask questions. He laughed his head off when I told him, near the start mind, how I got the weird groove in my scalp. He laughed harder when I told him about Thump's generous offer of handjob insurance. By the end of the tale, all caught up, we just sat there smiling at each other – some kind of giddy rapport in our new triangle of horsepeople.

After a while, Shirley had a good question for the team: 'So how do *we* stop it? I mean, there's you – an immortal agent of God – and Susan, and I guess the two of you have got to where you are with some skill and a dollop of good fortune, but how do I fit into this?'

'You know about war, right?' Susan asked. 'You know all about this stuff. What else do you know about?'

Shirley smiled. He was a handsome guy. Not quite as good looking as me, of course, but he was much younger anyhoo. Thirty years old, a science graduate with a physics major. Knew his way around computers too and spent a little time in his teens and twenties learning a bit about hacking.

It was all starting to make sense. Me and my varied yet kinda vague skill set, Susan the psychologist with experience in more fields than I ever knew existed, and now Shirley Bottom – the smart techie with a shit name. A girl's name.

'When those nukes fly,' he said, 'a lot of people are dead. If that's what's going to happen, as you say, then when it does it's game over, or kinda the beginning of the game over. Years ago there was this fad for people building their own bunkers underground, but these days most people think the nuclear threat is over. You've got the UN anti-nuke guys going around doing inspections. The nukes have all supposedly been deactivated. But that's just what they want you to believe. Far as I can see, the world and his wife have nuclear capability, right down to some fat kid with no friends who's found out how to build a dirty bomb on the internet. As for the governments, they're all loaded and staying that way. There's no way the Russians or North Koreans are giving theirs up, and here in the States... well, we've probably got 'em stacked high in a cupboard somewhere in the White House.

'Once the order's given, the silos and subs and bomber command go into action. It's an instant thing, no hesitation after the directive. Missiles and bombs will be prepped and you'll see birds in the air in minutes. The silos will launch and the bombers will take off, even satellite nukes if they have them. But that would be M-A-D: Mutual Assured Destruction! Those who aren't hit directly get the fallout. Their skin falls off. They puke. They die.

'It could go another way though, which I reckon is more likely. Most of those nukes could never get used. We're not talking hundreds all at once. It's not like the whole of the Earth's sky is gonna light up like fireworks and lightning. They'll probably launch one or two tactical nukes at most, then go conventional from there. Guns and grenades.'

I felt elatered and deflatered all at once, realising as I listened to young Shirl that I'd always just taken my life for granted. I was born post-pocalypse – I lived in the aftermath, not through it. I didn't have to watch anyone die. But Angie had shown me what was gonna happen, how it went down – and how it was going to happen to my future too, if I didn't complete my mission.

All of a sudden the enormity of it hit me again. With my old memories clashing against all these new ones, my emotional state was not unlike a spinning room. But I had to hold it together.

The three of us and some other woman – how could we really hope to stop it all? For all the influence me and Susan had, it was just among a few million people, and I gotta admit that despite my obvious appeal I wasn't sure it was the type that could save mankind. The world was billions of people. And stopping Thump might not have been the solution after all. For all the down-to-earth normality of sitting here, watching the sun set over Odessa, we were talking about grand concepts I wasn't sure I even believed.

Shirley wasn't privy to my private thoughts, but what he said next settled me down a little: 'Odessa is bang in the middle of the Bible Belt. We got Christians, Mormons and Muslims living side by side. Sometimes that ain't an easy alliance, but one thing's for sure – round these parts, people believe in the higher power. You go up to New York or hang around in Los Angeles and it's different. People are their own gods. It's a state of mind. People believe different things. Over the border to the west you're in New Mexico, with the Navajo guys. Now they are some deeply spiritual dudes. And to the south you've got the real Mexico. There's some voodoo shit going on down there, I reckon. Black magic in some parts.

'Way I see it, you're born in Iraq, you're a Muslim. You're born here, you're most likely a Christian. You're born in India, you're a Hindu. Look at sports too: you're born in France, you're not gonna support the German soccer team. It's all about geography. You wanna know what I believe?'

Me and Susan nodded. This guy was eloquenked. I liked the way he spoke. He sounded a little bit like me, but more soothing. The kid had a smooth way about him, even when plunging his speculative brain stick into the deep, dark hole of spiritualisement.

'I believe there's something out there, but what it is I don't know. If there's a Christian God, he's gone to a lot of trouble to hide that, hasn't he? You're supposed to run on faith, right? Nothing else. Where's the evidence? And that God, who's supposed to be all about love for his human creations, seems OK with flooding and burning and cancer and AIDS and everything else that's bad in the world. I mean, if he loves us so much, why doesn't he do something about this stuff?

'The *Bible*'s full of really scary shit, like smiting and God-sanctioned genocide. That ain't no loving, caring attitude as far as I can see. But at the same time, I see the evil of man, of people like Thump and just about every damn politician on the planet. It's the power that corrupts them. They start out with good intentions but then the power gets to them. They're given free will just like the rest of us, but the power they wield to use that free will is dangerous. Maybe the best thing for the planet is to let this stuff happen anyway. Let us destroy each other. Maybe that's what this God – your God – wants.'

We were all wrapped up in Shirley's thoughts. He continued: 'Hey, I try to keep an open mind, but I'm a scientist. I've learned a lot of stuff that goes directly against all that religious stuff, from whatever angle. But the stuff you've just told me, well I can either believe all of it or none of it. I ain't gonna pick and choose to suit my own belief system. If you're telling me time travel is possible, that's something science doesn't allow for – at least not yet. So maybe the stuff I think I understand turns out to be false, or maybe you turn out to be false, but so far you've got me half way to convinced. I'm not seeing a whole lot of proof of what you've told me. I mean, that's quite the story. But I have faith, I guess. It feels right. Mad as shit, but right.

'Whichever way, I'm happy to come along for the ride. The way I see this, well… either way, there's a result. Either we live or we die. You've got that on your shoulders, Marty, and I'll help you carry that. Which leads me to my next question: what do we do next?'

I felt a smile break out on my face, all the way across. I'd known this guy for less than two hours and he was already exactly what we needed. Our quest was on the right track.

I was half expecting to be plucked away and into darkness as usual when Shirley got all the proof he needed. A silhouette appeared against the sunset.

'Shit on a sandfly,' the other 'me' said as he came into view, 'so it all worked out then?'

10

Shirley's jaw stayed slack for a good couple of minutes before he managed to get his head straight.

The other 'me' shook my hand, doffed his cap to Susan and just smiled at Shirley.

'I don't have long,' Me said, 'but I just had to check this was all going to plan. And – I've got a message for you.'

'So it was you who left him the note?' I asked. Me nodded. 'Were you one of the *me*s sat round the table with Angie?' Me shook his head. 'Then you're the one who saved me at the hospital?'

'That's right,' Me said. 'But listen, I really don't have much time. You have to listen carefully. This shit is mad-mega-important. War is coming. A big war. Not the *really big* war – hell, that's not even a war, strictly – but America is about to cut itself in half. You need to get ready for the part you'll play. And you need to find your final horsewoman.'

'OK,' I said, apparently comfortable with taking directions from a rogue 'me'. 'Who is she? Where is she?'

'Don't worry about any of that,' Me said. 'I'll put you in the right place. The rest is up to you. Just follow me.'

'But how can you do that?' I said. 'I can't.'

Me smiled at me. 'I'm a messenger,' he said. 'I deliver messages. You sent me here to deliver this message to you. *I* don't even know how that works. I've got another message to deliver in about ten minutes, so get a fuckin' move on. Follow me.'

With that, we all stood up. I regarded this other 'me'. He was different, somehow. Me, but not. The others had all been like mirror images. This one was off though, like maybe younger or even older. In the fading light it was hard to tell which.

Shirley closed his trunk and stepped up to me. 'Marty – do you promise me everything you told me today is true?'

I nodded. 'Course it is, Shirl.'

He turned to Susan. 'And you – you vouch for that promise?'

She nodded too. 'I do, Shirley. Entirely.'

'OK then,' he said. He picked a bag up off the ground, one he'd packed with what he called 'a few essentials', and we set off with Me.

Once we were far enough away from the base camp, Me stopped and motioned for us to do the same. 'Stand in a circle around me,' he said.

I looked up to the sky, seeing the Sun fading under the horizon as my gaze turned up to space – the vast universe ahead of us, all seventeen-trillion stars looking back at me.

Then there was a weird tearing sound, like harsh TV static hanging in the air and ripped in half. The tear opened.

'Wait!' Shirley grabbed the other 'me' by the arm. 'How is… how is this even possible?'

Me fixed him with those soft yet intense eyes. 'How should I know? I sent myself back to do this. I've done my bit, and I've got a lot more to do. It's vital that you do your bit too.'

Me spoke one last time before we all stepped in. He fixed me right sternly: 'This is the last time you'll see me. The absolute last time. Remember that. And good luck.'

We watched in awe as the tear expanded around us like a bubble, then almost as suddenly began to contract, as if about to squash us together. But that didn't happen, thankfully. We were plunged, what a surprise, into darkness again. Shirley's first time, mind. I was used to this shit. A pro.

11

Oh no. I couldn't believe my eyes. This was not happening. I turned to Susan, then to Shirley.

'Supercalichickenbiscuitsexpialidouchebag,' I said, vocalising abstractly my strong internal opinion of the non-happenisation of the situation at hand. Shirley looked scared. Susan looked confuzzled. I guess I looked spazzwazzed too.

'Where are we?' Shirley asked. 'This place is grim.'

Right he was. It sure was a freaky place. 'Welcome to the future,' I said. 'This is where I come from. This is Kingston.'

Susan gasped. Course she didn't recognise it until she realised what we were standing opposite. There we were, right across the street from The Oubliette. It'd been there a hundred and fifty years or more. Back in her time she'd been there.

We were back to square one. Back in fuckin' shitty South London, back to where my life got turned upside-down, inside-out, and wiped its arse on my eyebrows.

We crossed over the road. It took me a little while to realise not where we were, but *when* we were. There, a poster on the wall announcing the live acts at The Oubliette, was mine. The night I last played there; the night Sally and me, not forgetting Georgio, had saved that little angel. I put my face up against the window to see inside.

Hoooooooooly-shriekin', shrimp-eatin' sock puppets! I grabbed Susan's hand. 'This is it,' I said perhaps a little too excitely. 'This is where it all started.' I got my bearings, taking the scene in. 'It's obvious now. You know – I've told you about this. In a minute I'm going to step out of that door, light my pipe and hear a little girl screaming up there. We can't let that happen. The screaming part, I mean.'

That shit was fresh in Shirley's mind. He'd only heard that part of the story ninety minutes ago. 'I'm in,' he said. 'What do we need to do? Which window was it?'

I pointed up to it. 'That one. I don't know how much time we have until I come out. Until whatever happens happens.' I thought back to it, that night.

How long had I been outside before I heard those screams? A minute; two maybe?

Susan grabbed my other hand. 'Then there's no time to waste. Lead the way!'

We ran across the street, into the alley. 'Oh shit,' Shirley said. 'Look back there. You've just come out the door.'

I didn't want to look back. I ran even faster down the alley, round to the left and straight up the metal staircase up the back. Susan arrived just after me.

'What now?' she said.

I was about to bang my fist against the door, but I stopped myself. Something held me back. Shirley wasn't waiting around though. That guy had some balls for sure. He strode up to the door, pushed me aside and was about to thrust his boot into it. Just then, sheesh, I realised the guy was still dressed as a Nazi. Shit, we all were!

'Wait!' I said, tugging him back. 'I gotta get this straight.'

As I held him, thoughts flooded into my head. Thoughts from just a few nights ago – if I intervened now, that would stop me from hooking up with Jessie (and eventually Angie), going to the police station, to Kingston Hospital, and probably to all the rest of it too. If I stepped in now, maybe none of that would ever happen, which might even wipe us out of existence. Angie had been clear from the start though – up to this point everything had always been the same, and it'd just taken that one small change for the butterfly effect to lead to this point. Making this change to it all now would lead to… what, saving the world?

Shirley clearly wanted to follow his instincts. 'Listen, Marty. I know what you're thinking, but why else would we be put here? This is the pivot. This is the fulcrum.'

Damn, that word again. I liked it even less amid this confuzzlement. Susan put her palms on my cheeks – the upper ones, mind, given that although such situations of unbrindled exciterness would potentially lead to some arousal of sorts, I wouldn't imagine that kind of business on the agenda there and then – and spoke slowly and clearly: 'No, Marty, you're right. Stepping in now would change everything. It'd stop us being here in the first place. Think about it!'

I thought about it. Again. This was my decision. I felt like the turtle's head, peering down from the anal cave of quandary at the pool below – a deep, dark pool of uncertainty and potential regret beyond anything ever imagined before. The fate of the world in my hands. Or, to follow the metaphor, hanging out of my arse.

'You're gonna have to trust me, guys,' I said. 'I mean it – someone's playing us here. If we step in now, we'll never come back to this point, and that means everything just happens as it did. Which brings us back here. Maybe. But this is my one chance to change all that. We need to get out of here. Now!'

12

It was too close. By the time we'd made it off the metal staircase and found the hiding place yonder – a bunch of burnt-out cars and shopping trolleys to crouch behind and peer at the action – my other self and Sally and Georgio were already well in motion.

From what Angie had told me earlier, I was just watching an echo. It played out just as I remembered it. Susan and Shirley knew what was gonna happen too.

Sally went down as before, the red beast blasting from Jessie's throat and knocking her out. It was OK – we knew she'd be up in a few seconds. Then that little demon took a shot at me too; the other me, that is. Sure enough it streaked right across my scalp. Even from there, crouched in a dimly lit recess of the back-street parking, observing myself being attacked by that slimy red demon with the eyes of eternal ballache, I could see it clearly for the first time.

It was breathtaking from that angle. That little girl opened her mouth and this fleshy rod came out of it, its end opened up and it spat this air-bullet at me. Georgio then came running up the steps and lobbed a flash at her – and it was over. Then the other me and Georgio carried that girl down and out of sight. Just as it happened before.

Susan, who'd been a few metres away hiding and peering from her own rapidly-chosen vantage point, crouch-walked over to me. I hadn't seen her much from that angle. Lordy, she was arousing in that position too.

She tapped me on the shoulder. 'That was incredible,' she said. 'Utterly incredible. I've seen some things but… the way you told me and then actually seeing it, well… that was something else. Really *something else*. So what do we do now?'

My eyes were still fixed on the scene. Something didn't feel right. Was it really exactly as it had happened the first time?

Shirley waddled over to join us. 'I know what you're thinking,' he said. 'I was watching for it too.'

'Watching for what?' Susan asked.

'For anything that deviates from the path,' he said. 'Remember – the whole reason we're here is because stuff changed. Now other things are changing, but we're still here. We need to change something too maybe.'

'What's changed?' I said. Yeah, I figured something was off, but I couldn't pin the tail in that donkey.

Susan got to the conclusion before Shirley could: 'It's Sally. She's still down. She told you she got up just after you left and checked the apartment out. But she's still down. Something's wrong.'

Those words churned my stomach. Poor Sally – I guessed this time she was dead. My tear ducts opened. I'd adored that woman for so long. Not sexualised, but sincere appreciation. And she had it back for me, I knew.

I'd known Sal for years and she'd always been straight. By which I mean you knew where you were with her, always. I'm not commenting on her potential lesbiosity. The most reliable old gal, she was. Sure, she had her struggles, but she'd come good. I just couldn't believe it.

Shirley took the initiative. He got up and ran out of the shadows then up the steps and crouched over Sally. Me and Susan exchanged a look of 'what's he doing?', then joined him up there.

I looked down at the poor girl. My stomach churned again.

'I think it's because we're here,' Shirley said. 'Somehow just being here in the same space is warping the continuums, or something.'

Continuums joined fulcrum in the naughty book. Geez, having these stupid big words wiped on my vocab-curtains was getting to be too much.

'OK, so whatever the continuums are up to, Sally here is dead. And I feel really bad about it,' I said. I was about to burst open. Waterfalls.

Then, out of nowhere, an eagle of fortune flying overhead shat a miracle onto the lot of us. Sally lurched up, her head bobbing between her shoulders as a sharp grunt came out of her mouth. I instantly put my hand on hers and held it tight.

'It's OK, Sal,' I said. 'You're OK. Just breathe.'

She fixed Shirley and then Susan in her gaze. A minute later she started to breathe normally.

'Marty,' she croaked. 'Jeez, Marty. Who are these guys? What the hell's going on?'

Truth is I didn't have any idea for a few moments. Then it hit me. 'Sally,' I said. 'You busy tonight? How do you fancy being a horsewoman?'

13

We ducked back behind the wall, level with Georgio's shop. Now Sally had a choice: she could either catch up with me and Georgio and continue the story as it was first told, taking them into The Oubliette, or she could come with us, listen to our long story, and save the world.

She made the right choice. We needed to get the hell out of there. I started running, beckoning the others to follow me.

'Wait!' Susan called. 'Your guitar.'

I stopped in my tracks and followed her gaze. There it was, my beauty, standing proud against the wall, where I'd left it. Shit, I couldn't stand the feeling, but could I risk me seeing myself and tipping the apple cart of continuity too much? Heck! I rushed over the road, grabbed the case, and legged it back the other way. 'We have to leave now!' I shouted. With that guitar case clasped tightly in my hand we got just up to the end of the street when the police car came around the corner. It sped past us and screeched to a halt outside the bar. We still hadn't seen Future Me and Normal Georgio come out of his shop with Jessie. The ramificaters were unknown.

We took the corner to the left and kept going. After a while, we took another left into a small park. It wasn't lit at all, so we stayed close enough to the road to give us a little visibility from the street lamps.

As soon as we got our breath back, I told Sally properly what had just happened. When I stopped talking, she said: 'I got this message… this weird message about a week ago, from one of my aug suppliers saying I should turn off my shield aug as it was faulty and dangerous. So if what you're saying is true, when this originally happened to you I was using that aug, which better protected me. So I sent that aug back and installed a lower power one I got from Georgio just temporarily, which didn't protect me as well. I get it. Totally fucked up, but I get it. Same event, different eventuality.'

Then we explained everything to Sally. Susan and Shirley interrupted me several times, telling me I was rambling and going off on tangents. Maybe I was. We got through the story faster with them pitching in anyhoo, and by the end of it Sally signed up just as Shirley did before: the awesome foursome. The circle complete. More like a square. Or a rhombus. Or…

Naturally, Sally had questions we couldn't answer. One of those kinda had us on the wrong end of the ignorance stick: how were we going to get back to the past?

After a few minutes, some speculative progress: 'OK,' Shirley said. 'I've worked it out. Tomorrow afternoon that tear's going to appear back at Eden, if that's still on the cards. So that's how we get back. That means we have to spend the night here, then make our way to Eden tomorrow.'

I thought back to that night again: yeah, I'd escaped the police with Jessie, then ended up after the crazy police station massacre incident in hospital, and then been abducted late the next morning and taken to Eden. The time line was sound – assumerising it hadn't been altered by past interference. I had to hope it hadn't.

'Well we need somewhere to stay,' Susan said. 'We can't stay out here. We need to sleep somewhere, get something to eat and I wouldn't mind getting out of this bloody uniform!'

'We'll go to my place. There's no hotels around here, just squats,' I said. 'I've got enough room – just. But excuse the mess. I've been away.'

'New Wimbledon, right?' said Shirley.

Sally laughed. 'After all these years, I finally get to see where you live.'

14

Sally dialled a taxi on her wrist aug. We stayed out of sight until it arrived. Although the cars were driverless, they required an implant scan. That's how we were supposed to be charged for stuff in the future – straight to our implants. Sally scanned hers. All business owners were chipped.

First we dumped our jackets. That was Susan's idea. A bunch of Nazis riding towards London might attract some kind of attention. I told the taxi where to go and it set off. For the first couple of minutes we were all silent – processing our own thoughts, trying to put a small condom of understanding on the giant bell-end of life.

I felt like I'd lived a lifetime between then and now. Hell, I kinda had. But I'd done my thinking. I'd made my decisions. I took my quiet time to watch the outside world, the dimly lit streets of Kingston leading out to the A3 and towards the old City. People in their cars, following their noses. A few driverless taxis here and there. The distressed dystopia of South London visible everywhere with only thin rays of hope bleeding from the dirty net curtains of the last remaining humans.

Fifteen minutes later we got to my turf. New Wimbledon was different to Kingston – not quite as grim. A shade or two less brown on the shit scale. It had more space too and a more mainstream, respectable night life. Well, relatively speaking.

'Let us out here,' I said. The taxi stopped. We were on the main thoroughfare, just outside the old railway station. Back in Susan's time, it was still doing its job. In my future, it was a bar: The Womble.

'You know what I need?' The others looked like they did. We strolled into the wide entrance and me and Sally stood ahead of them. I was glad to be back somewhere I knew, after all this time.

I heard Shirley gasp. Susan was silent. We turned around. Shirley was turning pale while Susan just looked rooted to the spot.

I turned back to survey the main bar and it hit me: guys out in the open smoking their Digis, a bunch of heavily augmented guys and girls over the other side just minding their own business… but to someone from the past, it must've been a shock. And to Susan, she was looking at what a hundred years did to a place she used to know. For Shirley though, his first visit to what used to be England hadn't been great so far.

Realising they were getting funny looks, Shirl and Susan joined us and we headed to the bar. I ordered for us: 'Fuck on, sir. Eight firesnaps.'

The burly barkeep poured them out. Shirley looked uneasy.

'Just pick it up and chuck it in,' I said. 'There's no new way to get drunk.'

We did our two shots each, then ordered some more. We did them too. We were headed half way to Shitfaced Island.

'We shouldn't do any more,' Sally said. 'If all you told me was true, we gotta be sharp tomorrow.'

'You're right,' I said. 'It's late anyhoo. We gotta get some sleep. You know, I'm tired. More tired, actually, than I've felt in a long time.'

Susan nodded. 'Me too,' she said. She flashed me a beautiful smile. Now firesnaps once or ten times had got me into lady trouble of the sexual kind, and I could see the night headed in that direction. Her expression told me the same.

'How far from here?' Shirl asked.

'Round the corner,' I said. 'Five minutes.'

We made for the exit. My heart sank at the sight of red and blue lights outside. The pigs had turned up.

The doors flung open. Five officers rushed in, their aug visors scanning immediately. The centre one made the announcement: 'Fuck on, ladies and gents! This is a raid!'

I looked at Sally. She looked at me. We shook our heads.

It all happened too quickly. A hand yanked at my arm, pulling me down to my knees and then both arms were grabbed and I was dragged away from my horsepeople.

'Martin Molloy, you're under arrest.'

It wasn't only me. There were three other dudes sailing in the boat of justice.

'What for?' Susan said, rushing over to me.

One of the officers got in front of her. 'Lady, step the fuck back please. He's wanted for...' He looked down at his wrist aug. Then he started laughing. 'Oh man, this is good. He's a seedless.' He showed his wrist aug to the officer who was forcing me down. Then *he* laughed too.

'What's your problem, mate?' he said. 'Got better things to spend your spunk on? Says here it's been three years since you fed the harvester. You a jaffa or something?'

His colleague jumped in: 'Yeah, you got something against enriching the human race of the future, or just got feeble nuts?'

Shirley, who it suddenly occurred to me had probably never drunk anything as strong as firesnaps, stuck his oar in. 'Actually, we're all trying to preserve the future of the human race, if you don't mind. You can't arrest him. He's an agent of God.'

The pigs burst out laughing. Pig One was the first to settle down. His face looked like it hurt from the laughter. 'Riiiigggghhht. In that case, how about this? Tonight you're coming with us. You'll enjoy the hospitality of The Council in a tiny cell with a toilet that doesn't flush properly. Tomorrow you'll get to empty every last iota of your middle-aged jizz into the wall, and then you can pay your fine and get out and get back to saving the human race. Or, if you haven't got the means, which I suspect is the case, well... you get to shit in that toilet a few more times. Let me tell you – you *never* get used to the smell.'

Sally knew how to deal with these guys. Ignore them. 'Marty,' she said, 'it's OK. I've got stacks of credits. It'll be fine. I'll get you...'

'Whatever,' Pig Two said. 'All of you – shut it.'

Shirley threw his hands up in desperation. He leaned in to whisper in Susan's ear. I couldn't tell what he was saying, but it was kinda obvious. If I was gonna have to ejacterise the entirety of my reproductive orbs into 'the harvester', how were we gonna make it to the tear in time? I mean, not that I'm a heavy lifter in that regard, but in my experience getting it *all* out isn't a quick process.

With the officers bustling about, I tried to get Sally's attention without calling out. Telling Susan or Shirley wouldn't have made any sense. Once we had eye contact, I mouthed my password to her: *Lizards*. Clutching my guitar case close, she nodded. The password would get them into my humble apartment. By humble, let's be clear: I mean shit.

Still, it was what it was. I'd always been OK on the booze. It made me feel happy, not aggro. I knew I was immortal, but the situation was too sensitive to introduce that level of craziness into proceedings. I'd learned that just because I couldn't be killed didn't mean I could solve any problemised situation with that knowledge.

As the pigs led me out of The Womble to the carrier out front, I waved to my colleagues and thanked the barkeep with a sincere 'Fuck on!' Outside, I felt eyes on me. The eyes of no-hopers, milling about in a future that never needed to happen. Heck, if I couldn't take my horsepeople safely back in time, this was going to be the end anyway. This and then nothing. Those demons Angie'd showed me, devouring anything that drew oxygen.

15

I had to hope they'd be OK. Sally's aug would lead them back to my place. She had the password. They'd be safe for the night.

I guessed I was safe too. I was processed quickly, at least. The carrier drove up the hill to New Wimbledon Nick. It was an odd building, with two kinda curved walls coming out of it at the front and some kind of commemorating monolith on the top. The locals called it The Peach. Odd name for a cop shop, but an odd name really for anything that isn't a peach.

They walked me through the entrance, scanned me and within about two minutes I was in the cell. The toilet was there, as advertised. I could smell it already. A flashback to my last such experience reminded me of *that night*. That pivotal night.

It was a fuckin' bloodbath. That red demon horse-hound thing had torn through the place, shredding those *guys from another place*, to get to me. Damn, I reckoned by that time... if that shit was still happening in this altered future, it'd be happening around about then.

I should've anticiperized it. The police, albeit a different set and for a different crime as far as I knew, had found me. The red beast wanted me, wherever I was. The *people from the other place* wanted me too. If the other me wasn't in Kingston Nick yet, I was definitely sitting there in The Peach. Two plus two equals seven. Chocolate arse biscuits.

About half-an-hour passed before it happened. By the time that big plasticky demon smashed my cell door open with its weird hoof-trotter, I'd made my peace with it. I'd heard the screams out in the corridor, the crashes and smashes, and when we stepped out of my cell I saw a scene so similar to the last one: blood and entrails sprayed on the walls and spilled on the floor. The red beast regarded me hungrily, its tongue lolling.

'It's OK, feller,' I said, reaching up and patting it on the head. 'Jump in. The water's lovely.'

PART 4

1

Damn, that red beast being back inside me was two things: first, just as fucked up as before; second, plain and simple lucky. There was something oddly comforting about its presence, something hard to pin down. What with all the crazy shit that'd been dumped on me on this mad journey, finding things I knew and could hold on to kept me sane.

'What is handjob insurance?'

Ha! The beastly bastard had been scanning my mind, its mental protuberances linking up with mine. I didn't need to speak out loud to this thing. Our communication was all up top.

'Fuck on, feller,' I thought. 'Look deeper if you care to.'

It did. Man, I felt it. Like a worm slitherising around my skull, poking in and out of crooks and fannies, finding a way through my mind-maze. Then it reached the same conclusion I'd arrived at.

'We do not need handjob insurance.'

I nearly laughed my kidneys out. Odd as it was, surveying the carnage in front of me, all those bodies and blood. Just like the last time, those *men from another place* had come after me. They'd butchered those poor police folk, and the devil's dog had chewed those bones up in the aftermath. Saving me was its job. Last time it'd been some branch pig station in Kingston; now we were in The Peach of Wimbledon. The same scene in a different movie. A sequel where the director was too afraid to tread a new path.

'We must go. Tomorrow the Tremendous begin their harvest.'

Huh? They begin their what?

I felt that thing rummaging around in my mind again, but this time deeper and harder, as if it was a pig in a trough, greedily gobbling up all my memories and knowledge. Gotta say, of all the feelings I'd experienced on this journey, it was the most uncomfortable – the otherworldly equivalent of wearing loose trousers and accidentally sitting on your own balls.

Then, after a few seconds that seemed like much longer, the snout left the trough.

'Here,' the voice came from inside. 'You have already seen it.'

Up until that point, I'd been riding along on some idea that I was predestined to make a difference. I'd watched the world kick itself in the nuts over and over with the most important decisions made by people who either had all the facts and ignored them or made up their own and got away with it.

Where were all these political geniuses who shaped the world into something worth keeping hold of? Having been sent back and given a chance to witness a world I could only dream of in my future existence, I couldn't believe how easily it'd all been squandered. The history lessons of my future were little more than lies and interpretisations woven together to make something that sounded a lot better than it was.

Fuck me sideways with an ocean liner – now I got to really thinking about it, behind that veneer of a developing society was a festering turd covered in the flies of fuckdom. Sure, there were politicians who wanted to do good, but those guys were hamstrunged right off the bat. Those guys and their good ideas – yeah, but where's the money coming from? Who'll pay for it?

In my time in the UK of a hundred years ago, I didn't see much other than bluster. The news was as much about Thump and the US shit as that stupid Britout thing. You give the vote to the ordinary chumps on the street and you can't then be surprised when the outcome is similar to a laxative inserted into the anus of the insane, which is attached to a garden sprinkler.

Racists, bigotists, ignoranuses all over... man, when did people find all that energy to hate on each other so much? And almost always in the name of some religion. They had no fuckin' idea.

The American Dream was a lie too. All of it. You can be anything you want to be? No, you can't. Not if you have no money and your mother's a crack whore and your dad's in prison for stabbing some poor bastard in the neck. I looked at the geography of the place. Looked real deep. You got some States where no one ever leaves. They stay there their whole damn lives, like there's nothing anywhere else. There's no world out there. Shit, I'd been given access to that world, the chance to go back and see it in all its beauty. Yeah, I'd seen that beauty, but I'd seen the rotten meat left out in the yard too.

I remember someone telling me, a long time ago as a teenager: perception is reality. It doesn't matter so much how things really are as how people believe them to be. You tell a nation that there's fifty million murdering Muslims on the loose, or even just one, they're going to be afraid. That kind of smokescreen means they focus their hate on the wrong targets. Now I'm not saying no Muslim ever shot a man in cold blood, but I read somewhere that more people died from eating fuckin' biscuits than terrorist attacks.

Still, Red was right: I *had* seen the harvest; I'd just had no idea that's what it was when I saw it. The vision came back to me in an instant – those flying beasts spitting fire, melting people's faces off, consuming their souls… just as Angie had showed me in the beginning of this mad journey, I saw it all again in a fresh context. Those demons doing all that stuff – they *were* the Tremendous. The vision Roger had showed me, of he and his shit-arse colleagues marauding around the beautiful planet they'd been given – well, hell on holiday, they were those same beasts destroying everything at the end. And that end was coming faster than a fifteen-year-old at a peep show.

But enough of all that. As we stood in that corridor, all that blood sprayed up the walls and those guts spilled on the floor, I felt the beast pulling at my mind again.

In that low monotone, he said: 'Why would anyone need handjob insurance?'

2

I told Red to stop thinking about that nonsenserised bullspit from Thump. As I stepped over those bodies, Red crouching inside me, I suddenly realised: I didn't know what to do next. Should I go to my apartment and join up with the others? What was waiting outside The Peach?

There was only one way to find out. We emerged into the night, the main road through Wimbledon's centre still buzzing with activity. But there outside the pig station, it was too quiet. Red had done his job well, but that didn't excuse the feelings of supreme guilt in my heart and head.

'They came *from another place*. The Tremendous sent them to stop you.'

But no! Hey, hang on a second – Roger, a Tremendous himself, had been helping me. Hadn't he?

Without thinking it or asking for it, Red fetched the truth for me and stuck it in my brain like a flag on top of the mountain of revelations. Damn that bastard, Roger.

He'd sent some facsimilar of me to that fake battleground in Odessa and led us back to this place – back to the future. The future where I, along with every other soul still alive, was about to be harvested by Roger and his bastard dickless demons. Of course! How could I make a difference to the past from the future? He'd manipulated the whole thing. I didn't think my anger could get any more intense at that point.

It could. Red twanged the figurative flagpole. Oh shit, this was getting too much. Susan, the woman I'd come to love – she couldn't play her part either. Shirley M. Bottom, a guy with experience just where we needed it – transplanted into the future to suffer a fate we could've prevented. And Sally – there I was figuring she was part of the plan, but it was more deception by that charming bitch of a bastard.

And so here we were – hours from the end. But hold on again – if I was immortal…

'No,' Red said. 'You are not, not here. I believe that is why Roger put you back here. The *people from another place* can kill you. I can kill you too. In fact, anyone here can kill you.'

Standing out there on the street, a giant red horse-dog-demon-beast hitching a ride, I felt my bladder twinge. Like an anti-confidence condom pulled over the purple shaft of hope, the fear crept back in. My legs started to wobble.

'Stop it, weak human,' Red said. That voice was louder than before, filling my skull. 'Now is not the time for this. You can still do what you need to do. We will go to meet the others.'

I couldn't help it. My knees were about to buckle under the weight of the world, the world I couldn't save.

'You *can* save it. Your mission is the same. We *have* to get back.'

But I was all out of juice. I'd felt it seeping out. Not piss, I'm saying. I mean figurative juice. Like liquid enthusiasm. I'd managed to keep my bladder in check at least.

I felt Red shifting – his body detached from my insides, slithered up my throat and shot out in front of me. Immediately that thing turned on me and thrust into my chest, pushing me straight back into The Peach at the speed of light. I slammed against the wall, my feet catching corpses on the way.

Winded and breathless, I raised my dazed head. Red pushed his plasticky-smooth nose up against mine – his hot, hellish breath washing over my face. His mouth didn't move – but I felt the full force of his roar rattling my brain.

'Snap out of this, human. Right now. I can help you, but you are my master. You must lead.'

Pinned against the wall, my eyes stared into the deep black holes ahead of me. I dunno what it was – like I drew some power from those abysses, my battery recharging in the face of the giant horsey hellhound – but I felt *something*. As if he sensed my shift, Red backed off, clopping away from me on his weird hoof-hands.

Odd that it hadn't occurred to me before, but suddenly I realised I didn't know.

'Who sent you?'

'*You* did.'

Fair enough, I thought. I mean… I felt stuck, hopeless and resigned to being devoured by the Tremendous, but I still had a chance if I'd sent myself a care package. Red believed in me. 'Fuck on,' I said.

Red reared up and did that dizzying vaporisation thing, then darted towards me. As usual my head snapped back with the force. Inside my head again, his voice was back to normal, firm yet moderate: 'Fuck on.'

3

We legged it across the main road and darted down the hill past the bar I'd been arrested in earlier, around the corner past the old Centre Court shopping mall and across the road again. I didn't fix on any of the faces we passed – getting back to my apartment, back to my guys, was all that mattered.

Thoughts rushed through my mind like the wind beating against my face as I ran through the streets. Yet again I'd escaped justice, and yet again I'd managed to avoid emptying my nuts into a robot. It seemed even stranger to me now, what with the old wall-fuck being known as the harvest, and the end of mankind going by the same name. Either way, my actions were supposed to lead to preventing both of those things.

Two streets away from mine, I slowed down a bit, almost as if I was the horse and Red was my jockey, pulling on my reins.

'What's up, feller?'

'I can smell them,' Red said. 'The *men from another place*. There are more of them. And they are close.'

'So why are we slowing down?' It was a fair question, I thought.

Red's tone was steady – low and somehow hollow, yet big in my brain. 'To allow us to separate without incident.'

'Fuck that,' I said. 'From now on, we're staying together. Like the skidmark on the fabric of the pants of the future of humanity, we're inseparable.'

'Why do you speak like that? Why are you always talking about excrement and metaphors pertaining to your sexual organs?'

'It's just who I am,' I said. 'Besides, you already know that, don't you?' A bead of mistrust ran down my figurative column of confidence. 'But... if *I* sent you, you'd already know that.'

'Yes,' said Red, his monotone calming me. 'I asked the other you the same question. Your answers are obtuse. I am still puzzled by this behaviour.'

'Where is this other me?' I asked. Another fair question.

'In Eden, of course. There are many of you there. We must make haste.'

'OK,' I said. 'We'll tackle these bastards together. So... where are they?'

'Your apartment.'

Geeeeez, why didn't he say so in the first place? Despite my natural displeasement at the thought of what lay ahead, I felt a lightness in my step – somehow having that thing inside me gave me some kind of wings. We ran down the rest of Gap Road and across into Leopold – my street. It was quiet, too quiet.

'I really think we should separate,' Red said. 'You will be safer.'

'No way,' I said. 'But we need a plan.'

'My plan is to kill anything that wants to kill you.'

'OK, Red,' I said. 'So what's the best way to do this?'

I felt him wriggling around inside me again, as if trying different positions to get comfortable. Then, surpassering by some considerable distance the previous point on the *Official Scale of Holy Shit What's Happening To Me?*, I felt my neck snap outwards as my spine curved into an arc. I was thrust forward onto all fours.

'How's that?' asked Red. 'Like this we will be most formidable.'

'Um... can you put me back the way I should be afterwards?'

There was a pause. Bent over but primed, like a dog ready to pounce, I could feel Red's power surging through me. I felt his head inside mine.

'Maybe.'

That had to be good enough. There was no going back now. I started prancing forward. It felt odd for the first few steps, but then I could feel Red's influence pulling up the slack where my body tried to remain human.

We found our rhythm and picked up the pace, stopping outside my apartment building. Although in my own reality I'd been there only today, it was to me over a year since I'd been home.

Our thoughts, as our bodies, had become one and the same.

They're in the building. We walked up the steps to the entry lobby. *It could be a trap. So what? We'll kill them all.*

It happened so fast and man, it was awesome. As soon as we entered the lobby we were set upon by three of those guys. Now I'd never seen one (or three for that matter) up close – they had eyes just like Red, dark and empty and going on forever. And they were armed, quite literally: their arms fashioned into blades, sharp as thorns and primed to strike us.

I reared up onto my hind legs and in three swift movements danced across the lobby meting out fierce justice. The first guy got snapped in half with one

151

slice – my arm providing the motion and Red's flesh scything out of me like paint flying off a brush. We jumped up onto the ceiling and took the next one from above, reaching down and grabbing him by the neck, then squeezing his head into a paste. It was like jumping on a watermelon – that head just squished real easy, the blood and brain and bone splatterising to the floor as we moved to the third guy. For a split-second I looked into his eyes. There was nothing there, nothing at all. He went to raise his spiked arm up and we helped him out, snapping it off at the elbow and turning it back on him. That eye I'd been looking into took the spike so easily. It went right through his head and into the wall behind, pinioning the bastard on it. He hung there, dead as he deserved to be, like a doll on a clothes peg.

We reared up again, having conquered the lobby, with an almighty roar: my voice and Red's combining into some demonic, awesome howl.

We advanced up the stairs. Two more of those guys came at us. We ducked down and ran full pelt at the first, and as my head connected with him, Red's came bursting out, his mouth opening wide and biting straight through the guy's waist. With his bottom half hanging out of our mouth, we swung it into the chin of the second bastard like an uppercut. It sent him sprawling back onto his arse. Without a thought we pounced up, landing squarely over him. Red took him by the throat, ripping it open.

We let out another roar, bounding up to the first floor. My apartment was on the second. As we rounded the landing and made for the next set of stairs, a door opened ahead of us.

It was Max. He was a good guy. Kept himself to himself most of the time, but he was a good neighbour. For about ten seconds we stood there facing each other, his expression turning comically from shit-yourself surprise to absolute fear.

'Don't mind us,' we said in our newly demonic voice combo. He collapsed to the floor.

We got up to the second floor. The landing was empty, but we could smell more of them. They were inside. With my friends.

We reached our finger up to the buzzer next to my door and pushed it a little harder than it'd ever been pushed before. The usual bleep sounded. I said the word: 'Lizards.'

The door unlocked with a click. We knocked it open.

There were three of them there, in my lounge, each with their spikes ready to slice through my friends' necks. We looked from Sally to Shirley and then Susan. Each had fear in their eyes like I'd never seen. Their faces were wet with tears, and they'd been beaten too. Susan's face was caked in blood, the result of a gash above her left eye.

The *men from another place* spoke collectivised: 'Give yourself to us and we will spare their flesh.'

Susan's head began to shake, causing the spike to cut into her neck a little. A trickle of blood appeared from under the spike and trailed down sideways across her throat. She was trying to mouth 'don't'. It didn't take me long to make the next decision. The world was about to end anyway. It was everything or bust. Seeing that blood trickle out of her, well... I'd become pretty good at dealing with my anger issues, but this was enough.

I felt Red's power surge inside me, as if about to take over. We reared up again, my spine straightening and the bulge at the back of my head morphing back to its proper shape. Then I found myself taking a sharp and shallow breath in. *Pt-chhhhhhoooooo*! My mouth opened the widest it ever has – Red shot out into three long, red arrows. A blink of an eye later, those three bastards were on the ground, their skulls collapsed around those arrows. Then with a weird fizzing sound the arrows came up from the floor, began swirling around and reconstitutered there in front of us.

We stood in silence, the only interruption coming into my mind: *they're all dead. We're safe.*

Shirley, fixated on the red beast standing there in the middle of my lounge, was the first to speak: 'He's... uh... with us, right?'

Red swung his head over to Shirley and came nose-to-nose with him.

'Settle down, feller,' I said. 'We're good now.'

'We're good? GOOD?' Susan clearly wasn't. 'What... the... fucking...'

I stepped up to her, putting my hands on her shaking arms. 'It's OK, Susie,' I said. 'It's all going to be OK.' I looked down at those bodies, lying in a neat line but albeit bloody mess behind her. 'Red's here to make sure we get through this. And I'm gonna make sure that happens too.'

Sally was regarding Red with pure distrust. Hardly surprising. 'You the fucker that shot me down?'

He must've spoken direct to her mind then. She nodded and said, 'OK then. You're off the hook.'

Then she turned to me. 'Marty, it was *you*. You brought those men here. We were sitting in here talking about getting something to eat and then the door flew open. You came in and... brought those guys in. Then you left. What the hell's going on?'

I explained my take on it, based on what Red had showed me. Roger The Tremendous Bastard had taken his pants off and started waving his dick of deception around again. We'd been played almost from the start. We had to get back to Eden.

That night, Red was the fiercest guard dog of all time, not that he needed to be. We were safe, at least for a while. We needed our strength for the next day. Possibly the last day of all time.

Anyhoo, I got my guitar out of its case. Course it was still in tune. It'd only been a few hours here since I'd played a blinder at The Oubliette. Since this had all started. Before we got our possibly final night's sleep, I played us a song – one of those that'd gone viralised on UniTube in the old-new-old days. It seemed apt.

Something tells me this is gonna be electric
In all the seasons, every day
Brings a new sensation
There's truth in the fiction, and sometimes
There's a cloud hanging over us
A storm in a teacup
They'll never take away
Our reason to keep going
Our reason to believe
Kings and queens
Friends and fiends
We see the whole world, but
Don't know what it means

The light streaming in through my bedroom window was as welcome as any break of day, but my head sure hurt. A combination of those firesnaps and having Red inhabiterising me – the hangover from Hell, literally.

Breakfast was served. Half a slice of bread each, some beans and not a lot else – but it was something at least.

Shirley was confused. He pointed to the stains on the lounge carpet. 'Hey, uh... what happened to the bodies?'

Red, who was still primed as I guessed he had been all night, watching the apartment door and ready to squish the skull of anything that came through it, turned his head to face us and snorted. He'd cleaned them up. While we ate our bread and beans for breakfast, that shiny instrument of swift justice put the image in my head: he'd spent the night enjoying a new definition of the Full English. He'd cleaned up the corpses on the ground floor too. I felt a little twist in my stomach. Sally made a puking sound. Susan just stopped eating.

We talked some more over breakfast. Shirley had a lot to say. I'd told Susan so much about this future of mine, a mere sliver of what the world used to be in Shirley's time. He seemed to know a lot about it – about how the world had gradually eaten itself. He wasn't surprised how it'd ended up.

'I blame UniTube,' he said. 'It's a dichotomy.'

More big words that don't make sense to me. Hey, this is my story, I told him – stick to the plain and simple.

'OK,' he said. 'Well a dichotomy is like a separation of something, two sides of a coin where each represents something very different. And things like UniTube, well... they represent – or represented, I should say – a giant playground fight. See, at first it was just videos. Videos of whatever, really, just stuff to pass the time. Then it got bigger, and bigger, until just about the whole world were all just used to it.

'It's a normal part of life. You go on UniTube, you check what's new and you look up stuff you like and maybe watch some stuff you didn't know you liked. Well, Marty, it worked for you, and it worked for Thump. That's because it turned into some giant political machine. You've got guys on there uploading videos of like three or four hours just of them playing some videogame, talking bullshit while they do. Then there's all the channels full of ranting teenagers and people positing conspiracy theories and, hey, there's even stuff on there showing you how to make a bomb. It's just *everything*. While the rest of the internet is pretty much this giant *look at me!* directory, and the world's biggest repository of people having sex, UniTube is an active propaganda machine.'

The three of us were all tied up in his smooth style again. Shirley could probably talk us to orgasm.

He continued: 'The real dichotomy comes in the comments function. As soon as you let people loose there, it's a massive food fight. The racist scum come out to play. It's this relentless stream of foul-mouthed cussing and cursing, mocking and mud-slinging, and it's *that* shit that put Thump in power. There's no moderation there – you can say whatever you like. And I think someone designed that deliberately so that endless playground fight just intensifies by the day, people saying whatever the fuck they want without any fear of punishment. You ever read the comments on your vids, Marty?'

I nodded. I had, but only a few times. I too had been shocked by the level of hate sent my way, hate for what I was trying to do – just spread a good message. Most people didn't want a good message, so it seemed. They wanted to make me eat my own shit.

'They called it social media, but that's bullshit. It's *anti*-social media. Same as all those other places. You put yourself out there and there's this giant fizzing ball of fiery fuckin' negativity waiting to burn your ass and the ground beneath it. You know why that is? Because TV makes you want to do that. It's all drama and lies about Muslims and homosexuals and black people and giant asteroids and AIDS and paedophiles and there's always this *dun-der-dunnnn* music introducing the news, like you're supposed to think it's all super-dramatic and important when in reality none of that shit matters a bean to you.

'It doesn't mean you don't care about other people if you don't need to know everything that's going on all the time, everywhere. But they want you to feel bad about it. They want you to think there's a volcano about to erupt on every street corner. They want you to be on edge.'

I looked over at Susan. She was as entranced as me, but I could see she agreed with it all too. We'd talked about these things a little over our time,

156

but in her job she'd seen how people got all fuckered-up wading through the river of social shit. Sounded like the river was rising over the banks.

She jumped in: 'It's all instant too. No one has to wait for anything anymore, and on those *anti*-social media outlets it's all quick-fire – nothing's considered. That's the psychology of a fight – you take a punch and you deliver one straight back. Not throwing one is a sign of weakness. And the brain is wired to not feel good about losing.'

Sally had no point of reference for much of this. Well, a little less than me. But our world was so different. We had no internet like that. Our propaganda machine was blasted from speakers and put out on the intranet. Do this, do that. Do what The Council needs you to do. And most of that stuff was about the survival of the human race – rebuilding. Masturbating into a mouth mounted on a wall, guys lined up day after day chucking their seed into oblivion. It might as well have been. Now I hadn't spent any time researcherising what happened to our pearls of jizzdom once we'd evacuated them into the State, but I hadn't seen any boom in the population neither. There were theories I'd heard, like The Council was collecting our DNA for some other reason. I didn't care anyway. Over my thirty or so adult years I'd managed to mostly avoid emptying my wrinkly orbs of love into those machines. Shit, they didn't even try to make them look like women. Either a concession to the gay brigade or just lazy design. I remembered hearing about some guy early on who objectered to it as much as I did and instead of putting his icing on the cake, he let loose on the moose with the yellow dick juice. No one else ever did. The Council saw to that.

But some things hadn't changed, I realised, the more I thought about it as Shirley was waxing on. We still had the great divide between rich and poor, poverty and luxury. Even more so, maybe. And we still had racial hatred, though a little less of that I s'pose. Just a touch. But it seemed The Council, risen from the aftermath of our civil war and untouchable ever since, had an agenda it kept close to its chest.

I'd travelled a mile or two away in my own thoughts when Shirley leaned over the table and tapped me on the shoulder. It snapped me back into the room.

'Well?'

'Well what?' I asked. 'Sorry, I was kinda distracted.'

157

'Well what are we gonna do? We've got, what… a few hours to get over to this Eden place and get back in that tear in time.'

I nodded. 'Yep. Guess so. We'd better get a move on.'

Sally shook her head. 'Dorking's almost twenty miles from here,' she said. 'And taxis – *any vehicles* – that head out that close to the cordon are flagged. We can't risk that. They'd have the choppers out as soon as we got close.'

'Then we need an unchipped vehicle,' I said. 'Like the van they took me in, the first time.'

Susan asked: 'And where do we find one of them?'

'Ain't many that aren't chipped,' Sally said. 'But I think I know where we might get one. And I mean *might*.'

5

'He's got one. But we need to go now.' Sally looked more serious than I'd ever seen her, or maybe I just imagined a layer for dramatic effect. Didn't matter. She'd left the room, gone into my tiny kitchenette, then come out after a couple of minutes. She'd called some guy. I forget his name so we'll go with Mike Anic. Geddit?

Anyhoo, Mike had a little workshop the other side of Wimbledon, almost into Merton. Now while The Council did its best to make sure everyone and everything of consequence they used was chipped – although tolerating the underbelly of NoBodies who weren't contributing shit anyhoo – there were some ways people could avoid it here and there. And there was a small window of opportunity between refreshing a chip's data during the mechanical fixerising process. In other words, Mike started working on some car and downloadered its data, then fixed the fucker and uploaded the new data to the chip.

He'd told Sally he could put it down as a write-off. The car was not in great condition, but it was just about good enough to get us to Dorking. Apparently he didn't even ask why we were headed out that far. Sally said she needed something and had the respect of people for them to know not to ask.

Strapping my boots on in readiness to leave, Shirley sided up to me. He gestured over at Red, by the door. I shrugged. 'What?'

'Is he… going to hitch a ride too? I mean… back inside you?'

I made a face. A face of sudden realisation. Yeah, it meant that, if he was coming with us. And yeah, there was no way I was leaving that thing behind. Together, we'd been like a pint of prune juice to the constipation of evil.

'Cool,' he said. 'I want to watch. I didn't really see how it happened last night. I was a bit distracted, y'know…'

I tied my right boot and strode over to Red. He instantly swung his head up to look at me. 'It's time,' I said. 'Time to… y'know…'

Red awkwardly rose to his full stretch, filling that narrow little corridor with his plasticky presence. His eyes penetrated mine and then – as usual – he kinda fizzvaporised and shot into my mouth and nose. A few seconds later he'd wriggled into his usual position. I felt that boost of energy right away.

I turned back to Shirley. His jaw was dropped right open. He nodded in appreciation. Sally was busy tapping shit into her wrist aug. Then Susan appeared, dressed and ready to go. She'd found some of my clothes just about appropriate for her smaller frame. Well hey, really she was a bit taller than me but I guess not as wide of the waist. A belt around my best jeans did the trick, along with a plain blue shirt I hadn't worn for years. Gotta admit I had acquired the mild horn at that sight – seeing her in my bits and pieces. Maybe Red's extra jolt had my blood pumping better too.

Anyhoo, enough about that. Susan looked worried. She asked: 'How come no more of those things have come after us? And why haven't the police come?'

I thought about it for a moment. Then Red pushed his own thought to combine with mine: 'There's no army of them guys. We dealt with what there was. Angie told me at the beginning. Those guys come through the tears. Some make it through here and there. And they don't operate like we do. They're not human. They sniff people out, just like Red. I guess there are more out there, but we've done enough to be safe for now. As for the pigs, they think I'm dead, I guess.'

That answer seemed to settle her a bit. We left the apartment, me and Red leading. He'd cleared the bodies and blood away well. Red showed me how he'd dealt with the witness, Max. It was horrible, but the only way. Besides, this future was about to get changed big time, *if* we could get back.

We walked down to Gap Road, then along to the junction with the main Haydons Road. That led all the way down to Merton, but we broke away down All Saints towards Colliers Wood. Just inside the East Road estate, we found Mike's workshop. Sally made us wait outside, then a few minutes later drove the car out. I'd never been much for cars, but it was a pile of shit. Well, strictly speaking it weren't made of shit, but it might as well've been. A TK Lancet, maybe fifteen years gone, there was no front bumper and the front windows were out too. The seats were hard and stained. At least it wasn't chipped.

Most of the way, Shirley dominised the conversation. He told us more about his work in computers and how he'd once won an award for cracking some crazy hack set up specially for a competition. All the big brains from the US and some from outside too had gone in for it. He wasn't like some brilliant hacker, though, and there was a bunch there far better than him. But he figured something out – spotted a weakness before anyone else. He talked about some advances in physics too, and how the world was always changing shape – really slowly, mind – from an egg shape to more like the sphere everyone thought it was. That was some billion years off though, he said. And we all knew by then there'd be no one around to see it. Well, no one but the Tremendous, if that was where shit was headed.

We avoided a couple of checkpoints pretty easy along the way. Security wasn't so tight down these parts anyhoo, but the unwary could be nabbed. I wasn't about to be dragged off to the harvest again. No sirree.

I got the feeling on that journey too that Red was sleeping. He'd switched off, or something. While I could still feel that demon's presence lurking within, the usual 'knowing' was silent. I kinda liked it that way.

6

'Stop here,' I said. Sally pulled over. We were about half-a-mile from the Eden entrance, and I'd decided we weren't just going to crash in there. No, we needed to take things slow and sure. We left the old banger by the road and walked with determination until we came within a couple of hundred yards of the tree break.

If we'd got there early enough, I had it in mind we would see me and Susan watching the other me arriving in the van, then see us escorted down into the complex where we'd meet up with all the other *mes*.

'What are we doing here?' Red had woken up. He read my thoughts and answered his own question, then questioned his own question.

'This is not the right place. This is not the Eden I came from.'

Shit – another complication we didn't need. 'How can you tell?' I asked him.

'It smells wrong.'

'You can smell it from this far away?'

'Yes.'

That was good enough for me.

'OK, guys,' I said. 'Listen up. The latest skidmark in the underpants of our plan, rubbing against the scrotum of mankind's survival: Red says this ain't the place. This isn't the Eden he came from. Nor, by that extension, the one I did.'

Sally was defiant. 'Well, let's find out then.'

We scarpered fast as we could the rest of the way, hesitatered a little when we got to the dirt track, but seeing it was all clear we carried on.

Strange – the hatch was open. Something was wrong, *very wrong*. I could sense Red knew that too. We descended into the Eden entryway, down the short corridor and stopped again. The door was open too. The camera above it was out, by which I don't mean not in, but rather off. Guess I shoulda said off in the first place.

As we entered Eden proper, the fist of truth punched me in the face as the boot of astonishment connected clean with my knackers. Bodies – soldiers and their guns lying in pools of blood; heads disconnected from their necks;

and silence apart from the low hum of distant machines. Some power was active, somewhere, as the lights were still on.

Susan tugged at my arm. 'We should go check…'

I knew what she meant. We followed the route we'd been taken along before, to the room where we met all the *me*s previously. The door was slightly open, a light flickering inside. Sally and Shirley hung back. They'd picked up a gun each, figuring the corpses wouldn't miss them.

Now I've seen some of what used to be called horror movies. I've seen hundreds of them and consequietly I've had my fair share of scares, becoming somewhat accustered to witnessing the worst things those writers could dream up. And on my personal journey I'd witnessed a hell of a lot of real horror, but nothing prepared me for what came next.

Susan edged the door open. Under that flickering light, clicking like some deranged tap dancer, around that big table – there I was. *Seven of me*, in various states of dead. The United State of Massacred *Me*s. I couldn't look. Susan pulled me away and closed the door tight. I leaned back against it, breathless with shock.

Sally came up to me, concerned. Susan put her hand up. 'Don't. You don't want to see in there. It's…' The look on my face told her what she needed to know.

A minute or five passed. I got my breath back. Shirley had been twitching his rifle, checking it out and flicking bits up and down. He was clearly impressed with its manufacture.

'So now what?' he said, looking to each of us in turn. 'Anyone?'

I chucked all the variables into a pot and started stirring it with Red's help. Angie! Where was she? Damn manipulative bitch. No angel, Roger had said. Angie was no angel. No – she was one of them. One of the Tremendous. At that point it all made sense. *All of it*. The gradual realisation had been bubbling in the cauldron for the last day, pulling the recipe together. The ingredients for this shit pie: marinade a handful of raw human turd overnight in arse sauce, then bake it for twenty minutes. Do a massive shit on top. Eat.

Angie? Sounds enough like angel to make us think she's one. Likewise that Gabe prick. Archangel? *No. Prick.* Roger – harmless human name attached to the most devious demon I could imagine – and a prick. All of them, and whoever else, playing me like a piano.

Red spoke quietly into my brain: 'Is this why we needed handjob insurance?'

7

There was no going back: only forwards. Eden's twisty geographising was still fresh in my mind. I led my horses through those passageways, past those labs and the medical centre and the armoury and eventually – *and let me drive home the horror of the amount of dead flesh we had to step over on that journey* – arrived at the mansion end, buckled up against the radiation barrier.

We went straight up the stairs to the main ops room, the very same one where Angie'd 'revealed' my mission to me. The lights were on, but the monitors were off.

We searched all those upper rooms, a bunch I hadn't been in before too. There were bodies everywhere. I recognised a few of them. Then I remembered that bit down in the basement, like a dungeon, where all those other red demons had been caged. I led the way down there. What we saw when we got into that room damn took my breath away again.

Red leapt straight out of me and began pacing around the room, swinging his head from side to side. He let out a howl to end all howls. The room vibrated – that is to say the air was moving with his cry, like heat from a hot stove, somehow breaking apart right in front of our eyes. The room shook and the four of us were thrown backwards.

The cages were smashed open and there, lying in each of them, piles of empty red, plasticky skin – it was a dichotomy, I guess: on one hand those guys were shit-yourself freaky fuckers, but on the other this guy was my *friend*. My guardian.

I picked myself back up and tentatisingly put my hand on his neck, reaching up and gently stroking it. Red snorted, then turned to look at me. For the first time I saw something other than eternal blackness in those eyes; there *was* emotion. His friends, or maybe even his brothers and sisters, his cousins or whatever they were to him – well, now they were nothing. He'd been betrayed too, so it seemed.

Shirley got up and went to one of the cages. He reached in and picked up the skin. It was heavy, I could see, and he draped it down with both hands like a man sizing up whether he's too short and fat to fit into some elegant slacks. There, it looked like some kinda costume. To Red though, it was so much more.

'Put it down, Shirl,' I said. 'There's nothing here for us. Nothing. We're damn stuck.'

Red howled again, not so loud this time. Susan came to face me and moved in to embrace. I held her so tight. This whole scenario had just kept going from bad to worse. A downward spiral.

There was silence for a few seconds. Then Sally spoke: 'OK, so this future is different. We've been stitched up. The world's gonna end in a few hours, for real. Everybody's dead. What do we do?'

I thought about that for a minute. 'Red,' I said. 'Jump back in. I need your thoughts on this too.'

Red shifted from left to right, let out another slow howl, then did as I asked. I concentrated real hard on the problem at hand. The tear. It kept going round in my head. The tear. A while ago I'd found myself thinking about it – how come sometimes there was a tear and other times not?

Then it hit me. The Tremendous – they created the tears. *Of course* they did. These guys did whatever they wanted. Lies and tears, mostly. Our voices came out combined again: 'We should check for that tear. Although Angie is gone, the tear may still appear.'

Sally, Susan and Shirley were freaked. Course they would be. That voice was not mine; it sounded demonic because it was. Partly.

Red delved deeper into my brain. I could tell he wasn't entirely supportive of my rationale and, after a few moments, the fruits of his research became clear: 'It won't appear. The Tremendous create them for effect. They want us to think that's the only way we can get about. It is a trick. Even if it is there, it would likely put us right back to the beginning.'

I was back in control of my voice: 'See, they gave me immortality and took it away again. The whole thing is some kind of master plan. I'm just the puppet. And they've got us right where they want us, ready to be devoured once those beasts get in. Hell, they've even got us as close to their first feeding spot as possible. That's the whole point of drawing us to this place – to Eden. The whole thing's a sham.'

Red stopped my rant, speaking just to me. 'It is and it is not. Both. I am here for a reason. Perhaps I can take you back. Perhaps that is why you sent me to save you, to make sure you escape from here before it is too late.'

166

I kept my question internal: 'How?'
Then Red had an idea.

8

Back up in the ops room, after moving the bodies off to one corner in a pile – a grim stack of death – Shirley managed to get the monitors on. It took them a few seconds to all flick into life. Those horrifying images were just the same as I'd seen them before, as if I was watching them at the exact same time as I'd seen them originally. That coulda been possible. No reason why not. Say Angie and her hoons had gone all killy on the population of Eden just after the other *me* had arrived, that would've made sense. But where she was now, and what she was doing, were the things that mattered.

I'd never had any intention to hit a woman before, but once I caught up with Angie I was going to punch the bitch's nose right out the back of her skull. She wasn't no woman, certainly no angel. She was a demon, pure and simple.

'These beasts,' Red said to me, 'are trying to get in. They are waiting for something.'

Holy hot chicken's tits, he was stating the obvious. We were *all* waiting for something.

Susan hadn't heard Red, but jumped in anyway: 'In your memory you leave through the tear, right?' I nodded so. 'Which means you don't know what happens after that. We have to assume these things actually get in.'

Red spoke to me; my voice broadcast his idea: 'When they come in, we will go out. They have come from somewhere that is not of Earth. They have come through some kind of tear too. We will find that tear and use it to go back.'

Shirley wasn't convinced. He said: 'How can you be sure there is a tear out there? And won't it just send us to some demon realm or something?'

Sally, who was looking intently at the monitors, shot a bolt of brilliance at us: 'There! I can see one. And another out there. Wow... there are loads. They keep opening and closing. Look – some of them are spilling out those demons, but others are just appearing and disappearing.'

I strode over to join her. Shirley and Susan did too. It felt good – all of us there. A team. We watched as Sally pointed them out, just as she said, appearing and moving like lips parting and closing before disappearing.

Red used me again: 'It is our last chance. But as soon as they break through, time will be short. They will devour anything close. They will feed on us immediately.'

Sally pointed to her wrist aug. 'I can use this,' she said, 'to give us some protection until we make it into a tear.'

Shirley was curious: 'Are there even any at ground level? Can we reach one? I mean... if it's just a matter of time before one appears at ground level before we get eviscerated, how much time do we need?'

'There's no way of knowing that,' Susan offered. 'And look at them – it's a suicide run. But it's also... our last resort.'

'Either we do it or we die anyway,' Sally said. 'I could blow my brains out right here, or we could fight for our future.'

Lord, if good ideas could start a fire, the whole place would've gone up.

Me and Red combined again: 'We have guns, and more. The armoury.'

I love being right. Sure, that feeling comes often, perpetual like on some days, but I'm not one to brag. When we made it to the armoury there was another little boost of hope: pistolas, machine guns, rifles, grenades and... rocket launchers.

'Anyone know how to use one of these?' I asked. I had it perched on my shoulder.

'Just press the red button – and make sure it's pointing the right way first,' Shirley said. 'This is insane. I've never seen anything like it.' He was looking over one too, holding it up and touching areas on a small screen that seemed to hover above it. 'This thing is fully automated. I mean... it has really sophisticated targeting. DNA settings... blood type... this is seriously insane.'

'Then this is the plan,' I said with a little help from my friend. The others now seemed a tad less willied by my demon-dude tones. 'We go out all guns blazing. And I mean all of them. Whatever you can carry, you aim it and you fire it and most important, we stick together. As soon as one of those rips opens, we're in.'

'But how,' Susan asked, 'do you know what's on the other side of those tears?'

She was quite right. 'It doesn't matter,' Shirley said. 'If we stay here, we're fucked anyway. Through one of those tears, we can't know. But it's

169

somewhere else. Maybe it's Hell. Or Heaven. Or nowhere. I'm happy to go find out.'

So we tooled up. We put whatever weapons we could find in our hands and over our shoulders and in our shoes and pockets. We walked back out of Eden and travelled over-ground to the edge of existence. There, with the mansion just behind us and oblivion to the front. Out of the ground rose those barriers, protecting us from the greatest extinction. And then, when the time came, the barriers just vanished. A switch flicked off by some unseen finger.

9

'Run!'

Oh, we ran. Those giant, winged, fire-spitting demon scummers wasted no time – like greyhounds leaving their traps, racing towards their goal of ending everything.

Shirley was the best shot, his chosen submachine gun rattling off rounds which thudded into a bunch of whatever he aimed it at. The noise was deafening, but not just the gun shots – those demons screamed and squealed and shrieked like nothing I'd heard before.

'This way!' shouted Sally, her shield aug deflecting fireballs. We all tried to keep close as we headed towards an opening mouth. Before we got anywhere near it, it closed again, the air around it warping and fizzing. Another opened back where we'd come from. Overhead, a cloud of beasts had come together, primed to zoom down at us. That's exactly what happened. All four of us opened fire on that swarm. Our bullets (and fire – Susan had taken a makeshift flamethrower from the armoury) thwacked into the dense demon blizzard, thinning it out as some fell slain to the ground and others broke away, wounded.

One made it through though, swooping down and slashing at Shirley. Its mouth opened wide to reveal a horrifying state of oral affairs, but as Shirley ducked just out of the way, its claw caught his shoulder. He was sent sprawling.

To make matters worse, the ones we thought we'd killed starting flapping around on the ground, moving towards us. We kept firing. I slung the rocket launcher off my shoulder, aimed it straight ahead and watched the screen. Red dots danced around on it, with a bleeping sound then turning to a constant tone. I pressed the button.

The rocket soared forward and sent me careening backwards. I landed on my arse but rolled over to get up. I just managed to crane my neck to see that rocket slam into the regrouping swarm. It exploded on, over and around those bastards. The noise – their shrieking – was too much. I felt my ears just shut down into total deafness.

I looked over at the others, who were clutching their heads too. We'd all been hit by that cacophony. Then, like a shotgun blast, Red leapt out of me and reconstituted in front of us. In the sky we could see the full horror: hundreds and thousands of those beasts flying overhead and spitting fire and shrieking and on their way to end it all.

Red jumped up, pegged it away from us and beckoned me silently. I heard him loud and clear. 'Run to me!' the demon said. 'Do not question, just run!'

I grabbed Susan's hand and made a face that attemptered to convey the uncertainty in but commitment to my action. She shrugged back.

'Follow Red!' I shouted, but through my deafness all I could hear was a muffled hoot. Susan and me sprinted to catch him up, jumping over the stirring bodies of those unkillable Hell spawn. Where was he leading us?

As we drew closer, right in front of us, and right where Red was waiting, a tear opened. Red stood up in it, on his hind legs, and pushed his forelegs against the opening. If he hadn't done that, we'd never have made it. Behind us, demons were flying and galloping and gaining ground. Fireballs slammed into the ground around us. I turned only to see Sally and Shirley just to my side, pegging it as fast as they could too. I caught Shirley's eyes just for a second. That smooth, unflappable dude from Odessa was baking shit cakes right then, I knew it.

Up ahead the tear began to close, pushing against Red. I think my heart stopped for a second when I heard that single word in my head, a punch in the stomach and a sword in the arsehole. 'Goodbye.'

With that, Red deconstructed himself for the last time, but this time not inwards – his body began expanding, pushing back against the tear as it tried to close on him. The second before I jumped through with Susan, I watched his shiny red skin split into hundreds of thousands of pieces. Red's anguished howl cut out abruptly as the tear closed behind us.

10

'What is this place?' Shirley's voice was full of wonder.

I was too busy wiping the tears from my eyes, sobbing like an old fool at the death of a demon. *My* demon. Susan put her arms around me and pulled me in close, stroking my back and patting it like she was winding a baby. I didn't mind – I was kinda crying like a baby anyhoo. Couldn't remember the last time I'd felt loss like this. The death of my parents never really registered as I'd been so young, and I'd never formed any close relationships with anyone who'd died so far. But Red was dead.

Sally couldn't believe what she was seeing. As my eyes unblurred, I couldn't either. We'd come out of that rip in the future to an Eden long past. Things that looked like terrydactils flew overhead, their wings flapping gently and elegantly. We were stood facing an enormous lake, a pink sky setting down and reflecting off the water. All we could hear was our own panting – we were still getting our breath back – and the weird but strangely soothing cries from those flying creatures. Then out of the water came this enormous thing, and I realised soon enough what it was: one of those beautiful creatures I'd seen in Roger's presentation. So he wasn't lying about that, at least.

The creature rose right out of the lake, beads and rivulets of water cascading down its brilliant, shiny scales and down to those fans coming off its tail.

We all stood there transfixered on that thing. Then another came out, like it was chasing the first one, but this one twisted around playfully and we saw its whole body, iridescent under the pink sky.

'This is the true Eden,' I said, almost not meaning to. My words came out slow and low. 'Man, it's beautiful.'

Beyond the lake and all around us were trees like we'd never seen, their leaves shiny like those creatures. They didn't look like they were made of wood; they had scales too, or something that damn near resembled scales anyhoo.

Further away, there were creatures on land too. They might've been dinosaurs. They might've been giant dogs. They were too far away to tell for sure.

173

Our attention was drawn back to the lake as Shirley had walked over to it and was peering into the water.

'Guys,' he said. His voice was clear and... I dunno... *free*. It sounded like he was right in front of me, but he was a good twenty metres away. 'Come and see this.'

We moved to join him, our steps soft and springy on the ground. Susan smiled at me and I felt so good about it, like she was caressing me with it. I smiled back, and somehow – I'm not sure I can describe it adequately – it made the feeling more intense. I saw she felt it too. We were transferring some energy between us. I saw colours appear around her, oscillating like guitar strings, and then the faintest sounds *appeared*. My hands started to buzz and fizz. I raised them up level with my face and saw the colours around them too, the vibrations bouncing around the tips of my fingers.

I swished my hands through the air, leaving colour trails as melodies literally danced through them. Susan began to do the same. I looked over at Sally, who was just frozen to the spot staring at us. She caught my smile and it took her over too. She smiled back – colours appearing out of her face. Beyond her, I watched as Shirley started walking into the lake.

My hands were still bubbling and fizzing as I put them down by my side. Shirley carried on, wading into deeper water, then got up to his neck and stopped for the shortest pause – and then he was right in.

Although I felt like I'd just discovered the greatest feeling imaginable, I'd just watched my friend wander into the unknown, diluting my univorgasm somewhat. Walking over to the water's edge, Susan close behind me on my left and Sally joining me from the right, we stopped there and watched; listened. We all felt it at the same time – that unimaginably beautiful feeling of warmth and joy and contenterment – and then it got even better.

Shirley came shooting like an arrow out of the water, the sound of hundreds of horns splashing in an explosion of colour over the whole scene and rolling as far as we could see and hear. He flew up and up, straight and true, then started to slow as he disappeared off into the pink sky. Then, and it's probably the coolest shit I'd ever seen – he floated down, still with beads of water falling from his majestic frame, scales shining through light feathers. We watched as he began to transform further, the colours radiating off him like someone farted a rainbow into his face.

And then those horns came back again, the most beautiful sound in the universe – stronger and longer and all-consuming. I felt something rising up from my feet, through my legs and up my whole body, encapsulating me in perfect harmony with Shirley's transformation as we saw his legs and arms and head retract so gracefully, like a drop of water returning to its ocean.

His head began to morph out of what used to be his chest, and there was that manta ray look I'd seen in Roger's special feature. Suddenly and with another blast from the horns his wings rose majestically from his sides, and with that he was away again, soaring upwards and weaving in and out of the rainbow trails.

The three of us just stood there, fizzing and buzzing with the purest energy. I looked at Susan and then to Sally.

'Fuck on, guys,' I said, my voice coming out crisp and clear in multi-coloured trails. 'Let's do this.'

11

Going into the water, it was dark but there were twinkling stars in there, all around us. We felt compuncted to walk further in until we came to a deep hole. We peered over into it – deeper than any hole I'd ever looked into, but with a light so bright at the bottom. So bright it should've burned our eyes out, but the only feeling was joy.

Sally went in first. Once she'd shot back up past us – a cosmic torpedo – Susan went in. As if the water lapped over that hole but not in it, I watched as she fell so fast into that light and then stepped back just as she went rocketing out of it. If I'd caught that in the chin, I wouldn't be telling this story.

I wasn't in too much of a hurry. I looked around, observing the stars twinkling in and out of view. One was just within my reach so I closed my hand around it then brought it close to my face. I opened my hand and there it was, gently rising out of my palm. It slowly rose up to my eye level and just popped – hundreds and thousands of tiny speckles coming out of it.

Next I grabbed a handful of them and did the same. I had about twenty of them and guided them all into a close cluster between my hands, then let go. They created the most beautiful, sparkling cloud there in the water.

OK, it was time to take my jump. It was time to become Tremendous. I peered over – triple-decker shit sandwiches! The light was gone. Something was wrong. I felt the warmth draining from inside me. The lake seemed to be getting darker, then more so. The stars were disappearing from all around.

I began to feel like I was panicking. I hadn't realised before, caught up in that euphoria, that I wasn't consciously breathing. Now I was drowning. Tits.

I pushed myself off the lake bottom and started grabbing at nothing, reaching up and swinging my arms through the water like a gorilla on acid. I reckon I only just made it up before I was a goner. As soon as my head emerged from the water I felt something lift me out. It carried me over the lake and drifted me gently down to the edge.

I turned to see that most splendid sight, of Shirley and Sally and Susan hovering there a hundred feet above the water. Their new bodies were resplendent. But mine... nope. Same as always. Hey, I'm not ashamed of it. I like the way I look, but I was not taking my time around getting peeved up about missing out on this.

Then my three celestial chums all turned their bodies together, their mantafaces twisting up behind them as if looking at some distant object. I saw it too: something, a tiny dot in the distance, was gradually growing, and with it a low rumble underfoot. The rumbling grew louder and the ground began to shake violently, like an earthquake was about to tear it apart.

It got ever closer, faster, and then shot forward like a bullet from some giant shotgun in space – or a meteor crashing to the Earth. But then it stopped dead. The rumbling did too, right away. Like closing a window to the howling wind outside, it was silent and still again.

That object, partially obscured by my three horsepeople hogging all the flying fish privileges, hung there as if filling the whole sky, as if the meteor had been halted by some unseen force field.

Slowly at first and then with greater force, a split appeared in the middle and opened outwards – a flower seeking the sun. I found myself walking around to my right, trying to get an unobscured view. And there it was, peering out of some giant rock: a single eyeball.

Now it's worth taking a moment here. Take a step back. When I saw it was an eyeball, that's exactly what I mean. Just like the ones in my head, there's no other way to put it. An eyeball.

There was no mouth. A voice boomed across the whole scene, as if coming from *everywhere*: 'What are you doing here?'

I couldn't think of anything to say. The voice came again.

'This place is not for you. You do not belong. *Seriously*.'

Something changed in that eye. It contracted a little, then blinked. Suddenly Shirley, Susan and Sally weren't hovering – they fell down and splashed into the lake. I realised all the colours had gone; the melodies weren't playing.

'You!' It centred on me. I could literally *feel* its gaze. 'You are not supposed to be here. Come on, spill the beans. How did you get here?'

I watched as the others swam towards me. I dunno how, but their clothes had disappeared – probably rainbow-exploded out of existence during their cavorting in the sky. Shirley had his hand over his squishy jewels. Sally and Susan let it all hang out. Gotta note here that although I'd usually find two ladyburgers appetising enough to squirt some mayo under the bun, it just wasn't the time.

'Chop-chop, sunshine. We haven't got all day.'

177

Was that an English accent? It sounded like some butler in one of those old black-and-white movies.

I didn't know how else to start. 'Fuck on.'

The eye remained silent and still, waiting for me to continue.

'We came through a tear, in the future. A demon held it open and we jumped on through. We were being chased by these flying Tremendous beasts, shooting fireballs at us. Are you...'

The eye focused even harder, down on me. It is difficult to describe the scene with enough gravity: this eye, filling the sky, somehow gripping me in place with its stare.

'None of your business,' it said. 'What difference does it make if I am... or not? You are trespassing in a sacred place, not for the living. A place that isn't a place, where there is no time or consequence. Nothing you can understand.'

But I *did* understand. Far as I could tell, I was having a chinwag – rather an *eye*wag – with the creator himself.

The others made it back to my side. They were wet and pissed off – their parade had been well and truly rained on.

'Erm... I'm sorry,' I called up. 'We were just trying to...'

'Yes, yes...' the voice interrupted me. 'I get it. Fine. OK. I know who you are now. I mean it's not like I didn't know about you, just that I was surprised to see you here, that's all. I mean... that wasn't expected, see?'

I just shrugged.

'Well, if you're here and not, you know... *there*, then that means it's changed. You've done it. The future is a blank canvas again. I cannot foresee...'

The eye closed, its rock lids silently sealing together. It opened then, just as slow as it'd shut. 'Do you know where you are supposed to be? No, hold on... I mean do you know where you'd like to be?'

Right here, I thought. *And turn that light back on under the lake. I wanna try some of that flying feathery fish stuff. Close yourself up again, giant freaky eye, and give me half-an-hour of rainbow explosions and fishy sky torpedoes.*

But no, I shook my head. I found myself speaking anyhoo: 'We are supposed to stop a great war. In the past... erm... the future... at some point.'

'OK – fine, fine. Yes, fine,' the eye said. 'Well, you can't stay here, anyway.'

For a few seconds the four of us stared up at the eye, watching as it seemed to be taking on some intense energy from all around. Then as before, its rocky lids began to close, and with them so did ours.

12

It seemed like waking from a dream. The most splendiferous, supercalifuckintastic dream of all time.

Shirley was already awake, I saw. Then Sally and Susan too, almost on cue as if simply looking at them switched them on. I guess I was half-pleased and disappointed to see they were clothed again. As my eyes adjusted to the room, I was flabbergunted once again – these changes of scene were all so stark and unexpected. Yet there we all were, reeling from the eyeballing to end all eyeballings, sitting quietly in a dimly lit room while outside, whatever was out there, was a wall of noise: some kind of thumping beat and a brass band playing, jostling for sonic position among a whole lotta whooping and cheering. And we were wearing… President Thump T-shirts. What the hell?

The room wasn't small, nor big. Seemed like a pretty standard dressing room. There were mirrors along one wall, above a bank of barber-style chairs, then on the other side several racks of clothes and hats and various props.

In the corner to my left was a mass of metal equipment, which on closer inspection turned out to be microphone stands and folded stools. A tambourine hung off one of them.

Sally said to Susan: 'Where are we? Any ideas?'

Susan thought for a moment, then answered: 'Don't know. But it doesn't matter really. We always seem to get put where we're supposed to be. And we kind of hit the ground running. That is to say, we… know what we're doing when we get there. It's like someone else's memories flood in. Someone else, but yours. I have to say, as a scientist, it's all mumbo-jumbo to me, but I can't argue with it.'

Shirley had gone over to the door. As he opened it, the noise blasted in. After a few seconds, mercifully he closed it.

'Shit, guys,' he said, grinning at us. 'Out there… I know where we are. It's only fuckin' Madison Square Garden. And you're not gonna believe this – it's Thump's inauguration.'

'So what are we doing here?' Sally asked. 'What's that got to do with us?'

I didn't know. Well, likely it was an ego thing – Thump'd invited us just to gloat, to shove his prize-winning dick in the astonished vagina of civilisation. There was only one way to find out.

I led us out, the noise hitting us like a tornado as we emerged into that giant arena. There were Thump's supporters everywhere, waving flags and placards and dancing to the band's soaring and thumping sounds. Gotta say, the music was good. Hey, the whole thing was great if I'm honest. A real spectacle. Shame the reason behind it wasn't worthy of celebration in any sense.

We'd come out onto a metal walkway high above and behind the main shenanigisings, with armed security guys at either end. Then I realised one of those security stations was mine – Hugo and Klein were chatting to each other, ignoring the spectacle below.

They stopped talking as they felt the rumble of our footsteps coming towards them on the platform.

Hugo headed us off. 'Sir,' he called, only just audible over the noise, 'we're not due to come for you yet. It's safer if you...'

I cut him short. 'Safer? We're fine, Hugo. Just fine, and we're bored in there.'

In that instant, all the context came rushing in. Although I hadn't seen either of those guys, or my campaign manager Tim, since the 'handjob insurance' encounter, back here while I was living my life without me all sorts had happened. I recalled back to Odessa, and while that other me had put us in that tear to the future, our 'echoes' had carried on without us.

It was an alternate line in the history books, although one which... oh shit, Sally. She didn't figure. I realised then why Klein was looking her up and down suspishickly. Course she didn't figure in any of those histories. She didn't exist in this time until now.

I had to say something. 'That's Sally,' I said, putting up a hand of reassurement. 'She's with me.'

Hugo wasn't quite satisfied with that. 'Sir...' he started. 'We led you up here. She wasn't with you. There's no other way up here. Who is she and how did she get up here?'

I was floored. Didn't have an answer for that.

Susan pushed in front of me. 'Sally,' she said, 'is *my* cousin. She's here visiting. *I* let her in. When *you* weren't paying attention.'

Klein's face betrayed what was going on north of it. He was bambuzzled all right, but also not one to argue with a lady he'd become fond of. Hugo, though, looked like he was going the other way. He leaned in close and said: 'However she got in here, that's not the issue. This is a maximum-security event. Even if *we* let her in, they won't.'

13

Standing up on that platform, with all that noise in the arena, I blocked it out and concentratered, searching my recently acquired memories for some context. Why were we there?

Thump had… persuaded me to play at his inauguration? Dog's cock on the doormat, that came as a shock. I recalled the moment as clearly as I could, seeing it for the first time: about a week before, while we were gearing up back at our base out in Boston – where we'd settled, mainly because Susan loved it there and said it was most like England, which I could neither agree nor disagree with considering my version of England mostly looked like every man, woman and child of Boston had shat on it – we got a house call from Thump and his enormous entourage.

He said he wanted to make a deal – a serious one this time. Nothing about handjobs or blowies or anything like that. So we let him in.

By then of course Shirley was part of the team, our preppy geek who was keeping an eye on things on the interwebs. He used InfiniNet, just like everyone else, for the mainstream stuff like maintainering our UniTube presence and working up our fan reach. And boy, he'd done a fine job. But behind InfiniNet, as he described it, he was on the DeepNet. That was the one that couldn't be tracked, he explained to us, where a lot of bad people were doing a lot of bad things. But he wasn't using it for bad things – he was monitoring what he said was 'really happening'. Mostly it seemed to be even more hate than you'd find on the mainstream channels, but he picked up on stuff we wouldn't have known otherwise.

So Thump came in with his guys, a whole load of them lining out on our porch while others went around the back. Five or six of them came in and swept the house with detection devices – checking to see if we were recording anything in there. We weren't. We were surrounded. It was like the C-I-A-holes had come to visit.

We led him into the lounge and Susan poured us each a drink – neat whisky. It was a nice living space, comfy chairs all around a low table on a fluffy rug. Susan took care of furnishings. I wasn't allowed my guitar in the lounge. She said it made the place look 'messy'.

We all sat down. Thump swirled his whisky around in the glass then necked it.

'Nice!' he said. 'That's *nice* whisky. Good to see you guys are living well here. That pleases me, really it does. Living the American dream. Now I'll get straight to the point, if that's OK?'

We didn't have a chance to say it wasn't.

'When we last met, I gave you a decent proposal. You do something for me, I do something for you. That's business. That's what I do. That's how I'm going to be running this beautiful country, this country I love more than anything else.

'Now I know you think something is gonna happen, but let me tell you something else: you think you're the only ones who've seen the future? OK – if you do, you're wrong. Marty, your history lessons don't mean shit anymore. That's all been changed. You see, you're on the wrong side. Whatever it is you think you're gonna do, and I'm guessing that because you haven't done anything so far you don't have a plan, as you say, anyhoo... well, I'm gonna put my neck out here and just say you ain't got shit.'

He'd been right about that, damn it. We'd been biding our time, or our echoes had at least, monitoring but not acting. That made sense – I was the original. I had to make the decisions. But this was just a memory, of something *I* hadn't actually done. The decisions would come later.

'So...' he continued, 'you might wonder why I've come all the way out here to see you.'

He looked around the three of us. We returned disinterestated shrugs.

'Now, now,' he went. 'That's not really very welcoming, is it? OK, I'll get to the point. In your world some stuff happened. There was a civil war, and I know you think that's gonna happen and yeah, I guess it is. That's inevitable. I'm a divider, not a uniter, and anyone who's on the wrong side of that divide is gonna get the long schlong of bad fortune up his ass. Now you're currently on the wrong side of it, kinda positioning yourself to be a player in there, get some groundswell of people to put a stop to whatever it is I'm doing – or just get me out of office, or assassinate me, or whatever. Hey, I don't care about any of that.'

'I thought you were getting to the point,' I said.

Thump laughed. 'Yeah, OK. The point. Marty, don't you see? The point is that you stopped it. You *already* saved the world. Kinda. I mean really, *I* saved the world, but you can share that with me if you like. I'm not proud. So in your past, I'm sharing the Presidency with Johnson. In my present, he's out of the frame. I take office in just a few weeks and I'm not firing nukes at myself! That's just not my style! We've re-worked things. We've got a handle on the Chinese now, and the Russians, and North Koreans. I've been briefed on your future, and it ain't happening anymore. No one's gonna be doing anything bad like firing nukes at anyone else. Well, until I say so.'

This guy loved his own voice. I asked him: 'Have you got to the point yet?'

He laughed again, louder and longer this time. 'Jeez, you're making this harder than it has to be. Just listen, Marty. There's a little way to go. I'll spell it out for you: I can't kill you. I'm not allowed to. Hey, I'm not in the business of killing people anyway, but you're the kind of guy I can't have doing what you're doing. I need people to support me, not buck against me. You could do with some perspective, I guess.'

'Go on,' I said.

'You wanna know who the Tremendous *really* are? They're the original beings. They're the most powerful creations in the universe. They've always done what they've done out of some selfish desire to hit back at their creator, to get him or her or whatever it is back for banishing them from the world that was created for them. I've seen it with my own eyes. I've watched the movie, eaten the popcorn, and had a champion blowie from Miss Venezuela in the back row.'

I imagined the deed, then quickly dispelled the disturbing image.

'But here's the rub, Marty. You know the old story of Adam and Eve, right? Well that's a simple way of putting it. That shit happened, just not the way the story tells it. And once those Tremendous were banished, there were certain rules put in place – rules to keep them in check, so to speak. The big one, the one that really matters, is what you and I have as human beings: free will. See, the Tremendous can try to influence us, but their real power is gone. They fed off the world, but it was taken away from them. Ultimately, they can't control what we do, only try to shape it.'

At last someone else spoke. It was Susan. 'And you've let them shape you,' she said.

'No, not quite,' Thump said. 'It's the other way around. I've managed to persuade them that my way is better!'

'So what's...' I started, '...what's my role in all this? You have a proposal, you said.'

'Indeed I do,' he smiled. 'See, when the shit hit the fan last time, it was all going to plan. They were wiping everything clean. If there's no humans left, it's theirs again. No rules to break anymore. But they can't kill humans. They just set it all up so it's humans killing humans. Free will to kill. And they reap their souls and feed off them. But they'd just not done a good enough job, and they'd not figured on the one you know as Angie. Now Angie isn't some *ordinary* Tremendous. No, she's more like God's pet. And she sat down there, put a big shield around all those people and protected them from *what was supposed to happen*. Now I'm OK with this re-run, because this time I don't get blown to shit along with everyone else, but what I'm not OK with is Angie. She's still out there somewhere – a tough turd stuck in my S-bend. And I can't have that.

'But all that's nearly irrelevant now, because you're gonna fetch her for me – for *us*. And then my good Tremendous friends and I will have this planet for ourselves. Feeding off souls creates far more power than feeding off some empty planet. There's no need to take some final revenge by destroying everything all at once.

'People die and babies are born. The longer we can keep that going, the better. The false 'pocalypse, as you call it, it's averted. Job done. You're employee of the millennium, and I'm the boss – hiring and firing and keeping the machine working.'

Course, obviously I wasn't about to make that deal. I told him so: 'You're out of your fuckin' mind, Thump. There's no way we're doing that. And I wouldn't even know *how* to do that anyhoo. I don't know where Angie is. I don't know her in this time.'

That's as much as I felt comfortable giving away. Truth was, as far as I knew she'd been killed back in Eden, but there'd been no corpse...

Thump elbowed his suit jacket away from his body and put his thumbs in his braces. He flicked them out, letting them snap back against his shirt.

'Course you are, Marty. You will because it's the only way you get any kind of future worth having. You're immortal, right? Thanks to Angie. But nobody else is – not Susan, not Shirley here. Which, by the way, is a woman's name...'

He looked at Shirley and snarled. 'You never thought of changing that? Shirley Bottom? Seriously?'

He turned his attention back to me. 'So think about it – we've changed our tune. There's no false 'pocalypse coming. The real one works better for everyone. It's fair and just. Everyone gets what they deserve and – *most crucially* – I get what I deserve. I make no secret I'm in this for me. And Susan's and Shirley's souls are gonna get reaped to shit just like everyone else's, so you'll be left without them, whatever happens. *Alone.*'

Toffee tits in a teacup, I wanted Thump to get what he deserved.

'And immortal as you are,' he said, 'you'll be powerless and just have to sit back and watch *everything* we do on this planet – a race so stupid they elected some racist, misogynistic fuckhead to the most powerful post in the world! That's funny, ain't it? Certainly tickles my balls.'

He went over to my drinks cabinet and refilled his glass with whiskey, necked it and gently put the glass back on the table.

'So here's the real meat of my proposal: you bring us Angie, we'll make you one of us. Tremendous. Goodbye eternal frustration, hello massive world-wank!'

I was feeling that rage coming up again. 'I get to be Tremendous too, if I flush the human race and an angel down the toilet for you?'

Thump stretched his braces out as far as they'd go, then snapped them back. That must've hurt. He hopped from foot to foot, chuckling, then sat back down.

'That's right,' he said. 'And we've got a little deal sweetener for you. Much better than handjob insurance.'

14

Now, I haven't forgotten Madison Square Garden. I'll get back to that. Patience is a virgin. There's more to this memory…

Still at our house in Boston, see, Thump was stood between me and Susan, a hand on each of our shoulders. Shirley was sat at his desk, bringing up images on InfiniNet. Thump was telling him what to do, like we all worked for him. I guess he thought *everyone* did.

Shirley brought up the map of the United States. Thump instructered him to zoom in a little on the west side.

'Stop there,' he said. 'Now look. Go in a little closer… See that? That's Yellowstone National Park. Yogi Bear lives there, but maybe not for much longer. Now go over a little to the left and you'll see Shoshone Lake. It's so beautiful there. *So beautiful.* Just above that, see there – that's the Yellowstone Caldera.'

Thump leaned forward and tapped the point on the map, although we could clearly see the words 'Yellowstone' and 'Caldera' on it. Condescenderising prick.

'Now that, which is something you probably don't know unless you've been there, is a volcano. But not just any common volcano. It's a *super* volcano. There's a chamber of magma under there about fifty-five miles long and about eighteen miles wide, and it's desperate to come up. All those little-bitty magma mice trapped underground, trying to get to the surface for some cheese. Some shit like that.'

'Fascinating,' Susan said with a smooth shot of sarcasm. 'There's a volcano. So?'

Thump clenched his hand firmly around her shoulder and grinned. 'That's right, it is. A *super* one. And you know what? Some scientists say they believe that could erupt at any time, although that's just bullshit – bullshit used to keep the fear quota up. Just like all the rest of it – terrorist attacks, drugs, the classic failing economy lie… See, there's a huge wall of rock in the way. But while it's not going to erupt on its own, with a little helping hand we can make it spurt.'

'Why would you do that?' I was a little slow in cottonising on, which is odd given whatever it was he was getting to, surely I must've known it would be bad.

Thump laughed again, his hands squeezing our shoulders even tighter. 'Because, Marty, you lame little duck, if you don't bring us Angie, we're gonna tug that volcano until it blows, pure and simple.'

He let go of us, reached into his jacket pocket and pulled out a small memory stick. He handed it to Shirley. 'Put that in, double-click or whatever, and you'll see.'

Shirley did just that. The screen filled with an image just like the last one – a map of the United States. Shirley wasn't controlling what happened next. Clearly a lot of effort had gone into the presentation. Thump stood back, folded his arms and smiled smugly.

His face appeared on the screen. It was some kind of news feature segment. We watched it all, for about six minutes. Thump, as a businessman with oil interests, had enterprises going on all around the world – the perfect guy to team up with the Tremendous for maximum coverage – where they were drilling down for the liquid money.

The feature focusted on one particular operation in Calgary, Canada. It was what's known as a deviated drilling operation, going about ten thousand feet down. The reporter collared some white-coated corporate parrot, who revealed that they'd hit a good supply and would be down there for years. Then the clip showed some more overhead shots of the drilling apparatums and zoomed out again to show the bottom half of Canada and the top half of the US, with a caption that said something about how Thump's oil discovery in Canada would help the US economy.

He made Shirley pause the clip on that frame. 'Nice, huh? So what you're looking at is a deep well that ends right smack-bang on a solid wall of rock, a long way down. Such a long way. I'm never going down there. No one is. Very dark. And that wall of rock, well... happily it goes a long way underground too, all the way in fact to the roof of the magma chamber under the Yellowstone Caldera. Are you following me?'

'You're gonna blow the rock down there?' Shirley got it before me or Susan. 'It'll fracture along the whole line and...'

'That's right!' Thump chuckled.

'But if you do, millions of people will die. Most of the US – Canada and Mexico too – will be uninhabitable. It'll be catastrophic!'

'Play the rest,' Thump said.

Shirley did. The clip returned to the facility, where the guy was asked some more questions. Then my heart skipped a beat as I saw who walked across behind him. Holy headlice, I'd recognise myself anywhere.

I finally understood what he was getting at. 'And you'll tell them I did it?'

Thump slapped his hand back on my shoulder. He grinned at me. 'Fuck on, dude. Fuck on!'

15

OK, we're back on the walkway overlooking Madison Square Garden. Having plundered my memory in that short space of time, much faster than it's taken me to explain it here, everything had become clear.

The first part of my task was to agree to play at Thump's inauguration. That bastard had me over a barrel. Looking down at the main stage, where the brass band was still playing its excellent song, I got that sinking feeling. I glanced at Susan to see she'd just remembered it all too. Shirley? Probably, but I couldn't see his face.

He spoke to Klein and Hugo: 'Guys, forget about her. There's thousands of people here. She's no danger. She'll just blend in. Say she's Marty's hairdresser or something. Get her cleared. We all need to be here.'

Truth was, I wasn't sure if Sally did need to be there. I'd picked her up and brought her back in time and for what? To be Thump's stooge? Not even that. A sub-stooge of mine, with me taking chief stooge duties. She was gonna die before she'd been born, that was all. Cheers.

None of that mattered anyhoo. I'd lost all credibility as soon as I'd announced I'd play at this event. Anti-social media went batshit-bananas over it. They'd gone after Susan too, calling her every bad word I'd ever heard before and some new ones too. Thump'd not overstated things when he said he was a divider.

Klein shouted over the music: 'We'll see what we can do. We won't get far going this way; the security's too tight. We should head down *that* way.' He pointed to the opposite end, where Thump's goons were gathered. 'If we clear it with them, we're good to go. Otherwise, she stays up here. OK?'

I nodded. That seemed to be at least a workable way to progress. Play the gig, leave the venue, go home and smash all the plates. Hugo led and Klein came up the rear. By the time we got to the other end, the band had finished. The crowd cheered and almost right away some quieter, placeholder music came on while the roadies went about setting up the next act – me.

My bodyguards engaged with Thump's goons. One of them pointed at me and said: 'The President would like to see you.'

He crossed the walkway and opened the door there. The room was buzzing with activity. Thump saw me and waved me in. The others started to follow behind me.

'No, just you, sir,' the goon said as he blocked them from doing so. 'They can wait out here.'

Hugo called: 'Sir?'

'Fine,' I said. 'I'll only be a minute.'

'My backstage is neater than yours, hey?' Thump was expectedly pleased with himself. And yeah, it was. Banks of TVs, a big clear-fronted fridge stocked with chilled beers and sandwiches, and a bunch of lovely looking women milling about carrying tablets and bundles of paper. In one corner sat a tiny guy with a video camera, filming the room.

Thump made for me to participise. 'Smile and wave, Marty!'

He slapped his hand down into mine like old friends might after years out of touch, then put his other arm around my shoulders and pulled me close so our hips were touching. Through trousers, that is, not naked flesh. That shoulda been obvious.

Anyhoo, I played along. I smiled as big and genuine as I could, slipping my arm around his back to reciprocise the manly embrace.

'OK,' he said to the camera guy. 'Shut it off for now. We got some stuff to discuss. This way, Marty.'

His backstage was far bigger than ours too. He led me out of the main room and through a short corridor into another, then closed the door behind him. The smaller room was still bigger than the single one we had. Course it was. Even the toilet I guessed was the size of a football field.

'So how's the mission going, Marty? Have you found her yet?'

'No,' I said. 'I haven't.'

'Hey!' he said, slapping my shoulder again with unearned affection. 'Maybe I wasn't clear. This isn't an indefinite offer. This runs out. I need Angie, or you know what happens.'

I did. 'I do.'

My name in the new history books above the entry marked, 'The man who killed three hundred million people.' That's what I was facing if I didn't shine this bastard's shoes.

'So let's strengthen that incentive, shall we?' Thump said. I dunno if I told you last time, but the way we blow that rock and start the mother of all chain reactions, it's a small nuke. Not one of those massive mushroom-cloud fuckers, but it's about the size of a football. That's all. And you know what? I had some guys place it down there. You'd be surprised what some people will do for money. These guys? Just no scruples! Now I know you think I'm lacking in moral fibre, but hey – I'd never even do something like that. Oh, and look at this.'

There was a tablet on the desk in the middle of the room. Thump picked it up and thumbed the screen. He navigised to some video link app and held it up for me to see.

'Marty, say hello to Marty.'

I didn't feel like doing that. I was looking back at another one of me. But that one wasn't *like* me. He was smiling.

Thump spoke to him: 'Is the package in place, Marty?'

The other me: 'All the way down to the bottom, yes sir, as you asked.'

'OK, and where's the rock that links up to the volcano?'

He pointed down. 'Right down there, sir. With the package. All present and correct and ready to blow, sir. *Kaaaaa-booooom!*'

I couldn't believe what I was hearing.

Thump again: 'And how long, Marty, between you setting that thing off and it going boom?'

'Oh, maybe about two hours. I'm gonna set it in place and leave in a minute. Don't want to be in the blast zone, sir!'

'And you can set that off remotely? Wherever you are in the world?'

'That's right,' he said. His grin was horrible – sickly.

'And... who else has that control? I mean, can I set that charge too?'

'Only me, sir,' he said. 'I'm carrying the torch on this one, sir.'

'Thanks, Marty. God speed.'

He put the tablet down and fixed me in his most serious gaze.

'How long have I got?' I almost predicted his answer.

'Tomorrow,' he said. 'Bring me Angie. *Tomorrow*. Or it's lights out America.'

PART 5

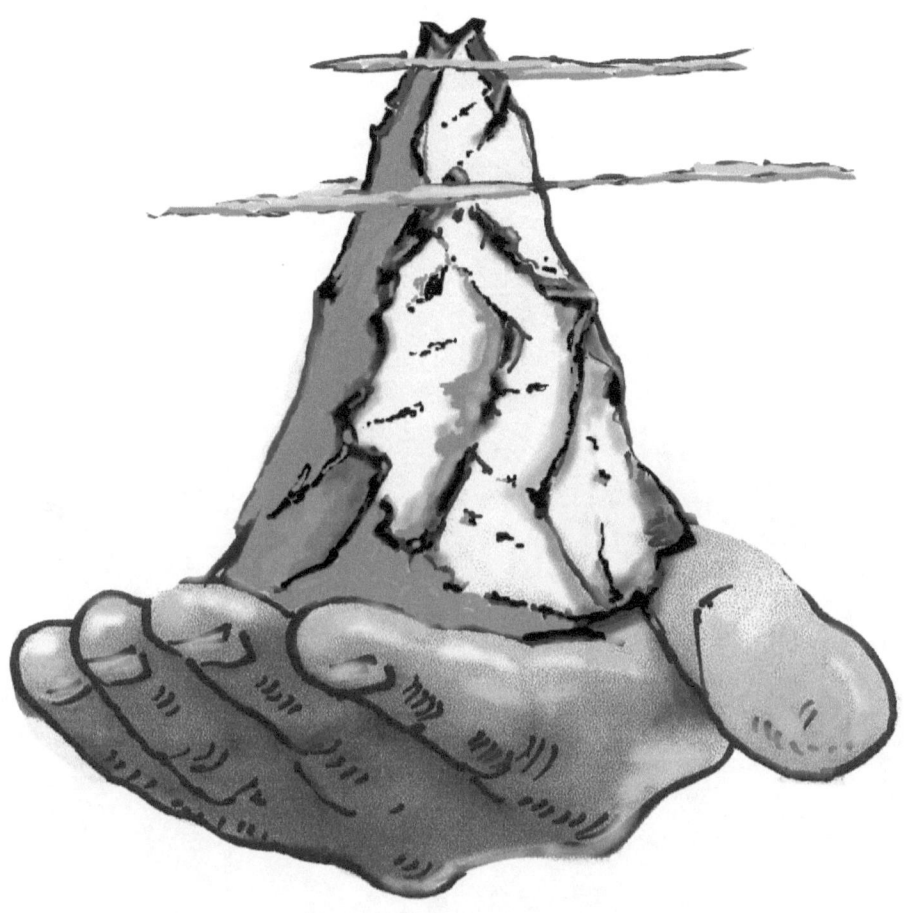

1

Shit-in-my-sherbet. A turd tornado was coming. An impossible choice. Not even a choice, was it? How could I turn over the Earth's last guardian to this monster? He wanted Angie. He wanted to destroy her. The Tremendous were going to make him one of them in return. And if I didn't bring Angie to this sick bastard, he was going to blow the super-volcano in Yellowstone Park, killing pretty much the whole of the United States and then blame it on me. Immortal me, living forever in the knowledge that it was my fault, even if it wasn't. He knew the kinda guy I was, and he was going to give me an indirectly guilty conscience.

Hey, I never asked for this. I could happily have gone on to my fateful end just like everyone else. If Angie hadn't put it on me, I'd never have known – I woulda just melted into nothing a few hours later when those beasts finally got in and devoured everyone and everything, just as we'd seen.

But she gave me a mission: stop the false 'pocalypse. It had sounded so easy. Just kill John Thump – a single, simple human. That's all I had to do, but I couldn't do it. Why? Because every time I'd had a chance I'd been pulled away. In an alternate time line I'd been accused of it, but in that dimension he'd been a good guy and killing him was a mistake – not that I did it then anyhoo.

And now, there was nothing I could do. He had me over a barrel. If I did anything except bring him the angel, he'd blow the biggest joint in the world. But if I did give her up, that would consign the whole human race to his rule of tyrannised testiclism. Stuck between a rock and a hard place, with Thump's balls resting in my eye sockets.

So there I was, my gut churning like it never had before, about to deliver my support via a song he'd made me write especially – a song so against what I believed in that I coulda vomited the whole thing onto the front row of his supporters.

But no. My opinions stopped mattering a long time ago. I realised that. So I left that bastard's office and walked down with Susan and Shirley while Sally – who of course was not established in this time line yet – watched from the balcony above.

I performed my song and those dummies cheered and clapped their stupid hands together like demented seals, whoopin' and hollerin' as if it was the best thing they'd ever seen and heard. Now normally I'd take the credit for that, being as I have a certain gift of enability for spreading the musical legs, but this crowd woulda cheered a limp dick in a bucket. Thump had these guys all riled up – his promises of economic upturn and crimonomic downturn, and that same shit every politician ever trotted out about making 'insert place name' great again… well, he'd tapped into something for sure.

But the Tremendous – hell, they *controlled* the media. They controlled what people thought and the things people thought they should think about. That's true of the way I was too, until my eyes were opened on this crazy journey. They controlled the music people should listen to, the TV they should watch, the jokes they should laugh at. And me – they controlled me now too.

I can't bring myself to recite the song. I don't think he even heard it – too busy suckin' his own balls.

2

None of that mattered. Reality – which was something I hadn't had much of recently – came to an end at that very point. I kid not: it broke up right there in front of me, as if a window shattering or a jigsaw breaking apart, the pieces falling away to reveal what lay behind it.

And that was... indescribably beautificated. All the noise around me vanished from sight, but I was still there on the stage, a spotlight coming from above and shining down on me, my guitar and my microphone. Gone were the thousands of people, the building, the ground beneath and the sky above. They faded out of view kinda spookily. Some light grey mist was rolling towards me, slowly and calmly, and I couldn't take my damn eyes off it.

Floating there, in nothingness, on my stage – my fingers began to strum the strings, but the sound that came was not of a guitar, more like a harp. And as I played, more harps joined in from all around, their melodies weaving in and around each other, not a bum note from any of them.

I watched that cloud intently as my entire being felt lifted and hot, but not uncomfortably so. And then the cloud began to disperse, gently peeling away from the figure within: the full, overwhelmerising beauty of the angel I knew as Angie appeared from it, gliding along in her own spotlight until it met mine. The two beams began criss-crossing in every direction, then finally exploded into a bright light that filled as far as the eye could see.

Angie reached out to me. I stood from my stool and let my guitar fall from my grasp. It floated in place. Then the stage and everything on it melted away beneath me as I took Angie's hand.

Was this really the end? Was she there to carry me away from all this madness, to tell me everything was going to be okay and lead me up to Heaven?

Er... no. She wasn't. We hovered there in the bright light together and did that weird 'think-speaking' shit I still can't get my head around.

'I have been watching you,' she said/thought. 'I have been sent to aid you.'

'Yeah?' I thought back.

'I am told I sent you back from the future.'

'Yes, you did. How come you don't know that?'

'Because I am not from there. I am from here, and now.'

'I don't understand.'

'I am an angel. Different to the Tremendous. I am an agent of the creator while they are agents of themselves. They are out of favour with the creator. They can move through time and see everything. I can see only what is past and present. This is why I sent you back. Probably.'

'Probably?'

'Indeed. I cannot know. So probably. It is probable.'

I found myself becoming a little quickened of the pulse with the sudden rememberment of my predicament.

'We're not safe here. You're not safe here,' I said.

'Why would that be so?'

'Thump is after you. And he's right *here*, so this is a dangerous place to be.'

'No, it isn't. Do not be concerned for my safety.'

'He wants me to bring you to him, or he'll destroy most of America!'

I should point out here that raising one's thinking voice is a strange concept, but it works.

'Will he?'

'Yes, I think he really will.'

'It is of no consequence.'

'*No consequence*?' I spluttered a little, mind-wise. 'Can we just get away from here?'

'There is no need. There is no here. We are not anywhere. Thump is not here. Neither are we.'

Little-fudgin'-potato-tits, this wasn't getting us anywhere. Angie seemed different. *And*, to boot, *in*different. Not just a little – entirely. She picked up on my confusion.

'As I said, I am not her, although *she* is *me* – me from a long way into the future, far from this point. It appears my future being is tarnished; as if she bears the weight of the world. *I* do not.'

Then I felt her rummaging around in my memories. It weren't neither pleasant nor unpleasant.

'Ah, then all is clear now. I see.'

Still, I couldn't shake the idea that this was all effed-up. 'You still seem very calm,' I thought, feeling not so calm myself. Thump was about to commit the worst atrocity of all time. He was about to dip his dirty balls in the mouth of human existence. And if Angie'd just seen all my memories, she woulda seen that. She woulda seen the carnage she'd left back at Eden, all those bloody bodies. And she woulda seen Thump making his threat and demanding I bring him the head of the last angel on Earth!

'But that is tomorrow,' Angie thought. 'In the meantime, and now that I understand why I've been sent to you, we can set about preparing you for the end.'

'The end? What do you mean?'

I gotta say, this version of Angie was twisting my ballbag. She weren't no patch on the girl who sent me back to stop all this shit.

'Is that not clear to you?' she asked. 'It is clear to *me*.'

'Hold on, lady. Just hold on a freakin' minute. How about you tell me what's going on here? Unless I hand you over to Thump tomorrow, he's gonna blow up the daddy of all volcanoes and blame it all on me. I can't let either of those things happen.'

For a moment Angie didn't think anything to me. Then she said, softly: 'You can give me to Thump if you need to. Remember, you have free will. But not yet. There are things you need to see.'

3

The bright light all around us faded into a view of the Earth – and we found ourselves right out in space, looking down at it. That strange sensation of not being able to, or even needing to breathe, came right back. I looked around, floating and moving easily as if I was swimming through some light, thin liquid. There and then, I took in all the majesty of the galaxy – the planets and their moons, and trillions of stars twinkling.

Angie got my attention by touching my hand, then took it again in hers.

'Watch this,' she said. 'And listen…'

I guess I fell into some kind of trance; my eyes seemed to set in place and focus. But more than that, my mind *fell open*. By that I mean it was as if I actually felt my brain just falling apart like a box folding down. And then my final lesson began.

Angie swept her arms in front of us, and in something like a puff of smoke but without any puff or smoke, Earth just vanished. She turned us towards the other planets and wiped them out just the same, and then all the stars too, until all we saw was *nothing*. She'd wiped the blackboard.

'And so it was,' she revealed. Then she clapped her hands together and there, out of the darkness a small planet appeared.

'That is Eden. You have been there, I see. No humans are ever meant to, but you seem to have found a back door. That is interesting. Nevertheless, Eden is the first. It has been forever, and will be forever.'

She clapped again, then again and again and as she did, the planets appeared one by one. But something was missing.

'You do it,' she suggested.

So I clapped – instantly the Sun appeared, shedding brilliant light across the whole scene. The stars had come back, and there the Earth was, right where it was supposed to be. Angie took my hand and we swooped towards it, entering the atmosphere with hardly any change in feeling. We stopped there, thousands of feet above the Earth.

Angie reached her hand out, closing her thumb and forefinger over a land mass, and then – *roger me to oblivion with a peach* – just picked it up! She held it up in front of us, dangling from her hand like a piece of bread.

'You try,' she said.

I did. I reached down to what looked like Italy and just closed my fingers around the tip of the land, then gently peeled it off the surface. I brought it right up to my face and as it got closer, I could see stuff down there on its surface. *What the hell?*

'That will do,' Angie said as she dropped her geographical biscuit gently into the Atlantic Ocean. It sent a ripple across the water, splashing up against the other land masses it reached. 'Now we will go into yours. Hand it to me.'

I gave Italy to her. She cupped it in her hands and blew on it. With an almighty rush of wind I felt myself thrown into her hands and the next thing I knew, I was hurtling at rocket speed towards the ground. Just as I was about to surely splat into it, Angie appeared out of nowhere on the ground and caught me as gracefully as a leaf falling from a tree and landing with no meaningful impact.

We stood together, looking out over a lake surrounded by beautiful buildings and lodges and with snow-capped mountains in the distance. Angie reached out towards one of those caps and again, just plucked the top off. She handed it to me.

'Open your palm. And watch.'

Without touching that mountain top, she was moving it with her hand gestures, rotating it in my palm. Then making as if to peel a banana, she began to strip away the mountain's sides.

'See?'

I looked beyond the thing in my hand and to the mountain in the distance. There, unbelievably, its sides were peeling away too. Then she clapped her hands together and the mountain collapsed – in my hand and out of it. I gasped.

'Do not worry. No one is harmed. This is not your reality.'

She turned towards one of the hotels, its glass exterior gleaming in the sunlight. Outside we could see a couple of hundred people, mostly in skiing gear, all fixated on that crumbling mountain in the distance.

Angie reached her hand up and plucked the Sun down like an orange from a tree. She held it in her hand, then cheerily chucked the thing at that hotel. It crashed into the glass, shattering it as it exploded into thick streams of hot lava, spreading down and all around in a river of hot death. No one had a chance.

'This isn't my reality? Whose is it then?' I was beginning to feel the full displeasure of genocidal angelic action unfolding before my eyes.

'It is *a* reality. But not yours.'

I wondered what she was gonna do next. Kinda obvious, really – she cupped her hands in the lake and threw a load of water onto the burning hotel and people. Then she reached down to the mass of dead bodies and plucked one up. She brought it right up to her mouth and kissed it. The body turned into a butterfly, *just like that*. It flew off her hand and away over the lake.

'You see now, yes?'

'Uh… maybe. I guess. Maybe.'

4

A few seconds later we had rushed back into space and Angie rubbed everything out again. Then she clapped a few times again, but this time a familiar sight came up – as I'd been shown before, a string of Earths, all looking much the same but with small, almost imperceptible differences were laid before me.

Angie pointed to each of the six examples in turn. 'That one is yours. These others are made from the same blueprint, but their histories are different. I know you have visited at least two of them on your journey. We shall visit a new one for you.'

Wiping the others from view, we rushed towards 'the new one'. Within a few seconds we were back just inside the atmosphere, looking down at the blue, green and white shapes on the surface. The land masses looked just the same as last time, but this version seemed lighter somehow; fresher. I couldn't pin it down.

'The atmosphere here is undamaged,' Angie said. 'On your Earth the ozone has been punctured. Here it has not because the people made other choices. Their options were the same, but their choices were different.'

'Better,' I suggested. 'Their choices were better.'

'No. Different, but not necessarily better.'

We rushed down to the surface and landed soft as snowflakes outside a large building – a hospital, I soon realised after seeing the word 'hospital' on the sign in front of us. Angie walked me inside. It was strange being there among those people, seeing us just as we saw them, but with no idea that one of us was Earth's last angel and the other was... erm... a doomed dipshit from the future.

We entered a lift and Angie controlled it without touching anything; just waving her fingers at the control panel. Kinda annoyed me a little bit. It was comin' across as damn lazy. *Angelazy*. Just press the damn button, okay?

We got out on the fifth floor and walked down a long corridor. The place was familiar, but also not. Although the surface details were the same, the machines looked different; the clothes people wore were different. I caught the eye of some no-hoper-lookin' guy, and he gave me this weird, unsettling wink. I shrugged back a little, and then he nodded at Angie, as if to say – I supposed in my body language vocabularisement – that he assumed the young girl to be my partner in the *boom-chicka-wow-wow* sense.

I shook my head at him. That was all. But then it occurred to me: this Angie was not like the young girl I'd met originally, now all grown up. This Angie was more like a late teenager or even in her early twenties. Her face was the same but older, and I gotta say yeah – prettier. Her features were soft and sunny and the billowy cream dress she was wearing suited her perfickly. She caught me looking at her and smiled, then thought at me: 'Stop it, Martin. What would Susan say?'

Higgledy-bollocks – Susan! Amid all this rip-yourself-a-new-brain-hole revelation of stuff I still had no real understanding of, I'd forgotten about my team. The Four Horsepeople of Failure, headed like a meteor of burning cat turds towards the human race's collective litter tray. Except now it was just me.

'No,' Angie thought. 'They have come to no harm. We shall rejoin them shortly and you will be on your way.'

'My way? My way where?'

'All in good time. For now, there is much more to see.'

At the end of the corridor, we followed a sign pointing to something called 'STRAIN CLINIC'. As we rounded the corner, I'd never seen anything like it: a waiting room packed, seated and standing, with grotesque figures. Immediately one caught my eye and fixated its gaze on me. Those eyes were burning in that skull, like I could almost feel the heat coming off 'em.

Angie said: 'Listen.'

In that instant, my mind filled with the voices of everyone in the room, but not like a cackyphone – I could hear what these people were thinking, clearly cutting through each other, but my brain processed them all. It was kinda like a song, their voices the instruments in an orchestra. And that orchestra tonight was playing the Symphony of Raw Human Shit. These guys were as fucked up as anyone I'd ever seen and ten times worse. Their bodies seemed to share some deformities – large, tumoured heads and giant boils coming out of their necks and arms and... well, they looked like fuckin' potatoes, to be honest.

Their thoughts were all sorrow through and through. And pain, a whole lot of it. So not just all sorrow, after all. Sorrow, pain and despair. Okay, that's three things now. There's probably more too. But let's digress no longer.

Angie explained: 'They were exposed to a rare element of human synthesis that occurred when they were conducting chemical experiments on soil. Unfortunately the pesticide in the soil reacted to the experiment negatively, although this was not clear – not for many years. The crops grown there went as they always did into the food chain. After approaching four years, people began to develop these strange tumours. Tests led to a particular chain reaction which explained the source of these, but by then the soil treatment had been licensed for use all over the world. It was just too late. This is one of thousands of clinics. These people number in the millions. In Africa, where almost all the arable soil was treated as a means to solve famine, it did only in the short term. Now Africa is full of these people. In other countries which did not take the treatment, there are still clinics. The food products travelled – and so did the disease. But then other people were resistant. An industry grew around making profit from these unfortunate souls, disfigured by human progress. They offer cures, special residences, insurance and anything else they can think of to profit from this. The Strain is unlike anything that has happened on your Earth since the plague, but it is very similar in concept.'

I nodded solemnly. Our ozone was fucked, but their whole food chain had been pissed on. Swings and roundabouts.

Angie went on: 'Yet in Africa on any number of other Earths, there is no such problem. On several it turns out that this deeply troubled nation in your reality is quite the opposite. They are leaders, free of your corruption. Their technological thinking is way ahead of the rest of the world. They are envied in almost all respects.'

I was getting that lame-duck feeling again. Did I really need reminders of the turd-brained, immoral arsewipes on my own Earth? In these other glimpses Angie'd showed me, I'd seen the simple reality: it was all down to the people and their decisions. Yet these weren't just visions of what could be – they actually *were*. These alternative Earths were as real as my own. A thought suddenly came to me: my friends – Susan, Shirley and Sally – where were they? Could Angie take me to their other versions?

'They do exist here, but you cannot interfere with them.'

'Why not?' That didn't make sense to me. 'If we're all hopping about between these realities, what's the difference?'

Angie sighed – yes, a thought-sigh. A *thigh*. Nah, scratch that. Sorry.

'I have searched your memories, but did not question this before. Now it is clear that you simply do not know. My future self was not, it seems, entirely honest with you.'

There, still standing in the waiting room while that weird Mutant Strain Guy burned holes in me with his laser eyes, she said: 'You are the saviours. The constants. It is now obvious I suppose that you haven't understood things as much as I expected, because you are lacking an important piece of information. On all these Earths, most of the humans are different. But the five of you were created on *all* of them. To be born at the same times, but into different realities.'

Hang on – 'Five of us? Who's the fifth?'

'Mr Thump, of course. Most everyone else is unique, so on each Earth your lineage is different, but you five are always born. That is surely why you had to come together. I can only assume, not being privy to the future, that what happens is a chain reaction caused by what happens on your Earth, or even others. There are many, *many* of them. More than could be counted.

'Perhaps it is a crunch time, as you might call it. Perhaps the apocalypse is *meant* to happen when it happens and isn't false as you say... or perhaps not that either. The future is unwritten, although you have seen it from the other side.'

Pretty as she was, this version of Angie was coming across like a real fuckin' drag. The way she *thought* this stuff to me was in this lazy kinda monotone, all matter of fact. Being the kinda guy I am, someone who likes a lady with a lilt, I woulda enjoyed a bit of banter. No such luck, fuck a duck.

Yep, I preferred the future angel, and she knew it, but she didn't care a masturbatered monkey either way. She was here now because she had to deliver a message. A damn long one, and although quite spectacular it was pretty boring if truth be told, but a message I had to receive nonthelessed.

Still, that crazy revelation – me and Sally and Shirley and Susan being these four constants in an infinited universe – hit me like a bomb going off in my brain.

'There is one final place I must take you,' she said, holding out her hand for me to grab. I did that. 'And then the end may begin.'

208

5

Zooming back out to space, revealing another Earth and spazzing our way down to it yet again, Angie swooshed us down – this time to South America. Now my geography ain't ever been great, exspecially given my upbringing was in a world smaller than a peeled penis, so I didn't know until we touched down and I asked the angel where we were.

'This is Venezuela,' she said. 'The Hope Hospital in Calabozo. Follow me.'

As we walked through the double doors, two ladies on reception clasped their hands together and bowed, their hushed voices uttering 'an hell'.

Angie smiled at me. 'It is my name – in Spanish. They know me here.'

As she led me through the hospital, past quiet wards, I could hear distant music, gentle and sweet like lullabies.

'It is a children's hospital,' Angie said. 'Here they treat children from all over Venezuela and Colombia, and some of the northern Brazilian states. The hospital is very special because it draws water from the lake north-east of here.'

Course I had to ask: 'What's so special about the water?'

Angie smiled again. It was kinda the first time I'd picked up a sense of personality on this version of her.

'It is blessed,' she said. 'Here on this Earth, loyalty is rewarded. Those peoples who come together in the spirit of their creator are blessed. Man, woman and child cannot live without water. All those who drink from the lake of Calabozo will be healed.'

'You shittin' me?' I regretted that crude crunk instantly. The smile disappearing from Angie's face registered her disapprovism.

'No, I am not. As I have shown you, all these Earths are different. The variables are the same, but the choices are often different. Here they are very much so, *very* different to yours.'

We were still making our way through the hospital until we came to a more modern-looking wing. Angie led me inside. There, just inside the entrance, was a sculpture that stopped me in my tracks: John Thump, done up like a doctor. My jaw dropped open.

'Come,' Angie said. She led me through some short corridors, past more peaceful wards, until we came face to face with the man himself.

As soon as he saw us, Thump leapt up from his desk and started towards Angie. Instinctively, I went for him. I knew it was stupid, but I couldn't let him get his hands on her – and why had she walked us into the lion's den anyhoo? Daft bint.

Angie put her arm out just as I was about to grab the bastard, stopping me dead in my tracks. I spluttered of course, winded a bit and confused as a cat with a cricket bat. Thump stepped back too, suddenly looking wary.

'It's okay,' Angie said. 'John – this is my friend, Martin. He was interested to hear about what you're doing here.'

Thump looked me up and down, then Angie put her arm down and nodded. He smiled at her, then at me.

'Okay then. Hello, Martin,' he said, extending his hand for the shaking thereof, a grin spreading across his face. 'Any friend of Angie is a friend of mine.'

I hesitantingly shook his hand and as I did, I realised my folly – he simply was not the man I knew. This Thump was *softer*. His features were gentler on his face, and he just seemed younger in some way.

Over the next hour or so we walked and talked, the three of us, having the kind of easy conversation only old friends might naturally slip into. This John Thump had never been touched by the evil hand of greed, or big business. He'd studied medicine, served with the army overseas for many years, and had finally – twenty years previous – set up this hospital in Calabozo. Through his own faith and that of the Venezuelan peoples in the city, there had been a coming together, some kind of serendipstick happening – where they united in faith and hope and, as he said it, 'loads of great things began to happen'. Children with giant tumours who were on the brink of death had been healed; those in queues for transplants were treated without needing them – and the whole thing was funded from Thump's own pocket and the trusts he set up. A few wealthy donors had helped, but this was the man's own gig for sure.

At one point he stopped, regarded me with inquirising eyes, and asked me what I did for a living. I told him – hey, I'm a songwriter and a singer, and I try to bring joy to my eager audiences.

His eyes widended and he looked like he was unsure of what to say. Then he took his hand in mine and said: 'Sir, I admire you creative types. You've got something I'll never have – an ability to make something. Now I can make someone well, but I can't make someone dance. There's a beauty to that. I can mend a heart, but people like you can make it fly.'

Eventually we said our goodbyes. I'd witnessed these things with my own eyes, and seen a man I thought I knew through a different lens. Once we were outside, Angie and I walked up to the lake.

'The lake has no official name,' she said, 'but the locals call it Las lágrimas de Dios – the tears of God. John does not know the truth of this, the divine water – only his faith carries him forward.'

I looked over that lake, half expecting Angie to pick up a handful of blessed water and extinguish the Sun with it. But no – I realised the fun and games were over.

'But this world,' she went on, 'has big problems too. There are great wars raging across Eurasia, for example.' She paused, smiled at me, then continued: 'So now you must understand. There is always a balance. You cannot pull something without something being pushed somewhere else. For every birth there must be a death. For every right there is a wrong. For every good choice made somewhere, a bad one is made somewhere else. It cannot be any other way. But also you must see that morality is a construct, made by man. On either side of the line, one must make one's own mind up. That is the nature of free will. What you do next with yours is always what matters most.'

'So...' I started, 'what should I do?'

Angie sighed. I realised what a stupid question that'd been. It was *my* choice. She couldn't and wouldn't suggest anything otherwise, but she did have the good grace to lend a little context.

'If you hand me to him, I will not be there to safeguard the future – should that come to pass. But if you do not, he says he will commit an atrocity of unparalleled impact in your name. That is a threat, but not a guarantee.'

I wanted to ask her another question, but before I knew it I was right back on that stage, the colours and the sounds and the cheers and the flashing lights fading back into my view. I was back on my stool, back in my reality. Back to business. Fuck on.

6

'Whoooooah! Just hold up there!' Back in the dressing room, Shirley couldn't believe the trip I'd just been on. 'We're actually, for real, the chosen ones?'

'Yeah,' I said. 'For real. Real as an eel suckin' orange peel.'

Sally was the most flustered. She couldn't get her head around it at all. 'So all... these realities, these Earths... I'm on all of them... *we're* on all of them... and this *always* happens? We come together like this?'

I shrugged. 'Way I understand it, yeah – we're supposed to be in this thing together, but maybe it hasn't ever happened quite like this before. This is truly the final shot we have. If we can stop the bastard, maybe it never happens.'

'And how do you intend to stop him?' Susan asked, ramming home the check-matedness of the situation. 'He's got us by the short-and-curlies. You can't do anything to him and he can't do anything to you, but he can blow the bottom out of the United States on a whim and we'll forever be blamed!'

'Calm down, girl,' I said. 'We are the chosen ones, so she says, and as that's the case there's got to be a reason why. What do we have, the four of us, and how come we did all come together like this? The chances of that happening, well... through choices I made, and some made for me, and choices you guys made too – here we are.'

Shirley was great at figuring shit like this out. 'That's easy,' he said, 'and yes, you're right. Through all the other time lines you've been through, although you didn't know it, you've been making proxy decisions on your own behalf. That's what led us to here and now.'

Sally piped up: 'But that doesn't explain the four of us, or this supposed destiny to stop Thump from whatever it is he's about to do.'

'Has our mission even changed?' Susan asked. 'How can we be sure it doesn't all just end up the same as before? If we've been here before, even if we don't know it...' She trailed off, clearly giving up trying to figure it out.

'No,' Shirley said. 'Some of the specifics have changed, but we're here for the first time. If Thump has made a deal with the Tremendous, we're not stopping the false 'pocalypse – we're stopping something far worse.'

The four of us nodded, simultanodesly. Does that work? Doubt I'll use it again anyhoo.

'Well whatever we do,' I said, 'we have to do it quickly. Far as I can tell, we're on our own now. Angie told me if I choose to hand her over, I just have to call her and she'll come. But I don't intend to do that.'

'Even if it means saving millions of people?' Susan asked sharply. 'How could you let them all just die?'

I put my hands up to stop her before she said something she'd regret. After all, this was *my* show. 'Make no mistake,' I said. 'I'm not gonna let anyone die at my hand. Well, maybe one person, if he doesn't make the right choice. I've got an idea, see – how about we turn the tables?'

My companions flashed me a look of confuserment. Naturally they wanted to know what my plan was. I ain't gonna set it all out here, because the anticipationment is always proportionisely measured by the joy at the end.

Three hours or so later we were back in Boston, waiting up to see the sunrise. Hugo, Klein and Tim had expected us to stay in New York, but we had plans – plans that required a little quiet time at home. Course through the airports we got all sorts of stares, a little cheering and a little booing given the divisive nature of playing celebratory music for a shitsucker like Thump, but once back at home we felt safe – insulated from the cold reality of what was going on back out in the world.

On the plane I'd revealed my idea, and what an idea it was. Ladies and gentlefolkers, here's how I saved the world...

Shirley – social media dude extraordinaire – had spent so much time ranting about the evils of UniTube commenters and the virtual racist riots raging online, it seemed so obvious; but we'd never thought of it before. A negative campaign went against everything I held dear. I'd always tried to be truthful; sure, every now and then I'd dip my dick in the den of deception, but to create something entirely untrue and present it as fact... well, that's what Thump had done to get where he was, so I reasoned I might as well employ the same tactics.

Sally, the good old girl, was the strongest of all of us – physically and psychologickly too. Now although it was my idea, I wouldn't have been able to do any of it without my horsepeople. That's a fact, sure as turd floats in the sea.

It was so simple in executionising, and so effective in deployment. A master stroke, if I do butter my own bread with it. Being as our house in Boston wasn't more than a donkey's dick from the Charles River, we had plenty of rope out in the back yard. Sally set it up while Shirley made sure the broadcast would be convincing. Susan did my make-up.

I felt like a movie star, I guess. Acting out my final, grim scene – but crucial like, just acting. Susan did a great job of greying me up. Sally tied the rope through the rafters in the back room while Shirley made sure the light in there was gloomy as all hell. Fact is I had to look *dead*.

See, here's the thinking: Thump knew I was immortal, but no one else did. And it's not as if anyone was gonna believe that wrinkly old scrote if he started telling people I was. Far as Average Joe and his dimshit wife know, there ain't no such thing as immortality. Putting that fact to work in our favour was kinda genius, huh?

Within mere minutes of posting the vid on UniTube, we had hits. And I'm talking major numbers – thousands, ticking up all the time. The first comment was a classic. Some guy or gal calling themselves TheRapist posted up: 'Always thought the guy was just hanging around anyway.'

Then the news reports came – lit'rally everywhere. Shirley monitored all the updates as they came in. We tuned in to the first big channel bulletin.

The anchor was all serious lookin'. 'Shocking news tonight as one of President Thump's chief supporters appears to have taken his own life, citing "irreconcilable issues" with the President's behaviour mere hours after performing a song at his inauguration,' she said.

Then her voiceover narrated the video. 'Marty Molloy, the celebrity singer-songwriter who controversially switched his support to Thump at the last minute – something that pollsters report helped the President to swing the undecided votes he needed – has been found hanged in his own Boston, Massachusetts, home. This footage may be too disturbing for some, so turn away now if you're easily upset.'

The video made its way from the view of Susan crying to the somewhat starker image of my body hanging on a rope. Shirley's work was the excellentist I'd ever seen. Now, being something of a movie guy, I've seen the world's best car chases and I've heard monilogs that nail the gonad of believableness to the table of far-fetcherism, but hell – this shit looked *true*.

Then as Susan held my fake suicide note up to the camera, we nailed the other bollock to that table.

'Molloy's note is chilling and specific,' the posh bint continued. 'It reads: "My heart is broken by the evil that runs through his veins. I'm sorry. To everyone. Remember me well."'

A flashy flash spread across the screen for seven seconds. Might've been eight, and really I don't give a shit as I wasn't counting, but the point is it was about that length of time.

The cameras came back on and focused back on the anchor. She was called Meredith Winters. She had the look and sound of someone who'd been raised just for this very thing – as if her entire existence was supposed to entail spreading thick bullshit jam on the toast of life.

'Thump's administration's first headache is setting in,' she said. 'Here we examine just how this Presidency can begin positively in the light of such a major embarrassment and we ask – just what *evil* is it that Molloy alludes to? We'll be back right after these messages.'

I almost popped a nut at that: embarrassment? My death was some kind of affront to Thump, rather than something to be mourned? I loved the way the media dealt with shit – and then I remembered who I was dealing with.

The Tremendous: cutting and pasting and making sure we all do what we think we're being told. They had the media. They had me. But hey, they didn't have *this*.

Shirley uploaded his next video. Clever boy, see, he'd seen right to make a copy of that stuff Thump had shown us – and his threat to blow that super volcano up – when he'd visited the house. And now Shirl had edited that into something quite compelling, I'd say. Compelling enough to make UniTube shit itself. For all its ills, we now had to rely on the rabid response.

And boy, did it come... those hits and views went up and up. We'd caught the bastards on the hop. Now this shit just had to play out.

8

He couldn't claim I was immortal. Who'd believe that? I hardly did myself. Thump'd kicked the football of fair discussion over the cliff of ridiculosity, and we had to take the fight right to his front door.

The reporters arrived outside the house very quickly, camping outside and almost blocking the street with their vans and equipment. All I had to do was lie low until they gave up. But how long would that be?

Course something we'd given some mind to was the police response. They'd seen my corpse hanging on UniTube and the news, and it didn't take long for them to decide to come looking for that corpse. Sally stayed out of sight too, hiding upstairs with me, while Shirley and Susan dealt with the press and then the cops. We didn't even take a peek over the window sill – anyone spotting me would unravel the whole thing. No, we hunkered down in a dark corner at the back of the house, watching the bulletins unfold outside on our phones. Sally monitored the comments flying in on those vids. They came so fast that she couldn't follow them all, but she read some to me, barely drawing breath between them. It wasn't much of a surprise that most of them were baiting each other – going off the topic, the not inconsiderable event of my grim death, and spitting bile instead.

Thump was on the spot: standing like a rabbit in the headlights. We hadn't fully cornered him yet though. Just as me and Sally were contemplating what his next move might be, the police came in. We saw them on the cameras then heard them downstairs, Susan and Shirley's muffled voices trying to tell them some quickly-made-up bull about what they'd done with the body.

They failed, just as we knew they would. Then the footsteps coming up the stairs... the whole thing coulda been over in that instant, if we hadn't taken steps to secure our spot. Those police, armed and ready, came in shining their torches on us – right at us! The lights streaked across our faces. If the croak that was threatening to escape from my throat had made it out, we might've been discovered, but those torches went right around the room and out again, and they left just as soon as they'd come in. There was some kind of shimmering in the room, so thin it was almost not there at all. Angie was there with us. She'd drawn some curtain across us, protecting our position.

'See?' Susan was outside on the landing pleading with them in her best 'upset' tones. 'I told you we put him in the river. That's what he'd always wanted.'

Good girl, I thought. She'd heard enough lies to know how to spin one. But then the snake of deceit bit her tit as the cop cuffed her. Still, this was all going to plan.

'You're going to have to come with us, ma'am,' he said.

Course they took Shirley as well. And as Sally and me sat up there, somehow unseen, we watched on my phone: my lady and fellow horseman led out into the glare of the world's watching eye and our computers carried out behind them.

The reporter was babbling something about what she was seeing and then the camera switched back to the anchor in the studio. It was time for some commercial messages, but not before that good lady Meredith Winters delivered her pre-break summation.

'Astonishing developments at Molloy's house then as his girlfriend claims his body is in the Charles River. Clearly something is amiss though – as the authorities take hardware from the house, we're left wondering if there's more to this story than meets the eye. After the break, we'll be examining another breaking story – what the internet is calling "Thumpageddon". Stay right here.'

I could imagine that sleazy bastard steaming over all this, storming around the Oval Office and barking incoherent orders at his underlings. This was our handjob insurance. He couldn't blow that nuke now. He couldn't blame anything on me anymore.

I had just one more favour to ask of Angie.

'You there, angel?' I called softly.

The room shimmered as she appeared into it.

'Is it time then?' she asked.

Yeah, it was.

9

Wham. There we were. Angie might've been a stony-faced ball of serious, but she knew how to throw a dart. Me and Sally, armed with her augs from a future we still had to ensure, were there in our house one moment then in Thump's domain the next.

Angie? Well, that was her last hurrah. She couldn't come with us – we didn't know what was gonna be waiting for us there, and the last thing we wanted to do was put her pretty head in the lion's mouth.

Now it was just up to us. We found ourselves in a dark office, somewhere near Thump's office hopefully. When Shirley had pulled up the White House floor plan earlier, we'd got a good idea of where we needed to be, but of course we didn't know where *he* was gonna be when we got there.

Sally was tapping stuff on her wrist aug, then she presented its display to me.

'Three bodies – one to the left, two to the right,' she said.

That was just our immediate threat; the aug only saw so far, and the White House was a big place. Still, one step at a time. Sally kept an eye on her aug while we sneaked the door open. The light of the corridor cast a thick line over us. Sally confirmed the goons' positions. Easier to take one than two, you might think, we went for the two instead. That way, if we messed up there'd only be one other to deal with. Always wipe the shittiest arse first.

Course, not being of the violent bent, I left that stuff to the lady. Two shots from her aug was all it took – sonic disconsciousment. They went down like sacks of shit, which I guess isn't really fair. These guys were just doing their jobs. But was it more than that? If you sit down to dinner with the devil, doesn't that make you party to his evil? Maybe, maybe not. I ain't privy to all those answers, but my own gut feeling is that it does.

Course the other side to that dirty coin is that these guys hadn't sworn no allegiants to Thump himself but to their flag. Guess I saw problems with that too – how can a man blindly follow a waving flag if he doesn't agree with the wind that blows through it?

Regardless, these guys had guns and comms and we had to find and stop that terrible tyrant before he could figure out what we were up to.

More dots appeared on Sal's display. We dealt with them just the same way, then rounded a corner into more dots. As we moved towards them, more and more appeared – until her aug beeped.

'Holy shit,' she said. 'There's gotta be twenty or more.' She looked at me and shrugged.

I wasn't worried. 'That means that's where he is,' I said. I could feel that he was too – like a turd poking its head out a little further as you get closer to the thunderbox, the pulsating peristalsis of my proximity to Thump was palpatable.

Sally looked nervous. 'Marty, I can take maybe three or four out at once, but any more than that just ain't gonna happen. It's military grade, but this aug's just a baby.'

Course I didn't expect the girl to waltz into a room full of guys and lay them flat, but we had to do something. Besides, there were still two corridors – busy they were too – and another large room between them and us. I couldn't call on Angie again; we were on our own.

Then I had an idea. We couldn't fight our way to him, but we could still get to him without any trouble at all. After all, the bastard was all ego – as self-centrised as it was possible to be. He wanted to hurt me. I'd kicked him in the balls, so he must've thought he owed me the same at least.

10

By then, of course, the guy was in trouble. By any estimation, that large gathering of people was surely gonna be a press conference. With Shirley's video nasty showing the world what Thump had threatened to do, he must've been shittin' himself with having to straighten it all out.

So, as I said to Sally, 'All we have to do is quietly walk in there. If we pose no threat, no one's gonna worry about us. The cameras will hit us, sure, but that'll work in our favour. It'll confuse the shit outta him. Dead man walking – right into his press conference. What's he gonna do about that? Then as soon as we're in, you concentrate your fire on him and him only. Stun the shit out of the room with a flash-bang, then put a real hole between his eyes.'

Sally shrugged at me like I knew she would. 'I don't wanna die,' she said. 'The whole point of this is to stop him so we can all live.'

'But what if that can't happen?' I returtled. 'Any great achievement comes with a sacrifice. And we don't even belong here. This is not our time. It's not our place either. We go out guns blazing, or maybe, just maybe… we get to survive.'

Course going out guns blazing weren't an option given I didn't have any guns, not even a peashooter, but the sentiment was right-on. The future of the human race depended on us.

With one last deep breath we made for the next room, heading around another corner into a corridor and down there a bit until we reached the source of all those dots. Holy shitballs, we weren't expecting to see that – the large room wasn't full of security guards after all. There were a few guys in uniform – serving and protecting – and the rest were people, just like us. The room was the central lobby into the White House, and all those guys were trying to get inside.

A TV screen in the corner of the room filled in some of the blanks. Outside, there was a horde of angry protesters bearing placards and shouting. Looks like our plan hadn't just rattled Thump himself but got the whole of Washington DC out of their pyjamas – baying for the blood of the man who'd threatened to cover them in lava and ash.

A couple of seconds later one of the guys in the lobby recognised me. Course I was supposed to be dead. He began rustling up a few more guys, then the bunch of them came over. I had some explaining to do. Turns out they understood my gamble, although I couldn't be entirely truthful with them for obvious reasons. Within another minute I had command of the room.

'My fellow Americans,' I announced in a confident tone befitting the man who's about to save humanity. 'Thump is an evil, rotten bastard. He must be stopped, and I'm here to do that. You may know me as a songwriter and performer of unusually high standard, but today I'm here to make sure this rat can't do any more harm. With my good lady friend at my side, we're going in. Now stand back.'

The throng parted just as it had, I guess, when that old *Bible* dude Moses took his chums through the Red Sea. Now it was my turn to lead my people to safety.

Me and Sally approached the main doors. They were shut tight. I nodded to her as she held up her aug and showed me all the dots appearing on the other side. One of those, well... just had to be Thump. I guessed there'd be some more surprises waiting for us too. He had, after all, the full force of the Tremendous at his beck and call. Damn it, I was right.

11

Sally let her aug do the talking as she fired off a sonic shot at the heavy doors. Like an invisible battering ram, they flew right open. She immediately let off a second boom, sending the guards flying down the corridor. We ducked into an alcove just as bullets started spraying towards us. Screaming from the lobby indicated those protestors were not entirely accustomed to being shot at.

We were pinned down. Sally shouted over the gunfire: 'My shield aug'll only stand so much of that.' I peeked out into the corridor. A bullet just missed my face and I drew back into the alcove sharply. The corridor was long and there were maybe six or seven guys, armed and ready. Something was odd about them – and then I realised: it was those *men from another place*. And the guns they were holding, why... they just vanished out of existence.

Course being immortal and all, I'd not really ventured down the road of figuring out just what that meant. When we'd jumped to our brief death off the hospital roof all that time ago, we'd died but been res-erected later. Was it the same now? If they killed me, I'd be killed for real but then given another shot later on? Or would their bullets bounce off me? It wasn't the time or place really to be testing the water.

Sally's sonic boom aug beeped – it'd recharged enough for another shot. Just outside the alcove was one of the unconscious guards she'd knocked out seconds earlier.

'Cover me!' I called.

Sally leaned out and activated her shield aug. I got up behind it and dragged the guy's body back into the alcove.

'Now get behind me!' I shouted. Sally did – reaching around in front of me and the unconscious guard I was propping up, the three of us waddling forward like penguins glued together, with Sal's shield up in front of us. Bullets bounced off the shield, richoshitting off onto the corridor walls. The shield began to flicker as the first bullet that made it through struck the guard I was carrying in the shoulder, then another in his chest and the next into his head. At least he got to sleep through it, not that I felt any sympathy for these bastards.

Sally let off another two boom shots, taking those guys out in fine fashion. I dropped my corpse and picked up another in case any other guys emerged from the next room. There were more dots in there. The aug beeped again to signify the shield was recharged, but at that low charge, Sally said, it was only good for a few seconds. It needed a minute or two to do the job it'd just done for us again. We didn't have that long.

I pushed forwards to the opening ahead of us and leaned the sleeping sack of flesh inside. A bullet flew right through his head and out the other side, thumping into the door frame and taking a bit of the guy's brain with it. I pulled the lifeless body back in, blood pouring out of the head onto my hands and dripping down my arms and legs to my feet.

Sally came up behind me. 'There's five in there,' she said. 'I bet we can take them. And there's just one beyond them, in the next room. That must be *him*.'

I *knew* we could take them. We were on a mission from God. And we had no choice. It was now or never.

'OK,' I said. 'How long on the shield?'

Sally checked her aug. 'About seven seconds, max.'

It would have to be enough. The dots were moving closer to the opening.

'Fuck on,' I said. 'Let's do this.'

Just like before, I held the corpse up like my own fleshy shield as Sally kept close behind me, shielding us all from the first shots. We advanced on them just the same, and as the shield began to fail those bullets came in and struck into the body. Then Sally sonic boomed those bastards down in two clean shots.

We were done! Looking at all those creepy fuckers sprawled on the floor, I felt a rush of relief. I'd never been in any situation quite like that. The place was all shot up to shit, corpses littering the corridor. Sally was clearly experiencing that rush too – she threw her arms around me and hugged tight.

There was just one door left to breach. There, a single wooden panel in front of us, beckoning the sonic boom. It seemed like I'd aged a whole year in the time it took for Sal's aug to beep. As soon as it did, she levelled it at the target.

We looked long at each other, right in the eyes. She was out of it, distanced, broken by the battle. I guessed I looked the same to her. And the grim realisation hit me, and probably her, too: the other side of that door, we were about to murder the President of the United States.

12

Sally was about to let the boom off when we heard the shot. She fell face-down like a sack of dead meat, blood oozing out of the hole in her head. The aug on her wrist, the tool from the future that'd got us to that point, blinked off as her pulse no longer gave it a reason to function.

I swivelled in some kinda slow-mo to see someone I'd hoped never to see again: that flaming bastard from the testicle of the Tremendous – Roger. He was holding a big revolver. Looked like a Magnum to me.

As I stood slack-jawed, he swivelled the Magnum around in his fingers theatrically like some sheriff in an old Western, then poofed it out of existence.

'You rat-bastard, cock-smoking bitch!' I shouted at him. My voice seemed to echo down the corridor as the atmosphere turned cold and dark, as if the life was being sucked out of the room.

Roger just stood there, grinning back at me with that same insincere, emotionless face. A face I'd come to hate anyhoo, without the extra bucket of shit he'd just poured over my head.

As the corridor's light continued to drain away, the air thickening around me, his grim grin was the only thing to focus on. At last he spoke: 'Such a shame, really it is. I kinda liked her. Not that I've seen much of her, mind, but I've been watching your little action movie unfold. Plucky old girl, eh?'

I wanted to put my hands around his throat and squeeze.

He continued: 'Yes, yes. I know how you feel. It seems like so much tragedy, all at once. Hardly fair, is it?'

I didn't answer.

'But you see, it's important that you're alone now. Just you and him. It wouldn't be fair to tip the odds in your favour now, would it? No, no it wouldn't. And this is, as you surely must realise now, the end.'

I remained still, my breathing low and deep, focused on the bastard.

'I suppose you'd like to do me some harm too, but that's not on the list today, I'm afraid. I just really wanted to wish you well – good luck, if you will. I've only ever wanted the best for you. And now here you are, proving that survival of the fittest rings true in all situations. So then… cheerio!'

And with that, Roger was gone. The corridor began to return to its previous state – the red in the carpet bleeding back in and the orange glow of the lights regaining its vitality. And there, at my feet, was my old friend Sal. I truly was alone.

I knelt down beside her and gently unclipped her wrist aug, then slipped it off her arm and onto mine. I fastened it and waited. Having never owned one of these things, I'd had cause to try them out on occasion at least. It booted up and then sounded a long beep, the only sound in that empty place. After a few seconds a shorter beep came, and then I tapped the screen where it said 'Format new user.'

Once the set-up was complete, I tapped the icon marked 'Recon'. And there it was – the single red dot the other side of the door. The geography of it, although rudingmentary in display, seemed to show another long corridor the other side of this one. I wondered what I'd find there – Thump, just standing there and waiting for me to kill him. But no, that wouldn't make sense, and for all I knew he was probably immortal too.

I tapped the icon I needed and waited for it to activate, then levelled the aug at the door. It flew backwards off its hinges and crashed into a structure behind it. There, just ahead, was a security gate, like one of those they use in airports. At the far end of it stood President Thump, smiling his idiot smile. We stood facing each other silently for a while, until he finally spoke.

'Neat trick you played there,' he said. 'The whole fake death bullshit. Very, very neat. Top marks for that one, Marty. Very, very neat.'

I shrugged at him and took a step forward.

'Hold on there!' he called, his smugness going up a notch. 'Are you sure it's safe to step inside?'

'I ain't carrying no weapons,' I told him. 'I'm going to kill you with my bare hands. Slowly.'

Thump laughed. Seeing him there brought back the memory of meeting the Good Thump on the other Earth, caring for sick people. But this guy was sicker than all them put together.

'Well come on then,' he chuckled. 'I'm right here. Come and get me.'

Now in hindsight I can say I shoulda really been more sensible about walking into such an obvious fuckin' trap, but walk into it I very much did indeed.

Halfway through the structure I was when with a howl of glee Thump pressed the red button at his end. In the blink of an eye those shutters came down all around me.

He walked up and pressed his hands against the thick glass. His voice was muffled: 'Neat trick of my own right there, Marty! Really, really neat, wouldn't you say? By the time the oxygen's all used up in there, it'll all be over. Time for my ascension to greatness! Well-deserved, I'd say.'

I shook my head. 'No. The only thing you deserve is my foot up your ass. And I'm going to get out of here real soon and make sure that happens.'

His laugh came through the glass loud and clear. 'Good luck with that!' he squealed. 'Well, I'd love to hang around and chat with you, but there's a few things I have to attend to, such as crossing over to the Realm of the Tremendous for my final transformation. I'd love to take you with me, but… well, no. You see, you may be immortal but all I need to do is snuff you out. When you die, you'll come back, sure… just not in time to stop me. And the Tremendous say it's you or me, and I choose me. So bye-ze-bye!'

Now I weren't officially up to date with the mechanics of my prospects, or his for that matter, but if they'd given him that choice then I could see why he'd want me trapped in there.

As Sal's wrist aug beeped again to let me know the sonic boom was back at full charge, I spotted another icon I hadn't really noticed before.

13

'Override' it said, and override it did. As those shutters came back up, Thump's face was a priceless picture, like his head just shat itself. I wasn't interested in talking so I just switched Sal's aug back to fire mode and made quickly towards the bastard.

He turned on his heels and ran, so I ran after him. I took a shot at him just as he rounded the corner at the end of the corridor. The shot connected with the flap of his suit and nothing more. As soon as I got round it myself, he was nowhere to be seen along the new corridor. There were a bunch of doors along it on both sides. He couldn't have made it too far down though. Course I just had to check on my wrist. As I made my way slowly up the corridor, pointing the aug left and right, his dot appeared. I didn't even try to open the door by conventional means – it came off its hinges real easy. I strode into the room. As soon as I was in, Thump pounced on me, sending me reeling back into the corridor with him on top. Immediately, he tore the aug tech off my wrist and flung it far down the passage.

'Now you're fucked,' he said, his hands gripping my throat and squeezing tight. I felt my eyes starting to bulge out. I managed to get a hand free from under his leg and went straight for his nuts, twisting them out and to the side as hard as I could.

Thump fell off me with a yelp as I rolled away from him and shuffled my way back up to my feet. I advanced on him and went to put my foot in his ass as promised. Somehow he anticiperised the move and swept my foot aside, putting me off balance. I fell backwards again into the wall, then down to the floor. I'd never imagined this bastard'd be such a nippy little scrapper.

Fatiggering as I was, I used all my might to push myself back up awkwardly against the wall and followed Thump back into the room. I shoulda been more careful about that – he brought a wooden chair straight down on my head, crumpling me back down.

I lay there, dizzy and defconbobulated, watching him move to the far end of the room, where there was a bank of monitors and controls underneath them. He turned back to me, my vision blurring him into four or more Thumps, swirling around. My vision weren't clear, but my hearing was.

'This… this is on *you*,' he panted. 'They know you're still alive, and you'll have to live with this forever.'

I mustered a little speaking gumption: 'But they know you're behind it anyhoo. They've seen the proof.'

'I don't care,' he snapped back. 'Me? I'm done here. I don't give a shit *who* they think did it. It's still on *you*. You're making me do this. Once I'm one of them, the Tremendous will give me power you cannot imagine.'

Although it was tough to see from my horizontal position, Thump flipped something open on the console. It didn't take me long to figure out what he was about to do.

'No!' I cried, managing to get up onto my elbows. 'You don't have to do this. Just kill me and let them live. Please.'

He turned back to face me, his face all lit up with the lust for blood. He'd really lost it. 'No, no, no! I'm going to make you watch. As soon as I put the code in and press this small button right here, you can watch the show in your personal private cinema. Then I'll finish you off.'

His final mistake was turning his back on me. As he reached into his pocket and pulled out the slip of paper with the code on it, I managed to get up to my knees and then stood straight up. He tapped the code in and just as he was about to press down on the button, I struck the side of his head with the chair leg I'd just picked up.

He didn't go all the way down and clung onto the side of the console with his fingers, trying to straighten himself back up. I struck him again, harder this time and kicked his legs out. He went down.

'You fool,' he muttered, edging away from me on the floor as I stood over him, ready to strike again. 'You utter, *mad* fool. Did you think for a second I wouldn't have a back-up plan?'

'Looks to me like you've got nothing but a sore head right now, you pigfucker,' I replied calmly, the adrenaline carrying me through this otherwise fraught encounter.

He began to chuckle again, punctuated with heavy breaths. 'Ever heard of voice activation?'

I'd never have had time in a million instances of replaying what happened then to stop him doing what he did. The spiteful, shitty maniac uttered just four words: 'Thump Foxtrot Nero Seven.'

As a disembodied voice confirmed the action, I forced that chair leg right down into his chest as hard as I could, my full bodyweight plunging the thing far enough in to kill him instantly. I lay there, my hands tight around the leg shaft and with my head just inches from his, watching the blood spew up from his chest and out the side of his mouth.

The countdown brought me back into the moment.

10... 9... 8... 7...

I managed to get myself back upright and examined the banks of controls in front of me. The console he'd been using before was only connected to the volcano bomb, it seemed. What he'd just activated was flashing up on the monitor in front of me as a 'Point Of No Return'. Seemed he'd primed it already, just in case, before he'd trapped me in the security station before.

6... 5... 4... 3... 2...

I just had time to digest what I was seeing on those monitors. Seven silos had opened and were ready to fire.

1... Zero...

And fire they did. At that moment, a cacophony of phones ringing in the room startled me out of the trance I'd found myself in, watching those missiles launching all at once. I looked over at them, at least ten and maybe as many as fifteen. I had no cause to answer any of them.

14

If I'd had any energy left, I might've jumped out of my skin when the hand clapped down on my shoulder. I didn't even care whose hand it was.

Roger appeared at my side. 'I told the others I thought it'd be you,' he said. 'Thump was… shall we say, a little too over-enthusiastic?'

I didn't say anything. I was busy watching the fireworks display in front of me.

'But you knew this was coming anyway, right?'

I remained silent.

'All along, you must've known this was coming. But you changed history. You did it!'

'I did nothing,' I said, slow and low. 'Just what is it I have done?'

Roger moved around to stand in front of me, blocking my view of the screens. He put his hands on my arms, then said: 'Let's get out of here. We can get much better seats for the show.'

In an instant the room went dark and for the final time I was whisked away from what I was doing. I could still feel Roger's hands on me as the colour drained back into my view.

We weren't in the celestial testicle this time, but stood on a platform of pure light, somewhere yet nowhere. Roger stepped away from me and waved his hand gently. The light seemed to ripple around his hand, and then from the well of brightness those creatures appeared, the ones from Eden with their beautiful scales and rainbow flourishes – weaving in and out of each other in the most wondrous cascade I'd ever seen.

Roger began to transform too, right there before me, until he reached his true incarnation. With a swish of his long tail, an area of the liquid light around me dissipated away. Roger's voice came softly in my mind as the images began appearing all around me.

There was never any way of stopping this…

At once I could see thousands of images, all there at the same time but visible individually too. The sky, light in some areas and dark in others, lit up by the trails of those nuclear missiles – Thump's seven silos launching at least ten each – soaring up and then down. And there, on the ground and in the workplaces and gardens and seashores and shopping centres were the pawns, those humans I'd done my best to save, pointing their smart phones up, capturing their final moments on film like tech-trained rabbits in the brightest, deadliest headlights; typing hurried messages into their devices; taking selfies and posting them on social media as the death rained down all around them.

You mustn't feel sad.

How could I not? There was no other feeling to have.

When you are one of us, you will never feel sadness again. It is not part of our reason. Look and see. See how they remain focused on themselves. While the world burns around them, they care only for themselves, their brothers and sisters, their mothers and fathers. But mostly themselves.

I looked and I saw. And Roger was right. Among all those hundreds and thousands of images swirling around before me, the overwhelming self-centredness was louder than the pockets of enlightenment. Those ladies and gentlemen watching the death on their screens, in their gyms and apartments and coffee shops, drinking their cappuccinos and fennel seed infusions, viewing the horror in a collective trance.

They'd known it was coming, every one of them. They'd seen the writing on the wall for years. How could anyone not have seen this being the final outcome? Dangerous leaders of populations too inert and passive to stop them; dangerous individuals spreading hate and poison on the internet; religious slaughter in the name of gods who would never allow such; a rampant global media casting fear and distrust into all corners of the Earth; and ultimately, the creation of weapons of mass destruction reaching their full potential and fired upon their very creators.

See how it was, too... how it has always been...

Roger swooped and swished around in front of me and slipped away out of sight as the images changed – images of history, from many thousands of years ago to recent times. The Tremendous, powerless to intervene with action but exercising its greatest power to influence, to tempt, to deal in the devilish – indirectly controlling the banks and the board rooms, the newspapers and broadcasts, pitching battles among the powerful and paranoid; distracting the core of humanity with sport and theatre and fear.

And yet, here too and all through was the complicity of those humans, tolerant of all those temptations yet signing petitions for tiny victories, one at a time, all the while not seeing how close the end was. Hypocrisy and hate

233

spreading like forest fires while the forces for good were drowned out at the bottom of the ocean. Births and deaths meaning so much and yet nothing at all. Charities and marathon runners shining the tiniest specks of light on a sea of black that swallows all.

That rapidly approaching 'pocalypse hidden behind a fog of millionaire footballers and pop stars, fashion and so many ideas born straight from the womb of the Tremendous – live, work, die. Rinse and repeat. Enjoy it while you can. And yet for all the billions of dead, those passed on to their eternal damnation or salvation, all was clear, as it was for me there and then.

So join us now. It is your right. Be with us and see the next stage. The reaping of the souls is nigh.

The images disappeared back into the blanket of light, rippling and warm. I stood on that platform, watching those beings in all their splendour for what seemed like hours, rapt in their chaotic patterns, entranced.

My thoughts came back to me eventually. There really had been no stopping it. One voice among billions. So why had I been sent on this journey, chasing the wildest goose of all time?

'It is always so.' The chorus pulled me right back to reality – well, the reality of unreality I'd found myself in anyhoo.

That was *my* voice.

From the light he appeared. Then another, and then another, and soon there must have been a hundred of *me* standing there.

'Humans have always searched for answers, although they refuse to believe the ones they are given,' the collective voice said. 'What is there is true. The truth permeates everything. If you do not see it, that does not mean it is not there.'

So now join us. Take your place among us.

I could've. Probably should've. But didn't.

'Put me back,' I said, my voice as clear as theirs.

'Why?'

'Because I want to go back. Put me back. Please.'

The other *me*s looked at each other, puzzled, as the Tremendous beings swished and swooped around them.

'What is there to go back to?'

'I don't care what's there. If I truly have free will, this is my will. Put me back. Right now.'

15

I stood outside Sally's bar with probably the most earned smile in all time. The good old girl was alive and well, and she'd just watched me play my best set in years – straight from a heart that had beat a hundred thousand more times than it ever should have; a heart full of understanding far beyond my years. And Sal? She was just like she always was, back to that day as it'd been. No knowledge of a world outside her own. Course I didn't go asking the girl no probering questions, but I surmised that if she didn't bring it up herself, most likely she wasn't going to.

I'd played my songs to those NoBodies and Digiheads, spliffed-up and happy in their hazes. Songs I'd written a hundred years ago; melodies tested on millions in a previous, privileged life. And my circle had completed.

I looked up and down that street and drank in the same view I'd had that fateful night. There I was, smoking my pipe outside The Oubliette, right under that neon sign, the 'i' bang-snap in the middle as a matter of fact. It was late, almost the turn of the day, and I could hear the thrum from the Oub behind me, sending a little rub up my bones.

Some folks came and went. I puffed on my pipe. And then I heard that noise that started it all, at least for me... *a scream*. A *child's* scream. Coulda been a car taking a corner in the near distance. Maybe it was someone's TV up too loud.

No – there was a clarity to it. Authenticitation. Not that I was overly familiared with screaming, children or not – although now I can profess of myself to being something of an expert – but the point I am trying to make is I felt it rather than just hearin' it.

I took my pipe from my mouth and tapped the bulb out. Charred tobacco landed at my feet. Then I scanned this way and that. It hadn't been raining, but the neon reflected a little off the street, and further down each way it streaked in lines, the colour kept alive by the street lamps a few yards apart. There weren't no children in sight, not so surprising for that period of proceedings.

Besides, that ain't a street for children at any time. Just in my view there were three whorehouses, two Aug shops, a Narcosuite and one of them new Nuface places I ain't ever set foot or face in. I like my face just as it is.

'Fuck on,' Sally said.

I put my arms around the old girl and kissed her square on the lips.

'Fuck on.'

Other works by Christopher Ritchie

FINALIST	Silver WINNER
Horror	Horror
2013 IndieFab Book of the Year Awards	2015 IndieFab Book of the Year Awards

TV/Radio news anchor Juliette Foster, *SURREY LIFE* magazine: This is a grippingly surreal novel with an edgy narrative and visual touches reminiscent of Stephen King's *The Shining*."

DANTE magazine, Juliette Foster: "Fusing horror, psychology and new age religion this is a novel that repels as much as it fascinates. Amidst the death and destruction lurk some nuggets of ironic black humour."

www.ingramcontent.com/pod-product-compliance
Lightning Source LLC
Chambersburg PA
CBHW020405210626
46816CB00006BB/2124